Someday Forever

John Moelaert has been a published author since 1958. He was born in Holland in 1930 and came to Canada in 1951. His writing has generated many comments of which one he values more than any other. In a face-to-face meeting a reader told him: "I don't always agree with what you write, but it **does** always make me think."

Several of John's short stories have won prizes including first prize for the Canadian Authors Association contest: Donovan versus Donovan, a.k.a. When Love Ends. He is also the former editor-publisher of the Canadian Conservationist and Insight. During the late 1970's he served as a participant in B.C.'s Royal Commission of Inquiry into Uranium Mining, and wrote the 1980 report, **Uranium Mining Is Not in the Public Interest**. His book, **The Cancer Conspiracy**, exposes the politics of cancer and continues to be a timely eye-opener. His articles have been published in newspapers and magazines across Canada and in the U.S., Japan and Costa Rica.

Someday Forever

Mr. John Moelaert

SOMEDAY FOREVER is protected by both Canadian and International Copyrights
COPYRIGHT 2014 @ John Moelaert All rights reserved No part of this work may be
reproduced or used in any form or by any means-graphic, electronic, or mechanical, including
photocopying, recording, taping, or information storage and retrieval systems without the
written permission of the author.

E-MAIL: jmoelaert@Shaw.ca

All rights reserved
ISBN: 1494270048
ISBN 9781494270049
Library of Congress Control Number: 2014901084
CreateSpace Independent Publishing Platform
North Charleston, South Carolina

Part I

I

The sudden transition from a warm and comfortable bed to a ruthless prairie blizzard was no uncommon experience for Dr. Lorne Parsons. Yet, as he piloted his car through the inky darkness of that hostile December night in 1929, he felt fear gnawing at his nerves. He had lived all his life in Alberta, but he knew that those forty-three years had provided no immunity against winter's fury.

His car crawled obediently through the powdery snow, the windshield wipers oscillating ineffectively in the on-rush of whirling snowflakes. With squinted eyes he searched anxiously for a landmark to determine his whereabouts, but the blizzard made a mockery of his efforts. The two light-beams, shortened drastically by the white precipitation, were almost more of a hindrance than a help since they made the snowflakes more blinding by adding glare to density. The whistling wind chased the snow furiously, building mounds and barricades. Trees, naked and forlorn, bowed in reverence, grateful for the firm support their roots found in the frozen earth.

Dr. Parsons glanced at the young farmer sitting stiffly erect beside him. Jim Caldwell felt very awkward: he had never before been in a car and he wished he were not in one now. Give him a team of horses and he could perform miracles; but a car, that was a different story.

You can't trust an automobile like you can a horse, his logic told him. But in this case the comparative values of the two modes of transportation were of little consequence since he owned neither a car nor a horse. Jim had not hesitated for a moment when he accepted Dr. Parson's invitation to accompany him to the Vincent farm. The urgency of this mission had given him the strength and courage necessary for the hazardous journey to Jake's and

Martha's farm. All he had thought of was the imminent birth of Martha's baby and the dire consequences should Dr. Parsons arrive too late.

The doctor reached forward and scraped the frost off the windshield. What a time to be born, he mused. But he was not referring to the weather alone. It was only two weeks before the bleakest Christmas North America had ever known. The tidal wave from Wall Street had lost little of its devastating force when it swept across the Canadian frontier. As he bent still closer over the steering wheel, straining his eyes for better vision, the blood-spattered face of his younger brother reappeared in gruesome detail before him. Suicide was fashionable in those days, but Dr. Parsons had never expected it to strike so close.

The wind tugged vehemently at the car as he steered it onto a narrow road that led to the Vincent farm. But Ray Parsons had died in vain. Only yesterday his wife had learned that the firm, which had insured his life, had perished in the growing whirlpool of bankruptcy.

The car inched convulsively forward in the thickening snow, the wheels nearly losing contact with the road, the engine sputtering in protest.

"It's getting worse," he thought aloud.

Jim nodded. This is no time to talk, he inferred solemnly. Doc needs all his attention to keep this confounded contraption on the road.

Dr. Parsons stopped the car and lowered the window in a desperate bid to see better, but the wind cut into his face before he could stick his head outside.

He pressed his face hard against his mittens to still the pain, wondering how long they could possibly survive this weather. Then he looked at his watch, illuminated by the light of the speedometer. It was twenty to three. He put the car again in motion and stepped a little harder on the gas pedal. He must hurry. Half an hour had passed already since he had left home. Jim stirred uneasily. He was convinced trouble lurked ahead.

"I can't see a thing," Dr. Parsons confessed. Jim bit his lip. His suspicions were confirmed, but he remained respectfully silent. He knew they were now heading straight into the blizzard.

Suddenly the car lurched to the right and Dr. Parsons bumped into his passenger as the lights went out and the engine stalled. A few moments later the two men climbed back to the road, Jim grabbing the doctor's satchel when it rolled towards him after Dr. Parsons momentarily lost his footing.

Dr. Parsons cast a doleful glance at his car that rested impotently on its side in the ditch. Then he put on his headgear, which was swept out of sight the moment his fingers let go off it.

Their bodies stooped against the vicious wind, their arched hands stiffening in the mittens, they slowly stumbled forward.

Jake will have the water boiling, the towels ready, Dr. Parsons thought confidently. He imagined Martha's bulging abdomen, the perspiration on her face. Then a frown creased his brow. What if the baby had already been born? What if Martha...

"The wind is changing again," Jim shouted. He considered it safe to talk again now that he felt the road reassuringly under his boots.

"Yeah," Dr. Parsons yelled. "Maybe it'll swing behind us." Strange thing, he reflected, how after ten years of practice in Inglewood he still so feared the elements.

Most of the town's residents viewed the atmospheric quirks of the area with stoic resignation which had always baffled him.

Inglewood could be bombarded by a devastating hailstorm less than an hour after the sun had smiled in a friendly summer sky. Or in winter, the temperature could drop twenty degrees inside an afternoon when a cold front from the Rocky Mountains blanketed Inglewood.

Suddenly the car stopped dead in its tracks. "Are you OK, doc?" Jim asked with concern.

Dr. Parsons pointed silently ahead, trying to catch his breath "There," he cried hoarsely, "a light." Jim Caldwell failed to see anything but snowflakes whirling hypnotically before his smarting eyes.

"There it is again," Dr. Parsons exclaimed excitedly. Now Jim saw it, too. The light seemed to sway erratically, the snowfall frequently obscuring it.

Then just as sudden as it had appeared, the light vanished and despite their fervent hopes did not return.

"Anybody there?!" Jim yelled impulsively. But the raging wind ripped the words from his lips and crushed them into nothingness. Dejectedly they stalked on, their feet ploughing sluggishly through the deepening snow. Dr. Parsons felt his strength ebbing and he knew that time was running out. Unless they would reach the farm in the next few minutes, he would succumb. Jim would probably try to drag him onward for a little ways, but then he, too, would collapse. In the morning their bodies would be found...

"Dr. Parsons!"

He looked at Jim. "What's the matter?" he asked in a failing voice.

Jim Caldwell looked at him questioningly. "I didn't say nothing," he confessed, his frosted eyebrows almost merging in a frown.

Was it a hallucination, Dr. Parsons wondered dismally: the beginning of the end?

"Dr. Parsons!"

This time it was too loud to be imaginary. They both recognized Jake's voice. The next moment they saw him.

"Good gracious!" Jake Vincent greeted them, using one of his milder expressions. "You're on foot."

"I ran the car off the road a ways back," Dr. Parsons explained as he fell in step beside the robust farmer. "How's Martha?"

"I think she's getting close," Jake replied solemnly. "The pain seems very bad."

Dr. Parsons nodded. When the lighted windows of the farm loomed ahead, he said a silent prayer of thanks.

Warm, moist air caressed their faces when they entered the kitchen. Dr. Parsons headed straight to the adjoining bedroom.

"How are we doing?" He asked as he took off his mittens and flexed his fingers.

"Ready any time you are," Martha Vincent said.

"Let's have a look at you," he said as he pulled back the blankets.

"I'm very happy you made it," Martha said gratefully, grimacing suddenly as pain racked her glowing body. "I was beginning to get worried."

"Old soldiers never die," Dr. Parsons smiled. "I think I'll have time to thaw a little before we get down to brass tacks."

Back in the kitchen the men awaited him with a pot of steaming coffee. Holding the mug in his cupped hands, Dr. Parsons could feel its warmth chase the numbness from his fingers.

"We weren't seeing things after all, doc," Jim said happily. "That light was real!"

Dr. Parsons smiled inquisitively.

"I was trying to hang a lantern on the gate post so you wouldn't pass us," Jake explained. "But I fell and broke the damn thing. I was just going back to the house when I heard your voices."

"It was sure good to see you," Dr. Parsons said. "I don't know about Jim, but I just about had it."

Jim Caldwell smiled nervously. Doc just wasn't made for this country, he thought as he returned his empty cup to the table.

"I want you to know I appreciate very much what you've done for us," Jake said.

"Think nothing of it," Jim said modestly. "That's what neighbours are for."

A few moments later a sharp cry brought Dr. Parsons and Jake to Martha's bedside. The blankets had fallen on the floor, revealing her swollen fingers clawed deep into the sheet beneath her.

"Jake!" She cried, lifting her head slightly, only to thrust it even deeper into her pillow. "Oh, Jake!" she cried. He took her hand, feeling her nails pierce his skin.

"I'm right here, darling," he said. "Everything is gonna be all right."

Dr. Parsons' hands reached forward. Jake closed his eyes. Slowly the head protruded. Martha pursed her lips as the pressure pains pushed her to the edge of unconsciousness. Now the shoulders became visible. The doctor tugged gently. Supporting the head with his right hand, his left moved forward to guide the rest of the body to freedom. After he cut the umbilical cord, he raised the infant by its feet. For a few seconds the silence that followed was heavy with suspense. Only Martha's breathing could be heard. Then Dr. Parsons applied the traditional slaps on the buttocks and the baby started to cry, filling the room with the promise of life.

"It's a boy!" Jake exclaimed, overwhelmed with joy. "We'll call him 'Lorne', doctor," he said gratefully. "After you."

Dr. Parsons gently lowered the child at Martha's side.

"Is he pretty, Jake?" She asked softly.

"The prettiest, darling. The prettiest baby in the whole world."

"I'm so happy," she said, her sensitive fingers gliding curiously over the baby's face. She sensed the softness of the skin, the beginning of hair on the baby's head. It seemed to compensate for her inability to see him. As she turned her head closer to her tiny son, Martha kissed him gently on the cheek, tears glistening in her unseeing eyes.

II

It was August, but only the calendar indicated it. To the people in Edmonton it felt more like late autumn. The mercury, which only a week earlier had soared to the stifling nineties, now had its ups and downs between forty and fifty degrees Fahrenheit. Thick, dark gray clouds bombarded the city with vast quantities of aqueous marbles which exploded into miniature fountains in the nearly deserted streets.

The weather seemed to accentuate the dreariness of the times, for this was the year of 1939 which, despite reports to the contrary, still bore the harrowing stamp of the Depression. Little was it realized at the time, that Germany was about to solve the economic problems of North America by plunging the world into its second world war.

Lorne, who had entered this cesspool of iniquity almost a decade ago, was still far too young to despair. Permeated with the ideals and hopes that characterize every new generation, he still believed in a promising tomorrow.

His robust appearance, the serious expression on his face, made him look considerably older than he was. But inside he was still a boy whose needs were primarily sensuous.

Grateful for the partial protection provided by the awning of a confectionery, he feasted his eyes on a tantalizing window display of candies, chocolates and nuts.

Just think, he inferred enviously, if you owned a place like that, you could eat that stuff all day long.

He loved sweets, particularly peanut brittle the way his aunt Eileen made it.

But Lorne did not see his aunt very often, because his father avoided Boris Dobrynchuk, her husband, with the same immutable contempt a monk employs in declining an invitation to a game of poker.

"I wasn't long, was I?"

Lorne turned around with a start. "No, dad," he said. And encouraged by his father's smile, he asked: "Did you get it?"

Jake glanced at the growing puddle of water that encircled his feet like a fallen halo. "Get what?" he said, stalling for time to formulate an answer, any answer - except the stock reply of 'no, not yet.'

"The job."

"Oh, the job," Jake said in mock surprise. "Yes, I've got a job."

"Really, dad?" Lorne inquired unbelievingly. "What kind of work is it?"

Jake hesitated. He wanted his son to be happy, but not at the expense of a lie. Still the truth was worse. How could he tell his boy that he was not wanted, that he would have to look for work again tomorrow and the following day and so on? How could he explain that he had to beg to sell his labor? Still it was the bitter truth, difficult to accept for an adult, but totally incomprehensible to a child. Tomorrow would be no different than yesterday, next month no different than last month: the future like the past. It meant roaming the streets in competition with countless other persons searching for the same fictitious salvation.

It meant frequenting the shrinking number of business enterprises, knowing the answer before asking the question, yet persisting because sitting in a bleak room was infinitely worse, even though that room was home.

No, one must never drift into idleness, for inactivity leads to contemplation and to meditate is like nibbling at the forbidden fruit of the Tree of Knowledge and thus learn that those resurrected from the gutter are small in number.

"What kind of work, dad?" Lorne repeated, impatience spilling over in his voice.

"Prospecting," Jake blurted. It was no lie, merely an ambiguous answer. He actually did expect to be prospecting: not for gold, but for work, which wasn't any easier to find.

"You mean we've got to leave Edmonton?" Lorne asked excitedly, visions of nuggets in a shallow mountain creek flashing before his eyes. "Maybe," Jake replied evasively. And eager to change the subject, he added: "Come on, let's go home."

Ignoring the drenching rain, they headed for their one-room abode on 97th Street in silence. Their reticence was unusual considering the past and regrettable in view of the future, for after today they would never speak to each other again.

Charlie Wong, their Chinese landlord, awaited them with a confusing monologue in broken English.

"Mistuh Vincent has lent, I hope," he erupted amid mystical gestures. "Me been vellee patient, no kidding. No more wait. Lent oh out. Vellee solly, especially foh boy."

"No need to worry, Charlie," Jake said with an artificial smile. "You'll have the rent next week."

"Vellee solly. No lent, no loom," Charlie explained stubbornly. "I gottuh pay bills, too, you know. Don't want to lose my house. Wuk hard all my life. Lailway. Got killed almost..."

"All right, Charlie," Jake interrupted," no use telling me your life story. You'll have your money tomorrow."

"What time?" Charlie asked, hope and suspicion blending in his eyes.

"Sometime before noon," Jake replied more confidently than he felt.

Without uttering another word, the retired railroad worker, with few fond memories to call his own, walked away to his modest quarters.

Once upstairs, Lorne asked: "How are you gonna get it, dad?"

Jake stroked his son's hair and smiled: "Don't you worry about it, my boy. We won't have to sleep out in the rain."

Lorne knew better than to pursue the subject any further. Instead he picked up his favorite book, sat down on the davenport and soon was absorbed in Tarzan's triumphs and tribulations in some remote danger infested jungle.

The smell of bacon, hissing appetizingly on the hotplate, failed to penetrate the imaginary vines. Even the sound of the crisping meat was lost in the din of roaring lions and snapping crocodiles.

"Time to eat," Jake announced a few minutes later.

After supper Jake announced that he would go out for a couple of hours. As he put on his shabby winter coat, he said: "Better give Tarzan a rest tonight,

Lorne. It's time you brush up on English. School starts in only two weeks, you know."

"Okay, dad," Lorne said without enthusiasm. English, especially spelling, was his weakest subject.

When Jake had left, Lorne picked up the soiled tea towel, flung it across his shoulder and started the dishes.

He turned around with sudden apprehension when he heard a knock at the door. Visitors were rare, especially at night, and he wondered if it could be Mr. Wong again. But when he opened the door he recognized Allan Batford, their next door neighbor, standing smilingly in the dim hall light.

"Is your father home?" he asked.

"No, he left about five minutes ago," Lorne replied.

"Oh, that's too bad. I must have just missed him," Batford commented good-naturedly. He was a corpulent man in his early forties with a receding hairline and a bushy moustache which usually displayed lost food particles from a recent meal. Noticing the tea towel on Lorne's shoulder, he remarked: "Doing dishes, eh?"

Lorne nodded with a blush. He liked Mr. Batford. On several occasions he had run errands for him with candy, or less frequently small change, as a reward.

Batford leaned nonchalantly against the doorjamb, his eyes scrutinizing the room, his mind mapping his strategy.

"Any idea when he'll be back?" he asked.

"He said he'd be away for a couple of hours, Mr. Batford. Anything I can tell him?"

"No, it's nothing important," Batford said as he pulled himself erect again. "I guess, I'll see him later."

He involuntarily recalled how only minutes ago he had watched Jake leave. "Say, don't let me stop you from finishing your work. You just go right ahead."

Lorne returned to the dripping plates and cutlery on the narrow counter near the room's solitary window. He wondered why the man did not leave. Batford stepped inside and closed the door quietly behind him.

"I saw you with Karen Dobie yesterday," he said as he sat down on the davenport.

Lorne felt his face redden as he wondered what precisely Mr. Batford had seen.

"Is she your girlfriend?"

"No, just a friend," Lorne said, shrugging his shoulders with feigned indifference.

"I bet you've kissed her," Batford continued, wishing he could sneak out for just a moment and have a beer.

Lorne hesitated. It's none of his business, he thought rebelliously.

"I bet you have," Batford insisted.

"Couple of times," Lorne admitted as he put the dishes away.

"Like it?"

"Not bad."

"I saw her just before coming here," Batford lied happily. "From my window I can look right into her bathroom."

Lorne remained silent, feeling increasingly uneasy by the presence of the uninvited visitor.

"She had just taken a bath and had no clothes on," Batford continued, getting excited by the products of his own imagination. "If you want you can come over to my room some time and see it for yourself. How would you like that?"

"I don't know," Lorne said noncommittally, fervently wishing his father would suddenly walk in.

"She's a very pretty girl," Batford went on. "Have you ever seen a girl without any clothes on, Lorne?" Lorne lowered his eyes.

"I thought so," Batford concluded. "Tell me, what is it that makes girls so different from boys?"

Lorne bit his lip, bravely suppressing the tears of anxiety.

Batford laughed nervously. "Come on, quit playing so dumb. I saw you two behind Wong's garage yesterday."

Lorne felt his stomach twist in agony.

"Girls pee differently, don't they?" Lorne nodded.

"Gets you all worked up inside to see that, doesn't it?" Batford suggested lasciviously. "I bet your father doesn't know about your games, does he?"

Lorne suddenly raised his eyes and searched his tormentor's face for a sign of mercy.

"Please, Mr. Batford," he pleaded, "don't tell him."

"Well, if you promise to be a good boy, I won't," Batford said magnanimously.

"I promise, Mr. Batford," Lorne pledged quickly, grateful for the surge of relief that swept through his tormented soul. "From now on I'll run to the store for you anytime you want me to and you don't have to give me anything."

"Come on and sit here beside me," Batford said, patting the davenport. Lorne swiftly complied.

"That's my boy," Batford said as he put his arm around Lorne's shoulders. "From now on we can share secrets, you and me. We are friends and we'll be nice to each other, won't we, Lorne?" Lorne readily agreed. He felt very grown-up now.

Carefully weighing the situation, Batford looked at Lorne's blushing face. Suddenly he asked: "Do you know what masturbating is, Lorne?"

"No, I don't," he confessed his innocence.

Batford grinned forgivingly, countless tiny beads of sweat glistening on his brow. "That's all right, Lorne," he said. And opening his fly: "I'll show you what I mean."

When Jake entered his room, he stumbled upon the most revolting scene his eyes had ever beheld. The loathsome sight triggered a fury that dwarfed his anger of fifteen years ago when he had found his first wife in bed with his boss.

The devil himself could not have enraged Jake as much as the debauchee who had defiled his son.

"You filthy, rotten bastard," Jake cried as he picked up Batford by the lapels. "You're gonna pay for this."

Lorne fled from the room as Batford stepped back and stammered: "No, Jake, don't hit me. You don't understand, I can't help it..."

The plea for leniency came to an abrupt end when Jake smashed his fist into Batford's face. The next blow tore into Batford's stomach, making him gasp for air as he doubled up. "No, no more," Batford lisped as Jake put his hands under his victim's armpits and straightened him again.

"Walluh hell goin on?" Charlie Wong inquired as he almost stepped into the room. But the sight of blood oozing from Batford's mutilated mouth made Charlie beat a hasty retreat.

Jake battered the pervert to vent the wrath that raged beyond reason, beyond pity in his shattered soul. Batford, who was too frightened to effectively defend himself, finally slumped to the floor. Several times Jake's fists crashed into the wall before he realized that Batford lay at his feet, bits of plaster covering the still figure. Before Jake could kneel beside him, he was roughly pulled back by a burly policeman who had arrived on the scene in response to Charlie's frantic summons.

The next moment was filled with the sound of many voices. The cool steel of handcuffs reminded Jake that the nightmare was real.

A middle-aged man with a stethoscope dangling on his chest, squatted beside Batford whose blood-spattered face was molded in a ghoulish grin, his eyes staring weirdly into eternity. A moment later the doctor rose again, announcing with condemning simplicity: "Nothing I can do for him. He's dead."

But the ominous implication of the words failed to register in Jake's dazed mind.

"Well, we'd better head for the morgue," the constable said matter-of-factly. Jake followed with the docility of a lamb.

At the doorway Charlie Wong gave a confusing account of what he thought had happened, while another policeman made a few notes. When Jake brushed past his landlord, Charlie asked indignantly: "Who pay lent now?"

In the hall the curious tenants parted to let Jake and his escort through, the noisy conversation of a moment ago suddenly reduced to a whisper.

Outside a small group of bystanders eyed him with the same peculiar delight people feel in Madame Tussauds Chamber of Horrors.

Before stepping into the police car, Jake intuitively jerked his head to the left. For only a moment his eyes rested on Lorne who sat on the sidewalk across the street: his face hidden by his folded arms which rested on his knees. The sight of the small, forlorn boy, huddled in utter hopelessness against the brick wall of another rooming house, was to haunt Jake for the rest of his life.

September 10, 1939, saw the opening of the Rex versus Hitler case in Canada. The beginning of military oppression in Europe spelled the end of economic depression in North America. The second largest nation in the world, in a deep economic coma only a few weeks earlier, flexed its industrial muscles impressively and promptly received a clean bill of wealth from the Toronto Stock Exchange.

Businessmen throughout the country suddenly found themselves so involved in preparing for the golden harvest of the future, that few paused long enough to pragmatize the lessons of the past. Instead they assisted the federal government in the planning and building of an economy based on war.

Things had never seemed better, except for those who had been assigned the unenviable task of dragging the products of the revitalized economy into the inferno of war, so that destruction would guarantee production--and profits, of course....

As in other wars, those who suffered most, profited the least, while those who profited most, suffered the least. It was all part of a gigantic attempt to create a better world by force. The scheme gradually gained momentum; news editors everywhere gratefully scanned the growing selection of headline copy. Events, which a month ago rated front page material, now appeared drastically abridged on an inside page. A good example in this category was the Vincent murder trial.

The only newspaper in Alberta to cover the trial was The Edmonton Sentinel, a biweekly tabloid in the midst of becoming a daily. If the metamorphosis had not been accompanied by an unexpected breakdown of the newly installed teletype equipment, the paper would have been filled almost exclusively with wire copy, but as it was, replacement parts could not be obtained too quickly and as a result local news regained its former popularity. The case of Rex versus Jake Leonard Vincent was described in great detail on page five between an illustration showing the latest in brassieres and an ad eulogizing a new brand of dog food.

But in all the hullabaloo about Hitler, no newsman had discovered the front page angle of the Vincent trial. When a man's life is at stake, he normally talks a blue streak to escape the noose, but Jake Vincent had said little more than his name during his six-week incarceration. This was particularly frustrating for Duane Thorneycroft, counsel for the defense. During the two weeks which had preceded the preliminary hearing, the brilliant criminal lawyer had exhausted his rhetoric in an all-out effort to make his client talk, but to no avail. In desperation, Thorneycroft had finally ordered a psychiatric examination, but the results had merely confirmed his own suspicion: Jake Vincent was sane, but incredibly stubborn. Mitigating circumstances can move a jury to return a verdict of manslaughter, evidence of extreme provocation can result in an acquittal. The lawyer knew that without either, a date with the hangman was virtually a certainty. Thorneycroft's only hope of saving Jake from the gallows now rested exclusively with the witnesses.

Duane Thorneycroft nevertheless continued the case and retained his sanity in the comforting knowledge that the handsome fee he planned to levy would be paid by Boris Dobrynchuk promptly and without a murmur of protest.

Toward the conclusion of the three-day trial, the astute lawyer began to dissect the evidence of Dr. Quentin Alsbury with such finesse and thoroughness that doubt manifested itself for the first time since the opening of the case. The pathologist's composure crumbled in the heat of Thorneycroft's relentless questioning. The presiding judge leaned forward with renewed interest, spilling some papers on the court registrar's desk below. Several jurors stirred in their seats, no longer certain of the accused's guilt.

Even Jake's interest was aroused. Until then he had followed the proceedings with the attention of a centenarian attending a lecture on sexual compatibility. He had never known how much rigmarole was required before they could hang a man. He failed to understand why all these total strangers suddenly took such an interest in him, when only a few months ago no one had given a damn whether he prospered or perished. Jake did not fear the possibility of being hanged: it was the waiting time he dreaded. Somehow the noose seemed less cruel than a long prison sentence: there was nothing left to live for except Lorne and he could not help his son from a prison cell. Jake was too much of a realist to hope for an acquittal and merely smiled when his sister mentioned the word.

The fact was he had killed a man and for a good reason made Batford no less dead nor the offense--to Jake's way of thinking--any less serious.

Now, as the trial approached its climax, Jake was surer than ever that he had been wise in refusing to explain what had driven him to attack Batford. He believed his silence was justified because it had spared his son the agony of having to recount and relive the revolting affair in public.

"Dr. Alsbury," Thorneycroft continued, leaning against the wooden balustrade of the jury box to make certain that the jurors could hear the witness, "you said in your evidence in chief that the deceased, James Kenneth Batford, died as a result of a brain hemorrhage, isn't that correct?"

"It is," Dr. Alsbury replied curtly.

"Now, isn't it true that there are several possible causes for such hemorrhages?"

"Yes, but..."

"And that an alcoholic has a greater chance of suffering such a hemorrhage than a sober person?"

"I have no doubt about the cause," the pathologist said testily.

"Please limit yourself to answering the questions I put to you, doctor," Thorneycroft advised authoritatively. "I'll repeat the question: 'Is an alcoholic more liable to suffer a hemorrhage than a non-alcoholic person?'"

"Yes." Dr. Alsbury almost spat out the affirmative. He seldom lost his temper, but nearly two hours of questioning had rubbed his nerves raw.

"Would you please tell the court why this is so?" the lawyer asked, smiling almost imperceptibly. We'll let him trap himself, he thought happily. It will look more convincing that way.

Dr. Alsbury took a deep breath as he collected his wits "If a person indulges in alcohol to an excessive degree," he started, "he stands a better than average chance in the long run of getting arteriosclerosis." He raised his hand to his mouth and coughed unconvincingly. Then he added: "Since the hardening of the arteries is often a contributing factor in hemorrhages, it is correct to say that an alcoholic runs a greater risk of suffering a hemorrhage than an average person."

Thorneycroft welcomed the silence that followed. Let it sink in, he advised himself. It was so quiet in the old courtroom that the stenographer beside the registrar could be heard turning a page of his shorthand notebook.

"Thank you, doctor," Thorneycroft said finally. After transferring his weight from his left to his right leg, his elbows still resting on the jury box's balustrade, he went on: "Dr. Alsbury, did your autopsy on the remains of James Batford reveal any evidence of arteriosclerosis?"

Crown counsel Ian Fenningham ticked impatiently with his pencil on the cover of the preliminary hearing transcript. He felt his leg muscles tighten as he prepared himself to jump to his feet the moment this would appear warranted and advantageous.

"The deceased suffered from an advanced case of arteriosclerosis," the witness volunteered wearily.

Thorneycroft acknowledged the legal plum with a faint nod. Time to move in for the kill, he inferred. "Dr. Alsbury," he said with apparent nonchalance, "a little earlier you testified that your autopsy also revealed damaged tissue on the back of the skull. Did you also notice any damage to the skull itself?"

"No, I didn't."

"Are you able to render an opinion as to how the skin injury was sustained?"

"No."

"Are you sure?"

Fenningham rose from his chair with the speed of a rocket. "I object, my lord," he announced briskly. "I submit, with respect, that my learned friend is belittling the competence of the witness."

"I am sure Mr. Thorneycroft has no such intent," the judge adjudicated. "Objection overruled. Please answer the question, doctor."

"I know I can't speculate what the cause of the injury was without resorting to pure conjecture," Dr. Alsbury said.

The defense counsel suddenly walked to his desk and picked up a thick manuscript. "Perhaps I can refresh your memory by reciting some of your statements at the preliminary hearing when you seemed less reserved," Thorneycroft said as he paged through the transcript. When he located the desired passage, he turned to the judge and said: "Second volume, my lord, page seventeen, question 342." A few moments later, the bulky manuscript balancing precariously on his outstretched hand, he continued: "Question: 'Dr. Alsbury, could you tell the court whether the skin injury on the back of the deceased's head could have been inflicted by a man's hand or fist?' Answer: 'Definitely not. The injury suggested the use of a blunt instrument, like a piece of pipe.' "Do you recall saying that, Dr. Alsbury?" "No," the pathologist snapped defiantly.

"Do you still hold the same view?"

The witness weighed the cardinal question carefully. Then he said with the solemnity of a wedding ceremony: "I do."

His path cleared of legal debris, Thorneycroft walked confidently to the witness box, rested his right hand on the edge while his left pressed the transcript against his side, and said in a loud and clear voice: "Dr. Alsbury, I suggest to you that James Kenneth Batford fell accidentally in the defendant's room, struck his head against the wood stove and suffered as a result the fatal hemorrhage. Judging by the injury which you said could have been inflicted by a blunt instrument, would you agree that this is possible?"

Fenningham scribbled some hasty notes to bridge the unbearable silence that followed the seemingly daring question. The prosecutor sensed the debilitation of his case. Even if Alsbury would say no, the defense would save its case by producing half a dozen other pathologists, if necessary, who would say yes.

Thorneycroft wondered how long he could stare at the witness without blinking his eyes. Dr. Quentin Alsbury secretly reveled in the suspense only he could end. It did him good to see his interrogator sweat+. Finally he said: "It is possible."

"Thank you. That's all," Thorneycroft said triumphantly. And turning to the judge he announced with a sigh of relief: "No further witnesses, my lord."

The prosecution summed up its case by describing Jake as a ruthless individual who had used his brute strength to vent his anger over Batford's refusal to lend him rent money. Fenningham called it murder pure and simple, then urged the jury to find the accused guilty as such.

Thorneycroft quoted the backbone of common law which states that no man is guilty of an offense until proven guilty beyond a reasonable doubt, then spent the balance of his summation planting the seeds of dubiety in the minds of the jurors.

"All we know," he said emphatically, "is that a fight took place. We don't know who started this fight or what it was about. The Crown's allegation that it was about money must be rejected, since there is no direct evidence to support it. But more significant than anything else in this trial is the fact that the Crown has failed to prove that the defendant actually caused James Batford's death."

He paused briefly as he placed his hands on the partition that separated him from the jury. If his words had hit home, the twelve impassive faces did not reflect it.

"You cannot send a man to his doom on the basis of assumptions," he continued with a sprinkle of fervor in his voice. "So let us concern ourselves with the facts. You heard Constable Robert Finnigan testify that when he entered the defendant's room, he saw him strike the wall with bare fists while Batford lay at his feet. A subsequent police investigation found nothing to suggest that any type of weapon had been used in the fight. No knife, no hammer, not even a piece of pipe. What the police did find was that the deceased's head rested against the kitchen stove. The Defense holds this as proof positive that James Kenneth Batford fell during the fight and accidentally struck his head against the stove, thus suffering the brain hemorrhage which subsequently caused his death. For that reason I ask you to find the defendant not guilty."

The judge charged the jury during a one-hour address. He explained the legal bases for the three possible verdicts - guilty as charged, guilty of manslaughter or not guilty. He commented in detail on the value of some of the evidence submitted, but terming Charlie Wong's contribution 'sincere, but confusing.'

After the jurors had filed silently out of the courtroom, a grim-faced guard led Jake to the prisoner's quarters.

"What do you make of it?" Jake asked as he sat down on a wooden bench below the room's solitary window, its heavy bars projecting a familiar shadow pattern on the floor.

"You'll hang," the guard prophesied impassively.

"I hope you're right," Jake said earnestly.

"The rope doesn't frighten you?" the guard asked, his beady eyes narrowing with incredulity.

"Life frightens me more," Jake confessed, and he volunteered: "If death differs from life, it can only be an improvement for me."

The guard creased his brow with a reproachful frown. Then he predicted in a reprimanding manner: "You'll change your tune when you mount the scaffold." And ploughing his arched fingers like a giant comb through his gray hair, he thought: don't kid me, you're scared shitless - like the others...

"Have you ever seen a hanging?" Jake asked. "Several," the guard replied, a peculiar pride permeating his voice. "I used to be a guard at the Fort Saskatchewan Gaol."

It was the prison where Jake had been detained during the past two months, a former post of the North West Mounted Police twenty-six miles northeast of Edmonton.

Jake studied the frayed ends of his shoe laces as he wondered aloud: "What's it like?"

"I think the waiting is worse than the execution. The actual hanging doesn't take long if you're lucky."

"Lucky?" Jake echoed apprehensively, recalling the scarcity of luck in his life.

"Yeah," the guard explained patiently, "usually the neck breaks after the trapdoor is sprung and you're pronounced dead a few minutes later, but sometimes the neck does not break." He paused, studying Jake's muscular neck, recalling a prisoner kicking wildly in mid-air: the contorted blue face with the bulging eyes.

"What then?" Jake asked, his stomach now twisted in dire anticipation.

"You choke to death, unless the hangman intervenes by adding his weight to yours and giving it a good jerk."

'If you're lucky.' The words reverberated with gruesome clarity in Jake's mind. 'If you're lucky.' He smiled cynically. How often had he been lucky? When was the last time he had been lucky? And the few times he had been lucky, were they not simply preliminary necessities to greater tragedy?

Without his promotion to foreman, would his heart have been scarred by Joan Bendrell, his first wife? Was not the love and devotion Martha had given him outweighed by the anguish he had suffered because of her death? And now Lorne, the very propellant of his life, had been separated from him through the perversity of a stranger.

No, Life had been unmasked too many times as an incorrigible villain to leave any form of hope in Jake's tormented soul. Instead Death beckoned like an unexpected friend, offering the only apparent way out of a labyrinth of painful bewilderment.

Perhaps the exit the gallows affords is a dreadful experience, but at least it is deprived of the uncertainty which makes life so often unbearable.

Jake sighed with resignation. The flash of fear the guard had ignited in his heart had dissipated.

Twice the jurors returned to the courtroom to have certain parts of the evidence read back to them. "...the waiting is worse..." Finally, after three hours of deliberations and interruptions, the court was reconvened.

As Jake returned to the prisoner's box, Eileen rushed to his side.

"We all pray for you, Jake," she confided, her eyes suffused with tears. "God bless you."

Unprepared for his sister's religious outburst, Jake merely smiled in response.

His smile was transformed to a grin by an impromptu vision of Thorneycroft praying on his knees in the privacy of the courthouse john.

"Order in court!" the sheriff barked.

Everyone rose to his feet as the judge entered the courtroom. The red-robed judiciary slowly ascended to his elevated seat. His step suggested regal dignity, but in fact it was a masterful cover-up for his rheumatic affliction. He acknowledged the salutatory bows of the two lawyers with two quick nods and lowered himself gracefully into his chair, his creviced face reflecting fatigue and boredom. It was nearly supper time.

A few moments later the court registrar inquired in a solemn tone: "Members of the jury, have you arrived at a verdict?"

A bespectacled door-to-door salesman temporarily promoted to jury foreman, shot up like a jack-in-the-box.

"We have," he announced with the same ardor he employed in cajoling gullible housewives to buy his brushes and spot removers.

"How say you," the registrar continued imperturbably, "do you find the prisoner at the bar guilty of the offense whereof he stands charged or not guilty?"

The foreman unceremoniously cleared his throat as he cast a furtive glance at the judge and said: "We find the accused guilty of manslaughter."

Jake stared at the man with a look of utter disbelief.

After the judge had satisfied himself that the verdict was unanimous, he turned to Jake and inquired formally: "Does the prisoner have anything to say before I pass sentence?"

Unable to push words past his quivering lips, Jake merely shook his head.

"Please answer the question, Mr. Vincent," the judge said sympathetically.

"No," Jake heard himself say and he thought: what difference does it make? Who gives a damn what I say or think?

The judge's voice reached him through a haze of bitter confusion. The words pierced his tortured mind incompletely, but the essence registered like acid in his heart: his wretched existence was to be prolonged in a penitentiary for twenty years unless Death would rescue him some other way....

III

An azure sky dappled with puffs of white clouds served as a halcyon background against which the tapestry of the trees exhibited their green splendor, the fresh leaves not yet stained by urban grime. The fragrance of spring made one appreciate one's olfactory sense, at least in those shrinking areas where the air was not yet polluted by the effluvia of traffic and industry. Birds provided their melodious music wherever trees were still tolerated and in dauntless defiance of the hubbub of city life.

George Foster, like most of his fellow teachers at Aldon High, continued his futile efforts to hold the interest of his pupils. The majority of students were obviously daydreaming. And why not? This was the first real spring day in 1945 and it seemed a downright shame to be penned up in a stuffy classroom when Nature was at its seductive best.

Even he found his thoughts wandering out of the classroom with alarming frequency. At times he had the distinct sensation of seeing and hearing himself as if George Foster was somebody else and he was merely an onlooker.

"Heat," he heard himself say, "is the energy possessed by molecules."

He surveyed the class with a surge of sympathy in his heart. He knew that many of the children's fathers were overseas like Bud, his son, giving the Jerries hell. He also knew that some would never return: Murphy, Stanfield and Vincent, maybe more. They were the few of the many who had made the supreme sacrifice to save the world from fascism.

"The hotter an object is," he continued stubbornly, "the faster its molecules move and the more room they occupy. This explains why matter expands when it is heated."

Thank God this was the last class of the day. Only a few more weeks and summer holidays would start. Now he could see himself stroll alongside his son discussing the depravities of war, comparing his experiences in the First World War with those of Bud in the Second.

"Heat can also change the physical or chemical state of matter," he said mechanically. "Can you give me an example of a physical change caused by heat, Dolores?"

Dolores Selby's face was the epitome of bewilderment.

"The molecules of an object," she started diffidently, then she paused in sanguine expectation of a helpful whisper, but instead the class exploded in boisterous laughter. In a desperate bid to save face, she asked: "Could you please repeat the question, sir?"

"Of course, I could," Foster said sternly, "but why should I? You're not suffering from a sudden hearing impairment, are you?"

A second salvo of laughter rocked the classroom, but the science teacher cut it short.

"Enough1" he said louder than he had meant to. Show them who's boss, George, he told himself. If you don't they'll walk right over you.

When the last giggle had been strangulated, he asked: "All right, who can answer my question?" Utter silence.

"1 didn't know that spring fever was that contagious," Foster confessed. "What about you, Lorne, did the epidemic get you, too?"

Foster was curious to know whether modesty or inattention was responsible for Lorne Vincent's silence. Lorne was his brightest student, but he wasn't a show-off.

"Did you hear my question?" the teacher prodded.

"Yessir."

"Well?"

"Melting ice is an example of a physical change caused by heat and burning wood produces a chemical change," Lorne said mellifluously.

"Excellent," Foster praised, "and thanks for the bonus. I only asked for an example of a physical change."

He glanced at his watch and announced: "For next week study sources of heat and answer the questions on page 307."

The bell rang a moment later and the students left the classroom with cataclysmic haste. The tumult of falling books and stumbling feet still echoing in his ears, he noticed Lorne at his desk.

"I've finished those equations you gave me yesterday," Lorne explained his presence as he handed the teacher a sheet of paper.

Foster, who taught chemistry in the higher grades, checked the results quickly. A moment later he shook his head and said: "What are we going to do with you next year?"

"Pardon me, sir?" Lorne asked, visibly baffled by the unexpected question.

"Next year you'll be in Grade X where normally the students receive their first year of chemistry, but everything I'll be teaching will sound so elementary to you, that I'll have a tough time keeping you awake."

Lorne smiled gratefully. "I take it then that my equations were properly balanced," he said confidently.

"Every one of them," the teacher said. "You know, Lorne, you've got a better grasp on chemistry than some of my Grade XII students." "Thanks to you, sir," Lorne commented modestly.

"Nonsense. I spend less time on the subject with you than I do with my regular students and yet you assimilate the stuff better than any of them. No, it's you, Lorne. You have a real knack for science in general and chemistry in particular. Has anyone ever mentioned the possibility of skipping a grade to you?"

"No, sir, and I don't think anyone will, because it wouldn't work."

"Why not?"

Lorne smiled apologetically "Because," he said, "I'm lousy in English and worse in history."

George Foster shook his head pensively. "It's a pity," he said, frowning slightly.

Lorne shrugged his shoulders. "It doesn't really matter," he said indifferently. "I enjoy school. I'm in no rush. The only reason I'm ahead in chemistry is because I spend a lot of time on it. It isn't really work or study, it's more like a form of recreation to me."

"In that case you may belong to the fortunate few who get paid for enjoying themselves," Foster said cheerfully. "Most people, you know, are interested in one thing and make a living at something else. The bookkeeper who excelled as a hockey player until a car crash changed his life, the cop who loved to play piano, but was never good enough at it to translate his talent into cash and," Foster added facetiously, "we must, of course, not forget the poor devils who simply don't know what they want and in final desperation become successful politicians."

Lorne laughed obligingly, then he asked: "have you got something else for me to work on?"

"Look," Foster said with feigned firmness as he walked Lorne to the door, "even chemists stop for a break now and then. You take yours this weekend and I'll dream something up for you in the meantime."

"Fair enough," Lorne said submissively as he stepped into the deserted corridor. "Goodbye, sir."

Ten minutes later Lorne parked his bicycle at the rear of Stenwey Drugs and walked into the store.

"I thought you had forgotten about us," Lorraine Phelps greeted him.

Lorne gave the pretty sales clerk the once-over and said rather saucily: "how can a rooster like me forget a cute chick like you?"

"Your chemicals came in today," she volunteered, smiling appreciatively. "I put them with your deliveries."

"Much oblige," Lorne said as he walked to a small desk.

As Lorne ripped the parcel open, a man walked into the store and Lorraine left to serve him.

Lorne listened intently to the ensuing conversation. It seemed all right. The customer bought some cigarettes and asked her about the new shopping center they were building across the street. Lorne did not believe in taking chances when Mr. Stenwey was away. He knew that some bastards came in to buy some rubbers simply to see what she would say if they asked her for a date at the same time. Or smart aleck questions like if the amusement tax was included in the price. Lorne hated guys who got a charge out of embarrassing a young girl. In the case of the amusement tax joker, he had dashed into the store and told the guy to beat it. The punk had sneered at him, but he had left just the same.

Lorraine had shown her gratitude for his intervention a few days later during a heavy petting session in the storeroom. It had rained cats and dogs that night and Mr. Stenwey had left for the evening. At first they had chewed the fat for a while, but it had quickly become clear that they were not discussing what they were thinking about. He had followed her into the stockroom ostensibly to help her carry some boxes of chocolate bars to the front of the store, but instead her proximity had set off a chain reaction of sensuality. If it had not been for a rain-soaked cop walking in shortly afterward to buy some gumdrops, Lorne might have been well on his way to fatherhood by now. Of course, you can't be sure. Some guys jazz around for years and get away with it, while others try their first shot and bingo!

Lorne quickly packed his deliveries into a double canvas bag while mentally composing the quickest route. He completed his errands inside an hour and made it home just before six.

Home! He had lived with his aunt and uncle nearly six years now, but he still found it often hard to believe that the stately residence on Gloucester Crescent really was his home. It was so much like a dream which could end any moment that he had failed to gain a sense of security.

There was something forbidding about the six bedroom mansion. Perhaps it was the ivy-covered brick wall that circumscribed it or the temple-like basalt steps that led to the huge front door which was seldom used. The tall stone columns that flanked the entrance to the two-story building and partially supported the roof together with the large wrought iron gates which filled the gap in the brick stockade made the house look more like an institute than a residence.

Lorne parked his bike inside the toolshed and entered the house through its side entrance. As he climbed the stairs on his way to his room, he heard a woman's tear-choked voice in the hall.

"Please, Mr. Dobrynchuk, no foreclosure. Give us a chance. We'll raise the money somehow."

Lorne stepped into his room without hearing his uncle's answer. He didn't have to hear it to know it, Uncle Boris didn't believe in compassion. To him ruthlessness and success in business were synonymous.

Lorne put his chemicals on a chair and walked into the adjacent bathroom.

He studied his reflection in the mirror while combing his hair with casual interest. He discerned a face that had largely lost its boyish look. It was not just the beginning of a beard that made him look at least two years older than he was; it was primarily the relentless bombardment of disillusioning blows which had accelerated his journey toward maturity.

There is no substitute for parental love. Love filters the harshness out of life and when it is reinforced by reason and discipline it gives a child confidence without which life is unbearable.

The Dobrynchuk residence was not a citadel of spiritual strength. It provided no more platonic intimacy than a hotel, making it a home in a physical sense only.

Lorne's aunt took a genuine interest in his welfare, but sincerity without insight is an impotent virtue. Eileen Dobrynchuk, never having had children of her own, was completely unprepared for the guardianship of her nephew thrust upon her by Fate. She was totally incapable of understanding the intricacies of a teenage mind and thus failed to foster the close relationship she desired so much with her brother's son.

As for Boris Dobrynchuk, the problem was far simpler. He saw Lorne as a pecuniary barnacle on the hull of the S.S. Ruthless Enterprise of which he was the captain. He took no more interest in the boy than he did in his wife's membership in the local garden club. It was a strange marriage of convenience.

Boris was twenty years older than his forty-one-year-old wife, but he did not look it. He was a short, stocky man with the face of a peasant and the mind of a mercenary. His bushy eyebrows accentuated the alertness in his dark brown eyes which were the focal point of his massive head. A pair of thick rubbery lips, trained to cling firmly to a fine cigar, was almost dwarfed by the enormity of a Negroid-like nose accustomed to the rich smell of garlic which saturated most of the food that passed his palate. His pate was covered by thick gray hair, except at the zenith where thinning vegetation failed to ensconce the pinkness of his scalp.

Eileen Dobrynchuk, who always wore dark clothes and never used makeup beyond the occasional lipstick. She was a slender woman with long dark hair tied in a Victorian knot, making her look more stern than she was.

To outsiders their conjugal venture seemed enigmatic, since they never showed signs of affection for each other and had very little in common. This was not a false impression. But where love was lacking, mutual respect was clearly evident. They complemented one another with remarkable success and so fulfilled each other's needs. They had both benefited from tying the nuptial knot. Boris had achieved the closest thing he could hope to attain in respectability and Eileen had found the financial security she had lacked in her youth.

As Lorne descended the wide stairway, the dinner gong sounded in the hallway.

It was exactly six o'clock. Punctuality was religiously adhered to in the Dobrynchuk household. Lorne seated himself at the side of the huge oval table and stiffly greeted his aunt and uncle.

Melvin, the butler, served the meal with his usual grace and dexterity. Dinner was always served at this time since Boris seldom came home at noon. The large crystal chandelier overhead silhouetted the butler's movements on the thick-piled Persian carpet. In addition to this enchanting source of light, three tall candles flickered festively along the prolate axis of the table.

The nutritious event passed in silence. Boris considered conversation taboo at mealtime.

Lorne thought about Lorraine and the big rock she had flashed before his eyes earlier that week. She had been pulled out of his orbit by some medical student who had put a deposit on her in the form of an impressive engagement ring. Lorne still felt pretty rotten about it, although he had secretly feared that something like that would happen all along. After all, what else can a fifteen-year-old boy expect from a girl almost eighteen?

Aunt Eileen glanced at her nephew, that product of ephemeral love bobbing helplessly in the vast ocean of Life. She thought about the striking resemblance between the boy and his father as she recalled her recent visit to Jake. Lorne's father was still alive, at least physically.

Instead of resting in his grave as a war casualty, he was slowly wasting away in the penitentiary.

When the last ray of hope had been snuffed out by the rejection of Thorneycroft's appeal to have Jake's conviction annulled, she had told Lorne that his father had been killed in the war. She had done so at the insistence of Jake who felt that it is better for a boy to grow up in the belief that his father is dead than be burdened with the knowledge of his father serving a twenty-year prison term.

Lorne had accepted the news without bursting into tears. Instead he had shocked her with painful frankness, asking her: "You mean I can stay here now for good?"

She had quickly pressed his head against her bosom so he could not see the tears that had sprung into her eyes. "Yes, darling," she had said, her voice betraying her emotion, "you can stay here as long as you want."

After dinner Lorne returned to his room, opened the bottom drawer of his chiffonier, pushed some underwear aside and gently lifted a two foot metal cylinder from its unorthodox hiding place. It was a small rocket with a bullet like nose and a perforated base. He placed the object on his desk in a vertical position and studied its simple shape with unadulterated delight. Tonight, he knew, would see a new altitude record in the field of backyard rocketry.

As he crushed and mixed his chemicals with his mortar and pestle, he recalled the thrills of his secret hobby. Secret because Uncle Boris would blow a fuse if he knew what went on at the rear of his estate under the cloak of darkness. It had all started a few months ago when Lorne had come across a book titled: Chemical Experiments for Fun.

Most of the experiments outlined in the book were too elementary to excite Lorne, but a chapter dealing with miniature rocket engines, greatly aroused his interest. His first model powered a toy car which traveled the twenty-foot concrete walk between the tool shed and the garage in record time, forcing the Dobrynchuk cat to increase the diameter of its tail to three times its normal circumference while en route to the nearest tree.

Subsequent experiments were conducted at the rear of the property which was less than a hundred feet from the Saskatchewan River. When Lorne hit upon the idea of vertical flight and managed to prepare a propellant that made it possible, he conducted all further launchings after nightfall.

His newest rocket, now pointing innocently at the ceiling, was in a class all its own. Until now Lorne had used odd lengths of pipe to fashion his projectiles, finding the waste heap of a downtown plumber a cheap and lavish source of such material. His latest model, however, was created by Dick Harman, a machinist who operated his own shop close to Stenwey Drugs. It cost six dollars and dwarfed its predecessors in size.

When Lorne had finished loading the chemical mixture into his rocket and furnished it with a fuse, he returned it to its hiding place He quickly tidied up his desk, then consulted his watch. It was just past seven o'clock. Wondering what to do next, he stared out of the window and noticed Harry Wenzel sitting in front of his small cabin.

Harry was the gardener who had landscaped and maintained the grounds since the mansion had been built some twenty-five years ago. Boris Dobrynchuk was his third employer here and the easiest to work for. The reason was simple: Boris did not know the first thing about horticulture and thus found himself in an awkward position to criticize Harry.

But Harry Wenzel did not take advantage of his superior's ignorance in botanic matters Harry loved his work and took great pride in keeping the grounds in tiptop shape. What Harry loathed were the winters when his responsibilities were augmented by innumerable tasks encephalically engineered by Boris and requiring the skills of a dozen craftsmen. Instead of cutting grass under a cheerful sun, he ended up cutting his fingers under a leaky sink. Instead of letting the fragrance of his flowers caress his nostrils, he held his breath while mixing paint and thinners. In addition he repaired locks, which he thought belonged in garbage cans instead of doors, fixed creaky stairs and performed a thousand other nightmarish tasks. At seventy-four such work can become mightily frustrating. Good Old Harry.

Lorne finally decided to study for next week's history exam. As he started to read, he wondered why he so disliked history. He remembered reading once that the only thing people learn from history is that people don't learn anything from history: *l'histoire sereatte*. People go right on making the same mistakes.

The First World War had been dubbed the war that would end all wars, but it hadn't. Wars don't end wars, Lorne reflected, only people can end wars. Now the Second World War was in its final stages, leaving millions dead, widowed, orphaned, maimed and mentally disturbed. Wars always exacted such an enormous price - for what? Nebuchadnezzar, Hannibal, Genghis Khan, Napoleon, and now Hitler. History repeats itself.

He started to read: "Canada obtained title to Sverdrup Island from Norway in 1931." Hooray, he thought, we sure needed it.

Around ten o'clock he went downstairs and bid his aunt good night, crowning the regular ritual with a kiss on her cheek which, as always, she returned with a motherly version of her own.

Back in his room he turned off the light and lay fully dressed on his bed in anticipation of his uncle's arrival. An hour later, on the verge of succumbing to sleep, he slowly and quietly opened his bedroom door. When he saw no light spilling under the door of his aunt's bedroom, he clamped his rocket and launching tube under his arm and managed to reach the side entrance of the house without making a sound. His hand on the door knob, he stood motionless for a few moments. When he heard nothing beyond his own breathing, he slipped out of the house with a dexterity that betrayed his experience in such endeavors. The sky was clear with a new moon adding to the pale luminosity of the night. Only the lights in Harry's cabin were still on.

He's probably reading, Lorne mused as he sneaked past the fish pond. The gardener had become an avid reader since his wife's death four years ago. Suddenly Lorne heard something rustle near a cluster of rhododendrons. He quickly ducked behind the vine-covered latticework of the arbor, holding his breath momentarily as he listened intently in an effort to determine the source of the sound. Just as he decided to continue his expedition, he saw something stir in the bushes. Stepping back hastily, his rocket fell with a thud on the ground. Lorne cursed silently. Now he could see a dark shape move towards him. He recognized the cat immediately. "You crazy nut," he muttered affectionately as he picked up the Dobrynchuk pet. "I should shoot you into outer space for scaring me like that." Tom purred appreciatively as he brushed his head with tender strokes against Lorne's face. The pure black cat had a well-earned reputation for living up to his name: hardly a cat for miles around wasn't fathered by him.

Lorne put the Gloucester champ of feline virility down and scared him home-bound with a hiss. He picked up the rocket and shortly afterward reached the weather-beaten door that provided the only exit in the rear portion of the brick palisade. After a moment of fumbling, he found the key on the ledge above the door, quickly inserted it and with considerable force managed to turn it. He slowly opened the door, thus guarding against the telltale sound of its rusty hinges. He closed the door with equal caution, but did not lock it.

A few moments later he forced the three spikes which were welded to the side of the launching tube into the ground. He carefully checked the position of the three-foot steel pipe to ascertain its perpendicularity which largely determined the proximity of the landing. Next he carefully lowered the rocket into the tube and pulled its fuse through a hole near the bottom of the launching apparatus.

When he had completed the preparations, he listened for any possible evidence of someone coming his way, but all he heard was the swishing water of the Saskatchewan River. Across the river, its rippled surface reflecting the silvery luminescence of the night in scaly blotches, he saw the lights of the University of Alberta.

A pair of headlights moved slowly along Saskatchewan Drive which bordered the other side of the river. Only a few of the houses along the drive still had lights on. When the car had moved out of sight, Lorne knelt beside his launching gear, struck a match and held it below the fuse.

Having lit it, he dashed towards the nearest tree and hid behind it. Peeking around the trunk he could see the fuse spit sparks as the bright flame ate its way toward the rocket. Then with a blinding flash and a shower of multi-colored scintillas, the rocket hissed into obscurity.

"Wow!" Lorne sighed ardently. "Did she ever GO!" But his enthusiasm quickly turned into anxiety when the awaited sound of the projectile crashing to the ground failed to materialize.

He rushed to the launching site and discovered that the tube was no longer standing upright, but instead pointed ominously at the river.

When his vivid imagination painted ghastly scenes in quick succession before his frightened eyes, Lorne panicked. What if the rocket had hit a house, or worse: a person? If it still had been burning on landing, it might even have started a fire and Lorne experienced a spasm of nausea when he realized that the wailing siren he heard was not in his head but across the river. The thought that it might be an ambulance on its way to the University Hospital as an aftermath of a traffic mishap never entered his throbbing head. Haunted by imaginary firemen, cops, blood-spattered victims, lawyers, judges and, most formidable: a raging Uncle Boris, Lorne quickly threw his launching tube into the river and headed for home in high gear. On entering through the side door, he noticed that his uncle's car was still not back in the garage. Lorne managed to reach his room unnoticed and sighed in gratitude as he undressed in record time.

But fear stopped him from fleeing into Morpheus' arms. Instead his tongue turned into a blob of parchment as he recalled some dreadful episodes in a book he had recently read about a boy trying to escape from a reform school

35

and the 'correctional measures' he had been subjected to after being caught in the act.

Boris Dobrynchuk arrived home around two in the morning. He climbed the stairs with the consideration of a berserk elephant and slammed his bedroom door shut as if to assure all within earshot that this could not possibly be a burglar.

A few minutes later he announced with a steady snore that he was asleep. Rumor had it that Boris Dobrynchuk occasionally snored so loudly that his dentures clattered as a consequence inside the glass of water that stood on the night table beside his bed. Lorne believed that to be the principal reason why his aunt and uncle slept in separate rooms.

Sleep finally overtook Lorne as well when he hit on the comforting thought that his rocket probably was resting on the bottom of the river.

In the morning he awoke with a start, his ears ringing with a loud knocking at his door. "What's the matter?" he yawned with perfect innocence, expecting some detective to furnish the answer.

"It's almost eight o'clock; that's what's the matter," Cora Tilden replied. "It's also the third time I'm trying to wake you up."

"Okay, Cora," Lorne said, grateful it was only the maid, "I'll get mobile."

He sat down at breakfast as the hall clock chimed eight times and the radio switched to the news. Uncle Boris apparently was still in bed, but Aunt Eileen was sitting fresh as a daisy at the table.

"Had trouble waking up?" she asked smilingly.

Lorne looked at her and suddenly it dawned on him how attractive she was when she smiled. "I guess, I must have dozed off after I woke up," he said apologetically.

"American troops have crossed the Rhine," the newscaster announced cheerfully, "causing the collapse of the German defense system on the east bank. The U.S. First Army crossed the vital river at Remagen. General Eisenhower has ordered General Bradley to put five divisions across in support of the military offensive...."

Slicing his boiled egg, Lorne suddenly wondered if he had locked the door in the rear wall and returned the key to its customary place. He decided to check after breakfast. He was just considering looking for his rocket near the river with the benefit of daylight, just in case he had missed hearing the landing, when it happened. At first the words did not register, but then suddenly the full impact of the news item hit him like a bolt of lightning.

"...police examining a strange object found in the garden of the T.J. Themussen residence on Saskatchewan Drive..."

Lorne, who had just taken a generous drink of milk, almost choked as he partially ejected the liquid through his nostrils.

"What's the matter, dear?" his aunt asked concernedly as she slapped him on the back in the firm belief that this would protect his lungs.

"I guess," Lorne stammered, his face beet red, "I was too greedy."

"Traces of explosives have been found inside the eighteen-inch metal cylinder, leading police to believe..."

Twenty-four inches, Lorne mentally corrected the announcer as he blew his nose in a critical effort to regain his composure.

A moment later he excused himself and went to his room. He was convinced he would be charged with God-knows-what inside a couple of hours. The police merely has to put two and two together, he reasoned as he stared outside. Harry Wenzel was sharpening a pair of hedge clippers. It was a beautiful day, but Lorne knew he would not enjoy it. What hope did he have? Mr. Stenwey knew about the chemicals, the library had a record of the books he had borrowed during the past few months and Mr. Harman could hardly be expected to forget that he had made the damn rocket.

But Lorne was wrong. The police never linked him with their odd discovery. Yet the event exerted a major influence on Lorne, for it taught him that chemistry, like any other science, is based on a sound foundation of facts - not chances. The erratic course of the miniature rocket signalled the end of his juvenile tomfoolery and heralded the beginning of a new phase in his life which ultimately would result in having his own thriving business.

IV

The status quo at the Dobrynchuk residence remained unaltered until a few days after Lorne's graduation from high school. It was 1948, a memorable year for mankind: Gandhi assassinated in India, start of the Berlin airlift, disastrous floods in Canada, birth of the Republic of Israel, execution of General Hideki Tojo and the arrest of Cardinal Mindszenty. But Lorne would remember the year for a more personal reason.

The day that was to change his life forever started innocently enough. He awoke around seven, his room aglow with the morning sun. He swung his feet onto the floor, yawned with such gusto that he nearly dislocated his jaw and stretched his arms as if he were trying to reach the ceiling.

Outside he noticed Tom moving stealthily toward an unsuspecting sparrow. When the cat was about to jump his prey, Lorne suddenly knocked loudly against the window pane, causing the bird to fly away safely. Tom looked up at Lorne's room, narrowing his eyes to express his disgust.

In the afternoon George Foster, Lorne's former chemistry teacher, showed him around at the university's Department of Chemistry. Lorne feasted his eyes on intricate laboratory equipment, listened attentively as one of the professors explained the synthesis of an organic compound and asked questions which often astounded his audience because of their advanced nature. The visit generated a sense of propinquity in his heart such as he had never experienced before and he realized with regret that he would not return to this fascinating world until September.

He would come back as a student - not as a visitor. In a matter of weeks this strange ivy-clad building would be as familiar to him as Aldon High. Already he felt at home here. Among the peculiar odors, the intricate instruments, the sparkling glassware laid his destiny. But September was still more than two months away. Suddenly he didn't look forward to the summer holidays. Just think of the terrific waste of time!

They only stayed a little less than three hours, but to Lorne it seemed like a full day crammed into a five-minute time capsule. The experience was like a magnificent vision, exposing the secrets of the future. His studies here would provide the key to a rewarding career. His chemical research would be creative: rather than testing the validity of old processes, he would formulate new ones. He would help unlock the mysteries of today in the crucible of perseverance. He would... His imagination painted a wonderful picture. Lorne had never felt happier: ignorance is bliss. He had failed to learn Life's most important lesson: nothing is certain, except death. How different the world would look tomorrow...

As Lorne drove his teacher home in his aunt's brand-new black Buick, he said: "There's one thing that really puzzles me, Mr. Foster. Why was Dr. Durack's lab so messy?"

George Foster laughed heartily, the more so when he saw how his mirth added to Lorne's bewilderment. "When I was at McGill we had a professor just like him," he explained gaily. "If you think Dr. Durack's lab is disorderly, you should have seen Dr. Cowley's."

He lit a cigarette, inhaled and reflectively blew the smoke toward the windshield. McGill, Cowley, Montreal: was it really 30 years ago?

"We were right inside Dr. Durack's lab, weren't we?" he said as if he were thinking aloud. "In Dr. Cowley's lab there simply wasn't enough room for three people. He piled his stuff on everything horizontal: the desk, the window sill, the fume cupboard and, worst of all, practically the entire floor. When you wanted to see him, you talked to him from the doorway. To venture farther meant courting disaster, since you were bound to kick something over and then all hell would break loose. How Dr. Cowley managed to move around in his lab without any major catastrophes is still a mystery to me. What's more, he somehow remembered where everything was. If he needed an Erlenmeyer which he had discarded two weeks earlier, he picked it out of his junk pile as if everything was in numerical order. Anyway, one day I had the impudence to ask him how he could possibly work under those conditions. I'll never forget his reply. He said that some of man's greatest discoveries were made by accident and that in a cluttered lab your chances of having such an accident are far better than in a tidy one. Of course, he had a point. For instance, the world might still be awaiting the blessing of penicillin if its discoverer had worked in a spotless lab. Just think, there was this used Petri dish in front of an open window in Dr. Fleming's lab and some aerobic interference which produced a mold that was to save the lives of thousands."

"The trouble is," Lorne commented, "that most accidents are more harmful than beneficial."

"Definitely," Foster agreed hastily. "Still much of today's research is based on the trial and error method."

The teacher was still extolling the virtues of individualism in science when Lorne pulled over to the curb and stopped the car.

"Well, what do you know," Foster exclaimed, visibly surprised, "home already. Splendid car I must say." For a moment he studied Lorne with fatherly concern, then he said apologetically: "Don't take what I said about untidiness too seriously. I merely mentioned it to illustrate my story. Dr. Cowley was a brilliant scientist and so is Dr. Durck. You see, what may seem like chaos to a casual observer is really no more confusing to Dr. Durck than an ant hill is to its inhabitants." "I understand, sir," Lorne said placidly.

"And if Dr. Fleming had not been the keen observer he was," Foster continued fervently, "the mold would have grown in vain and penicillin might still be unknown today."

"Well," Lorne intercepted, "I'm afraid I have to go. I'll be doing some biological research tonight, that is if my date doesn't object too much." And extending his hand, he said: "I want to thank you very much for everything you have done for me."

He was about to indulge in a brief eulogy to express his gratitude for the many hours of extracurricular instruction the teacher had given him, but Foster cut him short.

"Let me hear from you from time to time," he said as he opened the door. "You've got a head start, Lorne. Don't bungle it."

A moment later Lorne pointed the car west and drove homeward. Crazy world, he thought, why a guy like Foster, who contributes so much more to man's welfare than uncle Boris, has so much less to show for it: an old house, no car, a couple of cheap suits and little else. Still Foster seemed much happier than Boris Dobrynchuk.

During his nine-year stay with his aunt and uncle, Lorne had never seen his uncle laugh. A smile, a grin, a snicker: yes, but never anything resembling genuine laughter. Aunt Eileen, Harry, Melvin, Cora - they all had a sense of humor. If Tom pulled something crazy or if there were something funny in the newspaper they would show it to one another and join in a healthy burst of laughter, but not Uncle Boris. The closest he ever came to giving his face a holiday was when he learned that some business adversary had gone belly-up.

But although Lorne did not like his uncle, he hated to speculate where he would be without him. So he never spoke bad of his uncle and sometimes even jumped to his defense. For example if someone asked him what his benefactor did for a living, Lorne would use a choice selection of euphemisms to protect the illusion of respectability his uncle relished.

"My uncle is in business," he would say. If this standard reply failed to appease the questioner's curiosity, Lorne would mention the investment field and real estate.

Of course, most people knew full well what kind of scheming crook his uncle was. They just asked the question to see what he would say.

The unvarnished truth was that Boris Dobrynchuk had built his fortune on the adversity and gullibility of his fellow men. He was shrewd, but merciless and had proved his cunning particularly during the Depression when he prospered while others perished. In fact, he had amassed the bulk of his fortune amidst the ruins of financial chaos. His methods varied widely. Often he invested in business undertakings on conditions which, quite inconspicuously, precluded any chance of success. The money he invested was always covered by disproportionately large collateral which in the end invariably rolled into his lap because the terms of his short term loan could not be met. Another specialty was over-financing. This concerned primarily sound business enterprises which, often on Boris' advice, were burdened by unwarranted expansion or renovation programs. The end result was always in Boris' favor regardless whether his debtors succeeded or not.

Boris Dobrynchuk had a simple philosophy: in business as in politics you can't be honest and successful both. He had made his choice and stuck to it with a tenacity that allowed no exceptions.

As Lorne approached Gloucester Crescent, he recalled one of the few words of advice his uncle had ever given him: "If you should ever try your luck in business, never forget that the fellow whose neck you save today may be your executioner tomorrow."

Unlike other money moguls, Boris did not support charity to ease his conscience. There simply wasn't anything to ease.

"What does your uncle do?" There was only one answer: anything he would benefit by.

Uncle Boris, Lorne mused as he entered the Dobrynchuk's quadruple garage, would screw a chicken if the price were right.

Lorne was so deeply in thought that he climbed the basalt steps in a daze and entered the house through its front door, something he had not done since his first major smooching session with Lorraine Phelps. He didn't know why so much of his thinking concerned his uncle. He didn't even wonder why he should be thinking of Uncle Boris at all. This was logical. Lorne had no way of knowing that his subconscious furtively fed him these thoughts to cushion the blow that would hurl him a thousand miles from the very point he now halted to close the door absent-mindedly behind him.

Edmonton in 1948 was not much better off than other cities in the grip of Prohibition during the roaring twenties. In fact, when it came to drinking anything stronger than apple juice, there was little to roar about. A man could not buy his heart-throb a drink within the city limits of Alberta's capital. Men and women who wished to imbibe in public were permitted by law to drink nothing fancier than beer and then only in separate parlors. To any male with amorous intentions, this represented an impediment of formidable magnitude.

About the only public place a fellow could sit beside his gal without arousing the puritans' ire was a theater. So Lorne took Janet Darwin to a Clark Gable movie as a first step to reducing her resistance toward the advances he had planned for the conclusion of the evening.

Janet Darwin was a Grade XI student at Aldon High with voluptuous dimensions. The daughter of a prominent city lawyer, she frequented the finest fashion shops and chose the type of apparel that accentuated rather than concealed her most obvious feminine attributes. The girls at Aldon High practically ostracized her for displaying herself to such advantage, while the boys outdid one another in acts of bravura to curry her favors. But if Janet actually enjoyed her ill-balanced popularity, she never showed it. The boys who had succeeded in dating her could be counted on one hand with fingers to spare. Although no girl at Aldon High would believe it, a rumor persisted that Janet Darwin was a cool cucumber who had her libido well under control. The boys who had dated her wisely refrained from comment.

Lorne was neither strikingly handsome nor particularly athletic, but he did on occasion have his aunt's new car at his disposal, which in 1948 was a mighty weapon to woo with. As far as the other boys were concerned, this was unfair competition, but to Lorne the only thing that mattered was that Janet had accepted him as her companion for the evening. What did it matter what others thought? The summer holidays had started and by fall few at Aldon would remember their dates. At any rate, if anyone wanted to ask him the usual questions, he would have to come to the university for Aldon High was, as far as Lorne was concerned, already a thing of the past.

As Clark Gable planted a knock-out kiss on the lips of the film's heroine, holding her in a position that could be comfortable only to people with rubber spines, Lorne tried to find Janet's hand, but when he touched it she withdrew it icily.

This was no new experience for Lorne: he had had his share of girlfriends. He knew that some girls loathe what others crave for. In the privacy of his car she might be different. He hoped so.

After the movie they danced at the Shangrila, a bare dance hall where only the name was of a paradisal nature. The music was too loud, the lights were too bright and the decor was no more festive than a Protestant church's interior in the sixteenth century. Still it was known as Edmonton's finest dancing spot, which it was and goes to show what the rest was like.

To some couples it really was a bit like paradise since it beat dancing on the street where any such activity would be welcomed like the plague. Some of the more daring escorts brought their own pleasure juice which was fine as long as you didn't mind mixing your drinks under your table and taking a chance on being arrested in case of a police raid. Of course, some couples were in love and when you are under the spell of Eros, any place seems like heaven.

Janet Darwin fostered none of these illusions. She moved with the grace of a broomstick and spent the balance of her energy maintaining air space between Lorne and herself.

Around ten o'clock Lorne suddenly remembered that he had promised Mrs. Darwin to return her daughter not later than eleven. Realizing that this left little time for the exploratory maneuvers he had planned to subject her to in the car, Lorne suggested they'd leave. Janet's ready acceptance of this preliminary overture gave him confidence that she would respond with equal eagerness to more intimate suggestions.

Lorne knew an idyllic spot near the parliament buildings where cops didn't bother young couples with flashlights and stupid questions. Before he had found this secluded spot Lorne had frequented several of Edmonton's better-known necking grounds where lights were low and traffic was light. This was one of those places. While they exchanged various topics of discussion, romance was not one of them. While Janet extolled the attractions of foreign travel, Lorne tried in vain to elicit her views on marriage, birth control and related subjects. Suddenly they were startled by a loud bang on the car's roof. In the dark of the evening Lorne could barely discern the outline of a male figure. As he stepped out of the car he realized the pugnacious punk he had mistaken the intruder for was in fact a policeman on patrol. Shining his flashlight on Janet's face the cop asked: "Are you all right, Miss? Not doing anything illegal, are you?"

"No, I am fine, Officer," Janet replied blushing profusely.

Experiences like this were not uncommon in Canada during the fifties when every cop considered it his duty to double as a chaperone.

But when Lorne started the car, Janet moved away from him as far as was possible without pushing the door out of shape.

"What's the matter, Janet?" Lorne asked, audibly irritated by her icy conduct. "You act as if I've got something contagious."

Janet opened her purse and a moment later lit a cigarette with a complacency that nearly nauseated Lorne.

"I think you'd better take me home now," she said calmly before returning the cigarette to her pretty lips which Lorne no longer craved to kiss. His desires had been withered by the frigidity of her disposition.

They drove to the Darwin residence in silence. Why, Lorne wondered, does a girl spend a fortune and plenty of time trying to look sexy if her main aim is to prove that she isn't?

Mrs. Darwin welcomed them at the door, visibly delighted to have her daughter back half an hour before the stipulated deadline. "Won't you come in and have a cup of coffee?" she asked Lorne with such friendliness that he found it difficult to believe that she was really Janet's mother.

For a moment he deliberated whether or not common courtesy demanded his acceptance of the invitation; then he said: "Thank you very much, Mrs. Darwin, but I'm afraid I've got to be home in time myself."

Lorne reached home just before eleven and entered the house in complete silence, reminiscent of his rocket days. He was about to enter his room when he heard Uncle Boris mention his name. He turned around and discovered that the sound of conversation originated in his aunt's bedroom, a part of the house Boris Dobrynchuk normally fought shy of.

"Nine years we've been takingk care of him," Boris protested vociferously, anger thickening his Ukrainian accent. "It's time he goes workingk. I'm doingk all right with half his education, so he can do twice better."

Lorne's first impulse was to storm into his aunt's bedroom and tell his uncle off, but he dropped the notion a moment later when he realized that such rash action would only aggravate matters.

"Stop your silly arguments, Boris Dobrynchuk," Aunt Eileen said matronly. "Lorne is going to university and that's all there is to it. He's got the brains and we've got the money. How can you even think of denying him the opportunity?"

"In my days I made my own opportunities," Boris sputtered. "Nothingk I ever got was handed me on a silver platter: I had to work for it."

Lorne bit his lip. He's rotten to the core, he thought, but he is right. I've had it too easy. I expect too much.

"Your definition of work is a strange one, I know," she rebuked imperturbably. "University degrees don't come on silver platters. It takes a lot of work, but it also takes money to make such work possible. I owe it to my brother to do everything I can to save Lorne from the pitfalls of mediocrity."

"You don't owe your brother nothingk," Boris erupted "and I owe him less!"

Stunned and stung by his uncle's invective, Lorne entered his room and plunged dispirited into his armchair.

It's the truth, he thought bitterly, but why does he have to desecrate the memory of my father? He looked around and for the first time he saw his room as he had never seen it before. How much he had taken for granted! The soft bed, the splendid desk, the leather-upholstered chair he was sitting on. Why is it, he wondered, that you don't appreciate the comforts and pleasures of life until you're about to lose them? Is a tasty meal any the less wonderful because you're accustomed to the best? Can good fortune be appreciated only against a background of miserable memories or prospects?

What a first-class ass I've been, Lorne scolded himself. And to think that of all people, Uncle Boris had to open my eyes. For nine years I've sponged off them as if I was entitled to their hospitality. And what do I do in return: I sow discord! How short-sighted, how goddamn selfish I've been to even consider going to university at their expense. How terribly one-sided the advantages had been.

Lorne had never felt worse. There was only one thing he could do and that was to end his parasitic existence--now. He slowly rose to his feet, feeling as if he had just come out of a coma. He walked over to his closet and picked up a suitcase. It took only a few minutes to pack it with some clothes and a few books. To take more seemed almost like stealing. He opened the door and for a moment studied his room as if to memorize its every detail, then he closed it soundlessly and tiptoed to the staircase. As he went down he heard his aunt sob: "Why do you always have to judge everything in terms of money?"

How much I owe you, he thought. How can I ever repay you?

He reached Gloucester Crescent with a lump in his throat. He felt like a fugitive and he realized that he was a fugitive of his own past. Just as the mansion threatened to vanish out of sight, he halted and turned around. The light in his aunt's bedroom was still on. He looked at the forbidding wall and the capitals of the entrance columns just visible above it. A thousand memories exploded in his mind: the death of Harry Wenzel's wife, Melvin caught in the act of seducing Cora, the rocket experiments, the silence at mealtime, Tom's exploits...

How all these things would fade in time? Already he felt like an outsider. Nine years he had lived here, but he had never really belonged.

As a stranger he had come and as a stranger he now left.

Resolutely Lorne turned his back to the Dobrynchuk residence and started to walk towards Jasper Avenue. He moved out of the past into the future. He knew that though darkness enveloped him now, the dawn of a new era was about to break. The excitement of venturing into the unknown made him quicken his step.

Part II

V

Vancouver is Canada's third largest conglomeration of people. It is built on a stubby tongue of land tasting the saline of the Pacific Ocean.

It is an urban adolescent: eager to grow up, full of vigor and ideals, yet uncertain about its destiny - like a virgin approaching adulthood.

All embryonic characteristics inherent in a metropolis are evident in the restless city. Skyscrapers are springing up like mushrooms on a dunghill, prosperity is reflected by an exploding poodle population, but most significant: the first major shake-up in the police department and the consequent expulsion of its chief, is now on record. What could be more indicative of a city's growth than corruption at the helm?

From the air the city offers a fascinating panorama, particularly at night when its countless streets are lit up by myriads of multi-colored lights. But the pseudo gaiety of Vancouver is as deceptive as its gaudy neon signs which flash their empty messages with monotonous regularity, for behind the phony facade of make-believe the city sheds its many tears...

"Well, I'll be goddamned!" Doug Marcus exclaimed as he entered the backyard garage.

"Welcome to Vincent's Custom Chemicals," Lorne Vincent said with cheerful pride as he shut the door.

From the outside the building looked like an ordinary garage, weather-beaten and a bit ramshackle perhaps, but no different from a hundred others in Vancouver's east end. The surprise was inside: directly beneath the garage's solitary window stood a work bench littered with pipettes, burettes, flasks, clamps, tongs, test tubes, funnels and filter paper. Shelves flanking the window were burdened with neatly labeled bottles and jars containing a wide variety of chemicals. Near the door four planks linking two large crates served as the top of a makeshift desk on which stained notes formed a random pattern similar to nature's mosaic of autumn leaves outside. The floor was largely covered by barrels, crocks, jugs, demijohns, a woodstove and two tubs filled to the brim with dirty glassware.

"How much dough have you got tied up in this junk yard?" Doug asked irreverently as he waded toward the work bench.

"About three hundred bucks," Lorne replied, pouring a clear liquid from an Erlenmeyer flask into a shallow dish, "but the actual value is closer to a grand."

"Courtesy the University of British Columbia, unknowing sponsors of Vancouver's own Frankenstein," Doug quipped. "Tell me, doctor, how many lab robbers do you currently employ?"

"Don't worry, you're still the only one," Lorne laughed. "Now, may I have your shirt?"

Doug obediently took off his shirt and handed it to Lorne who promptly spread it over the dish, pressing the ink-stained breast pocket into the liquid.

Lorne and Doug were as different as day and night in appearance and character. Lorne was tall and wirily built, Doug was short and stout. Their clothes reflected both Lorne's poverty and Doug's opulence. But their outlooks on life produced an even sharper contrast. Lorne had confidence in himself and mankind, while Doug was firmly convinced of the futility of life. If they had held these views in reverse it might have been more understandable, for Doug was the son of a prominent surgeon and given little to worry about, while Lorne had suffered enough disillusioning blows to depress a saint. Doug was a confirmed hedonist who attended university only to evade the social responsibilities of life which he had managed to evade for twenty-two years of satin lined existence in the artificial world of the rich.

Yet both were firmly resolved to make the best of life, albeit in entirely different ways. Their friendship was puzzling to all who knew them and at times seemed even illogical to themselves. But several months had passed since Fate fused their friendship in the heat of an argument and their differences had nurtured rather than destroyed their enigmatic relationship. They had met at UBC's Campus Coffee Shop where Doug, in the company of some fellow students, had advocated the re-unification of Germany. Lorne, who had sat in an adjoining booth, had suddenly interrupted Doug by reminding him that between 1914-'45 such unification had led to two world wars. A lively debate had followed with two of the students siding with Lorne.

Now, as he stood shivering in the unheated garage, Doug studied his friend with unmistakable respect.

"How long is this operation gonna take?" Doug asked with a suggestion of impatience in his voice.

"Just a couple of minutes," Lorne said cheerfully.

"I feel like a naked martyr," Doug protested facetiously, "sacrificing the comfort of my shirt in the interest of science and risking pneumonia as a reward."

"I'm sorry the thermostat is out of order," Lorne said drily, lifting the soaked material out of the dish. Holding the shirt against the light for a brief examination of the results, he explained apologetically: "Actually the spotting agent should be mixed with pressurized steam and forced through the material, but due to circumstances beyond my control..."

"Skip the commercials, dad," Doug interrupted. "Let's finish the hocus pocus while I'm still conscious."

Lorne rubbed the stained area with a piece of cloth, transferring the ink onto it. "See, I told you it works," he said proudly.

"My compliments, professor," Doug said genially. "I must say, though, that the odor of your vanishing act is offensive to one's, proboscis."

"That's the amyl acetate you smell," Lorne explained. "Now what's up?" Doug inquired as Lorne reached for a small bottle. "I thought you were finished."

"I want to pour a bit of alcohol over it to speed up the drying process."

"Alcohol? You mean the real McCoy?"

"No, just methyl."

"Too bad, I could use a snort right about now to restore my body temperature. You know, Lorne, you should set up your own distillery. The mark-up on booze is fabulous!"

"I can see it already," Lorne laughed: "Vincent's Custom Gin. But seriously, what do you think of my spotting agent?"

"It looks like a technical success, but that doesn't mean that it will be a financial one as well."

"I can market it for almost half of what the dry-cleaning trade is paying now and still make a good profit."

"Provided your competitors will let you."

"What do you mean?" Lorne snapped. "This is a free country, isn't it?!"

"Yes," Doug said disparagingly, "it is a free country, but for those in the saddle it is a hell of a lot more enjoyable than for the suckers trying to make a bare living."

"Well, I am a firm believer in free enterprise," Lorne maintained, handing Doug his shirt.

"That's your privilege and probably your downfall," Doug commented. "The fact remains that free enterprise is neither free nor very enterprising. Success is like a pyramid: there isn't much room at the top. What's worse, those who occupy this choice spot, like to keep it that way. If you should somehow manage to build up a business to the point where it represents a threat to established firms, your competitors will simply drop their prices below yours until you're kaput."

"I have other products...."

"Sure," Doug intercepted, "you also got shampoo and God knows what." Then putting his shirt back on.

Doug continued: "but if you should be too successful, the same fate will await you. The reason is simple: your competitors have large financial reserves and you don't. You're living in 1952, not in the days of Henry Ford and Thomas Edison when a persistent pioneer could launch an industrial empire. Today it takes much more than ingenuity and elbow grease to succeed in business: it takes money--piles of it. Even if you manage to accumulate vast sums of money you will need high-priced lawyers to hang onto it."

"I have no illusions," Lorne said simply. "I just want to make a living."

"That doesn't alter the fact that you will be competing with those who want to make a killing instead of just a living and have the means to do it. Let's face it: whether it is a bottle of bleach or a bottle of perfume, what sells it is largely advertising. A ten-cent bar of soap costs more to advertise from wrapper to commercial than it costs to manufacture. To promote a new brand from obscurity to popularity is often a multimillion dollar proposition; that's why the advertising business is one of the largest industries in the world today. The cost of advertising often exceeds the vast sums spent on product research and development. Here you sit in a ramshackle tool shed with a bunch of discarded crap, thinking you can jolt the business world with a spot remover."

"Of course, capital is indispensable in business, but it can be generated as business volume grows and by responsible borrowing and reinvesting profits."

"I know what you mean. You think you can finance your initial outlay by sticking to your job until your profits will allow you to quit. I hope you'll live that long, because if you do, you'll make history as a modern Methuselah."

Lorne smiled forgivingly. "At least you no longer call my plans impossible," he said.

"You're a born optimist, Lorne," Doug confessed, "but optimism has no monetary value."

"I think it has, at least indirectly," Lorne countered. "Faith, hope, optimism, call it what you like, the real meaning is confidence and without confidence man is nothing but a vegetable. You've got to have faith, especially in yourself, or you'll perish."

"Amen," Doug blurted. "Brother, you sound like an evangelist."

"Well, it stimulates the mind if nothing else," Lorne responded and changing the subject he continued: "I'm going to the university in the morning. Can I borrow your library card again?"

"You may," Doug corrected, "although I hate to be an accessory to your downfall."

"I'll return it to you tomorrow night," Lorne promised as he slipped the card into his wallet.

"Just put it in the mailbox, because I won't be home. I've got a date with the most delectable doll on campus. I guess it's my absolute faith in sex that keeps me from developing into a vegetable."

"We all have to believe in something," Lorne agreed.

Terry Weldan applied the comb gently to her hair, watching her movements closely in the hotel's bathroom mirror. The rain was coming down with torrential violence, the big drops exploding noisily against the window. Terry glanced at the puddles and rivulets which covered the cobble-stoned surface of the alley six floors down. A large bread truck, partly obscured by an ugly maze of dripping wires overhead, squeezed its way between some battered garbage cans and an illegally parked car. As she continued the restoration of her platinum blond coiffure, she wondered what a bread truck was doing in downtown Vancouver at this time of night. It was nearly eleven o'clock.

Terry Weldan was the kind of woman whose face and figure are constantly used in ads urging people to buy some flashy sports car or quench their thirst with a certain soft drink. She was twenty-one and every inch a woman, especially in the circumference department. She was also sophisticated and witty, characteristics which most people mistook for a carefree disposition.

She applied her lipstick, rolling her lips inward to distribute it evenly, daintily plucked some stray hairs off her dress and looked over her shoulder to check her nylons. Satisfied with her appearance, she took her purse, turned the light off and walked into the adjoining room. She bent over the still figure of a man on the double bed and smiled when she found him sound asleep. Terry picked up her stole from a nearby chair, wrapped the fur around her slender neck and tiptoed to the door.

"Good night, George," she whispered sweetly. Then she left.

In the nearly deserted lobby she phoned a taxi which arrived a few minutes later. As Terry stepped outside she was pleasantly surprised to see the young driver rush to her side with a large black umbrella in his hand.

"Beastly weather," he commented as he escorted her to the car.

"With this kind of service it isn't so bad," she smiled gratefully and entering the cab with weather-defying elegance she added: "Thank you so much."

"Whereto, madam?" he asked a moment later when he joined her on the front seat.

"Rozano Apartments."

"I know," he said as he pulled away from the curb. The Rozano Apartments were well-known. It was one of the largest apartment blocks in Vancouver's West End. He turned the meter's 'vacant' sign down and picked up the microphone.

"Twenty-five," he reported, "fare to Rozano Apartments."

"You must be new with Starlite," Terry said as she observed him boldly. "I'm a regular customer and I've never seen you before."

"The misfortune is mine," he said without looking at her and he explained: "I've been with the company for half a year now. Do you usually travel at night?"

"Why?" she asked, suddenly cautious.

"Well, it would explain why we haven't met before. You see, I worked days until last week."

Terry watched the windshield wipers struggle in the onrushing rain. He's sure different from the other drivers, she mused in silent complementation. And, prodded by curiosity, she asked: "Do you like your job?"

Somewhat startled by her question, he glanced at her, but he failed to ascertain the motivation for her interest in him. "It's a living," he said noncommittally.

"I didn't want to be rude," she said apologetically, "but I just couldn't help wondering why you're pushing a cab. There's something about you that tells me you're cut out for finer things."

"Thank you," he said. "I must confess that I have similar expectations. I like to believe that I'm not wasting my time and that the taxi business is just a stepping stone to something more rewarding."

The car stopped and the driver dashed out to her side, his umbrella ready. When they reached the brightly lit entrance of the Rozano Apartments, she asked: "Care for a drink?"

"A drink?" he echoed with feigned incredulity. "Do you realize that company regulations forbid me to even consider such a thing? It could cost me my job, my stepping stone to a more lucrative career. A drink when my whole future is at stake? Okay, you talked me into it."

What a character, she thought as she led the way to the elevator.

"Swank place," he commented after they had entered her apartment.

He was not exaggerating. The spacious layout was ultramodern in both appointments and decor. The furniture was functionally sculptured without detriment to its aesthetic value. Several realistic reproductions of paintings by Van Gogh and Gauguin enriched the plain walls with their bright and contrasting colors. A huge picture window offered a fabulous view of the blazing city.

"What'll you have?" she asked as she opened a liquor cabinet which he had mistaken for a radio-phonograph combination.

"Rum and coke will be swell," he said, impressed by the extent of the alcoholic arsenal.

A few moments later they seated themselves--he in an easy chair and she on the edge of a settee. The drinks further loosened their tongues.

"What's the magic formula for happiness?" she asked suddenly.

He smiled to hide the fact that her question had startled him. "I'm afraid you've overestimated me," he replied. "I am not a wizard. If I were, I wouldn't be driving a cab."

"But you're happy, aren't you?"

"Yes, I am," he said instantly, casting a furtive glance at her shapely legs. He noted that the view gradually ameliorated as the hem of her dress crept upward.

"Well," she persisted, "if you're happy you must know why."

"I do," he admitted. "I'm happy because I appreciate the things I've got and I don't lament what I don't have."

"You make it sound so simple," she sighed smilingly.

"It is. Simplicity is the very foundation of happiness," he said philosophically. "Most people are miserable because they expect too much of life. I don't know why we were placed on this earth, but I'm sure it wasn't so we could have a ball. Since worrying tends to complicate problems rather than solve them, I feel the only logical alternative is to accept things as they come."

Terry suddenly burst into laughter. "No, don't get me wrong," she pleaded, "I am not laughing at you, but here we sit talking about life as if we're old acquaintances and we don't even know each other's name." And raising her glass, she added: "Here's to us. I'm Terry Weldan."

"My name is Lorne," he said, clinking his glass against hers. "Lorne Vincent."

"Only three books today?" the librarian inquired. "That's all," Lorne agreed.

The girl made the customary notations and asked: "Do you know you have a namesake on campus?"

Jesus, Lorne thought, she smells trouble. But he said simply: "Really?"

"Yes," she explained pleasantly, "the other Doug Marcus is the son of Dr. Marcus, the chief surgeon at St. Thomas' Hospital. He is also in his third year, just like you."

"What a coincidence," Lorne commented with feigned surprise.

"Maybe you'll run into him one of these days."

"I'll let you know if I do," Lorne said as he picked up the books from the counter.

"Okay, Doug," the girl said happily.

Well, it was bound to happen sooner or later, Lorne inferred as he left the library on his way to a nearby bus stop. Those librarians have a fantastic memory when it comes to names. She'd probably flip her lid if she knew that besides my name not being Doug Marcus, I am not even a registered student. Just think, he mused, how easily I could be exposed. A simple check of the records would show that there is only one Doug Marcus and that he reads a hell of a lot of chemistry books, considering he's a law student.

Since his arrival in Vancouver four years ago, Lorne had faithfully continued his chemistry studies. He had digested all textbooks on the subject used in the university's program and proven his proficiency by passing several third year exams with flying colors and well within the set time limits. The professor, who had permitted him to write the tests, later had invited him to attend some of the lectures, an offer Lorne had gratefully accepted.

How differently things had worked out from what Lorne had expected during his fateful train journey westward. He had planned to find a job and save enough money to pay his way through university. But after a few weeks' work as a twenty-five-dollar-a-week warehouse helper, he realized that this method would prove too time-consuming. His subsequent strategy had been more rewarding. He had utilized the major part of his spare time to study on his own.

To his surprise, progress had been faster than could have been possible at the university, enabling him to write third-year exams after barely two years of home studies. Of course, this was partly due to the fact that he was not burdened by a complete academic program, but instead could devote most of his studies to chemistry. The fact that his work would never be crowned with a degree had never bothered him. To Lorne the only thing that mattered was the acquisition of knowledge. He was convinced that the know-how to translate this knowledge into a source of income would come in due course.

But as Lorne sat in the bus on his way to his one-room habitat on Lorenzo Street, the subject of his thoughts was not of a chemical but of a physical nature. Terry Weldan followed him everywhere like a persistent apparition. When he read, the formula would blur and her smile take its place. When he angrily shut his book, he would see her across the street, her eyes melancholy, but her face no less attractive.

A pretty face and an enticing figure - big deal! There are millions like her. Well, thousands anyway. Why the hell do I keep thinking of her?

Maybe you're in love, it echoed in his mind. Lorne rejected the idea with a sneer-inspired grin. An elderly woman across the aisle, her lap burdened by a huge shopping bag, observed him with unadulterated wonder.

The whole thing is ridiculous, Lorne continued his silent soliloquy. I can't even think straight and she probably couldn't remember my name if she tried to save her life.

He got off the bus on East Hastings Street and a moment later found himself inside a telephone booth. He inserted a nickel into the appropriate slot, dialed the number vigorously and turned around to see if she was watching him. She wasn't. Then he heard her voice: "Terry Weldan."

The telephone voice hurled him back to reality.

"Is Mr. Lucas there, please," he half asked, half stated.

"Just a moment, please."

Lorne played nervously with the chain dangling in a loop below the directory.

"Paul Lucas here."

"This is Lorne Vincent..."

"Who?"

"Lorne Vincent. I left you a shampoo sample a week ago."

"Oh, yes, Lorne. We've tried it and we're quite happy with it. How much did you say it was?"

"Three ninety-five a gallon," Lorne replied matter-of-factly, but it was only with supreme effort that he succeeded in preventing exultation from spilling into his voice. He added: "That's the imperial gallon." "Well, we've got a fair stock on hand right now, but we'll be needing some shampoo in about two weeks. Could you ship us a couple of gallons, say the end of the month?"

"Certainly."

"Do you also handle shampoo for dry and oily hair?"

"Yes, we have those as well," Lorne lied enthusiastically.

"I'd appreciate it if you could give me a couple of samples next time you're around."

"Sure thing, Mr. Lucas and thank you for your order."

Lorne almost dropped the receiver in his excitement. My first order, he thought jubilantly. My very first order: the ice is broken!

VI

The black lettering was still wet on the corrugated glass: M.J. Nithdale. Western Division Manager.

Malcolm Nithdale paused in front of his office door to study the palpable evidence of his promotion, unaware the staccato rhythm of the typewriters had been interrupted by silence as the girls watched him.

"It looks very nice," one of them said in a congratulatory voice.

Malcolm abruptly turned around. "I trust your typewriter is not out of order, Miss Roberts," he snapped caustically. The work resumed immediately and Malcolm entered his office.

"How do you like that?" Lois Roberts whispered as she sped the letters to the paper at a furious pace. "Six years I've worked in this crap joint and still he calls me Miss Roberts. Probably calls his wife Mrs. Nithdale."

The other girls giggled in sympathy although they were amused by the fact that formality seemed more painful to Lois than sarcasm.

Malcolm Nithdale considered informality a vulgarity to which he seldom resorted. He firmly believed that familiarity destroys authority. He walked over to the large window behind his desk, his steps cushioned by a heavy broadloom carpet that covered the floor of his private domain. It was a beautiful, crisp October morning. Through the bluish haze of sawmill smoke that hung above Burrard Inlet, he could see the majestic Lions Gate suspension bridge which links Vancouver with the North Shore. Deeply engrossed in thought, his fingers danced erratically in his cupped hands behind his back. Despite his promotion - or more accurately because of it - he felt insecure. At thirty-eight he was the youngest division manager at Fentex Industrial Supplies and he could think of at least a dozen older executives who were green with envy over his promotion. Of course, the envy did not bother him. What did was the knowledge that his position was in constant jeopardy. He could afford no mistakes: there were too many eager volunteers to take his place.

Malcolm had fought a bitter battle to reach this coveted pinnacle, making considerably more enemies than friends in the process. His tactics were seldom laudable, but always effective. Even at home his conduct was always calculating and his wife and two daughters knew him as an undisputed ruler in the realm of family affairs. He appreciated respect more than affection and preferred obedience to understanding. His gaunt face rarely displayed a smile; his tall, slim frame never moved without personal advantage.

He had worked late the previous night and made the nauseating discovery that sales of some dry-cleaning chemicals had made an unprecedented nose dive during the past few weeks. Although this dangerous downhill trend had started before his arrival here from Toronto, he knew he had to arrest and reverse the trend immediately. Failure to accomplish this would, without a shred of doubt, spell his funeral at Fentex.

Malcolm turned to his desk, pressed a button and sat down. His secretary walked in a moment later.

"Miss McPherson, what time does Mr. Scott normally arrive here?" he asked, studying her appearance. He liked what he saw. Sylvia McPherson was a twenty-seven-year-old redhead who possessed the rare combination of sex appeal and office efficiency.

"Usually around nine," she replied, secretly surprised that her new boss had not been more observant during his first week at the Vancouver office.

Malcolm consulted his watch. It was ten to nine. "I want to see him as soon as he gets here," he said.

Wayne Scott walked into the Kenton Building with his usual ebullience.

"You're looking gorgeous again, Phyllis," he greeted the elevator girl.

"Thank you, Mr. Scott," Phyllis Gallagher said as she closed the sliding door.

"This must be my lucky morning," Wayne joked. "Just you and me in this cozy cubicle. Phyllis, baby, as soon as I succeed sourpuss as division manager, I'll hire you as my private secretary and I'll make passionate love to you."

"How romantic, Mr. Scott. You're sure your wife won't object?"

"Of course not. She's very broad-minded. As a matter of fact, so am I...."

The door swung open and Wayne stepped out, blowing the girl a kiss just before the door slid shut again.

"Hi ya, dolls," he greeted breezily as he entered the Fentex office. The girls returned his salutation with equal cordiality but in more subdued tones.

"Caesar wants to see you," Sylvia whispered. "He's in an extraordinarily foul mood this morning."

"He'll snap out of it," Wayne predicted. "I've got a couple of jokes that will slay him."

But Malcolm, never easily humored, this time was in his most unreceptive mood.

"Yeah!" he barked when Wayne knocked on his door.

"Good morning," Wayne greeted.

"To hell with phoney cordialities, Mr. Scott," Malcolm snapped. "There's nothing good about this morning, I assure you." And sweeping his hand over some papers on his desk, he asked: "Tell me, Mr. Scott, why is it that your sales have dropped dramatically in the past couple of weeks?"

"I meant to tell you earlier."

"For Christ's sake, man, get off the pot. If you meant to tell me earlier, why the hell didn't you?"

Wayne quickly suppressed an urge to punch his boss right in the kisser, but instead he explained with artificial serenity: "Bright-way Cleaners and several others no longer take our spotting agents because they can buy them cheaper elsewhere."

Malcolm plunged heavily into his plush swivel chair. "Surely you can be more specific than that," he said, his reptilian eyes nearly hypnotizing the young salesman.

"Apparently," Wayne continued, "there is a new company in Vancouver which manufactures a variety of chemicals."

"What's their name?"

"I don't know."

"Well, find out. How can we meet competition if we don't even know who our competitors are?" And after pausing a moment, Malcolm continued: "It can't be much of a setup or I would have read about it in the trade journals."

"I'm sorry, but I am unaware of the extent of their assets," Wayne commented impudently.

"Don't bother me with the obvious, Mr. Scott. You don't seem to be aware of a lot of things, such as not being indispensable. I want you to do everything within your power to increase your sales, because if they should continue to go down, you'll go down with them. Let me remind you, Mr. Scott, that you are in the employ of Fentex Industrial Supplies which is the largest firm of its kind in all of North America. We simply don't tolerate competition. We don't have to. Am I getting through to you?"

"I am reading you loud and clear."

"All right. Now I expect to see you tomorrow with the name of that company, a list of its products, all prices where these products compete with ours and the names of our customers who are now using those products."

When the salesman had left, Malcolm turned around in his chair. The haze had lifted and in the distance he saw the CPR ferry head for Vancouver Island. It looked like a beautiful day.

One of his rare smiles, supercilious and transitory in nature, spread across his face.

I'll squeeze the bastards out of business by fear or by force, he resolved.

Wayne Scott entered Malcolm's office the next day, brimming with self-confidence, carrying a cardboard box with glass bottles.

"Exhibit one," he announced proudly as he placed an empty bottle on Malcolm's desk.

"It doesn't even have a proper label," Malcolm said disparagingly. "Just a cheap piece of paper with a stamp on it." And bending closer to the soiled lettering, he read aloud: "Vincent's Custom Chemicals."

"Please note," Wayne said, "they sell their spotting agent at $3.95 a gallon compared to our price of $5.25. That's a saving of 1.30 per unit. Add to this that Canadian gallons are 20 per cent larger than ours and we are talking about a total price difference of about forty-five per cent."

"Quit showing off your grasp on arithmetic," Malcolm said with a hint of cordiality in his voice. "They're a bunch of dead ducks."

"I note," said Wayne with a touch of insolence, "that you're using the plural pronoun 'they', but all reports indicate that the firm in question is a one-man operation."

"A one-man operation?" Malcolm echoed mockingly. "It's gonna be a cinch. He'll be out of business before the end of the year."

Although Wayne did not share Malcolm's optimism, he knew better than to argue. Instead he said: "Next exhibit is a list of customers who apparently have done a bit of arithmetic themselves and consequently changed their suppliers." Malcolm added the names up quickly: "I count only twelve," he said disparagingly." Is that all?"

"It was at three o'clock this afternoon."

"I thought we had a problem."

"Next some incomplete information," Wayne continued, ignoring Malcolm's comment. "As far as we are concerned he sells only two products in direct competition with ours, but they happen to be our biggest sellers in the dry-cleaning line: Prestine and Boratex. Apparently he has a slew of other products on the drawing board, including a complete janitorial line."

"And where is all this going on?"

"The address seems to be a well-kept secret. I managed to peek at one of his invoices, but all it says is Vincent's Custom Chemicals Vancouver, B.C."

"Printed or stamped?"

"Stamped," Wayne replied, adding: "The items and prices were hand-written, so he probably hasn't even got a typewriter."

"Just a fly-by-night operation," Malcolm said, visibly relieved by Wayne's report. "It probably would die an early natural death on its own, but we can't afford to take chances. We must be humane and see to it that the suffering of our friend is not unnecessarily prolonged: the guy is obviously struggling."

After Wayne had left, Malcolm consulted several directories and phoned the Better Business Bureau and city hall. No one he talked to had ever heard of Vincent's Custom Chemicals, but an official at the city's license department thanked him for the tip and promised immediate action. No business enterprise can legally operate in Vancouver without civic approval and Malcolm happily realized that as a result of his phone call, the competitive light might be snuffed out without any further efforts on his part.

The Dungeon was situated in the basement of a huge rooming house in Vancouver's west end and served as a regular meeting place for young persons fed up with the pressures and hypocrisies of everyday life.

Clusters of chairs circled barrels which served as tables and were adorned by the intimate light of candles anchored in the necks of empty beer bottles. In essence The Dungeon was a sanctuary for a group of nonconformists who refused to surrender their individuality to the mushrooming mass of routine-addicted people. Painters, musicians, students and miscreants alike found here the freedom of expression denied them elsewhere in society. The atmosphere in this exclusive hideaway was exhilarating because it lacked the strangulating effects of uniformity, bigotry and self-righteousness which have poisoned society at large and pushed mankind to the verge of nuclear extinction. Here criticism did not produce the usual toxins of enmity and resentment--it was welcomed as freedom of expression.

Extremes in tastes constituted no threat to the group's cohesive character. The Dungeon resounded with the compositions of Bach as well as those of Previn and its walls bore reproductions of paintings by the masters of the Renaissance, the impressionists of yesterday and the abstractionists of the present.

George Shearing's Lullaby of Birdland ended prematurely as Doug Marcus climbed on a bar stool and surveyed the scene. There was a mixed audience of about thirty persons, most of whom continued their conversations. All chairs were occupied and some members of the clan were seated on the floor, their backs resting against the wall.

"Marriage," Doug started," should be abolished. Not because, as some suggest, it's immoral - for how does one define immorality? - but because marriage is hostile to love."

He paused briefly; taking pleasure in the silence that greeted him.

"Matrimony is unethical since it is a product of distrust rather than affection. Where love is manifest, red tape is superfluous. If two people desire to share their everything in bed and in thought, society has no right to demand a signed declaration. And if such a voluntary union ceases to be desirable to one or both partners, society has no right to deny such people the dissolution of that union."

"He's a card," Terry Weldan whispered. Lorne smiled obligingly.

"Of course, the clergy objects to this postulation, because free love and freethinking weaken its hold on people.

"So, in order to safeguard their parasitic existence, they spew their protests with the same boring verbosity sermons are known for. But negative thinking doesn't alter the truth one iota, and the truth is that if a woman loves another man more than the one she happens to be married to, she will gain nothing by frustrating her true desires and faking faithfulness and affection to her husband, while rejecting her lover. The rewards for such behavior are not peace of mind and family joy as the puritans would have you believe, but nervous strain, irritability and just about every form of mental misery you can think of. This is only logical, because you can't correct an error by prolonging it."

How can anyone who has been a student practically his entire life, utter such drivel, Lorne wondered. How can I be in such complete disagreement with him and still regard him as my best friend? What's happening to me?

During the past few weeks, Terry had played the peculiar dual role of frustrating and inspiring his experiments and sales.

A few days ago he had taken her out for dinner, a move he could ill afford. They had run into Doug who had promptly invited them to tonight's session at The Dungeon. Before Lorne had been able to formulate an objection, Terry had enthusiastically accepted the invitation for him.

"Of course, if Pasteur prefers to tend to his Erlenmeyers and test tubes, I will be pleased to escort the young lady myself," Doug had gallantly offered, winking at Terry.

Doug's obvious interest in Terry had alarmed Lorne, and now, as he sat closely beside her, he began to suspect that this interest was of a mutual nature.

"Why can't a woman love more than one man?" Doug asked as if he were reading Lorne's mind. "Why shouldn't a man love more than one woman? True love knows no bounds. Possessive love knows no happiness, for love--like happiness-- is multiplied by being shared."

As if there isn't enough chaos in the world as it is, Lorne mused, glancing at Terry. But Terry was palpably in another world: Doug's world.

"Only the immature will feel jealousy when love is not exclusively theirs," Doug continued, "but jealousy is a fragile shield, a moral vacuum created by a lack of self-confidence. Too many people minimize the importance of the physical side of love, but the truth is that taking sex out of life is like taking air out of a tire: it makes it flat! The peabrained bluenoses claim that pleasure is sin and that sex is the most egotistical form of pleasure. But love is an art and art is always a gift. For love to be sublime it must be the ultimate in giving. Love without consideration for one's partner is rape..."

Doug was suddenly interrupted by an irreverent blast on a tenor saxophone and all eyes focussed instantly on a small platform beside him which was now ablaze with the bright light of several flood lamps. The next instant a four-man combo began a jazz cocktail which quickly put the audience on its feet.

For nearly an hour everyone danced with gay abandon. Then--as if by prearrangement--most of the floor was vacated and a spirited melody slowly gained momentum. Encouraged by the audience's rhythmic handclapping, the pianist, drummer, saxophonist and bass player soon reached an intoxicating crescendo that left only Doug and Terry twirling.

Doug managed to wrestle out of his sweater while he guided Terry through a series of acrobatic contortions that made the crowd howl with approval. Only Lorne did not share the spontaneous enthusiasm. Jealousy gnawed at his soul as he stared at the spectacle before his baffled eyes.

After fifteen minutes of pushing, pulling, jumping and whirling, Doug capitulated to sheer exhaustion and plunged gracelessly on a nearby chair. Lorne sighed in relief, thinking the show had come to an end. But it hadn't. Terry kicked off her shoes and pulled off her sweater with a surplus of energy that astounded all. The music was nearly drowned out by a roar of cheers as she performed a fascinating series of gyrations, in the midst of which she dropped her skirt and slip for greater freedom of movement. The bass player plucked his strings hypnotically as he studied Terry's lithe body. The saxophonist, with bulging cheeks and perspiring brow, wailed bewitchingly, while the drummer hit the skins with a passion and precision he had never achieved before. Only the pianist had his back turned to Terry and the audience, hitting the ivory with an incredible combination of speed and calmness. The Dungeon clan had never seen anything like it before.

When she finally quit--the music still echoing in her ears, her body gleaming with perspiration - The Dungeon exploded with a burst of applause that threatened to deafen everyone. And Lorne, suddenly finding her in his lap, erupted into a fit of uncontrollable laughter that took him days to forget.

Doug Marcus took a step back, a dripping rag in his hand, and looked at his shining 1936 Chrysler. I say there, he mused, the old tank looks like new again. He had spent nearly two hours washing and polishing his car, planning to drive to Lorne immediately afterward. Doug had not seen Lorne since The Dungeon party a week ago and he was beginning to wonder if Lorne had been angered by the uninhibited festivities.

Doug had taken the afternoon off. He was one of the gifted few who can get top marks with little study. He had a photographic memory which is a major asset at any university, but particularly at the Faculty of Law. He never worried before or after exams and seldom felt surprised about the results. To Doug the university was not the gateway to a rewarding career, but rather a sophisticated playground where radicals and idlers, materialists and idealists, opportunists and artists mixed with amazing tolerance. Graduation, the climax for most students, was a plain nightmare to Doug, for he knew that this approaching day of reckoning would ruthlessly force him to accept the very responsibilities he loathed.

Doug was a confirmed hedonist. He considered life far too short to be anything else. To fight for some cause, to strive toward some lofty goal or even to work for a living was an inexcusable waste of time in his eyes. To Doug life was an unfortunate accident in which idealism was an exercise in futility and the only certainty: death. Still, sometimes he did not know whether to pity or envy those who mysteriously derived satisfaction while fighting life's ill-matched battles. Although he was convinced that such people had to be masochists, he was not sure whether to be right and miserable was preferable to being wrong and happy. Self-deception with its countless forms of fantasy is, after all, still life's richest source of pleasure.

A striking example of this ignorance-is-bliss herd was Lorne. Doug simply could not understand how anyone with Lorne's intelligence and history of hardships, could still hopefully search for security in a world that has never known it.

Doug stepped in his car and turned his exhaust towards the luxurious mansion that was his home. Half an hour later he reached the slum area of which Lorenzo Street formed an integral part. Why should it feel so good to be here? The stench of a toppled garbage can welcomed him as he approached the dilapidated tool shed. Do I like it here because it demonstrates how well off I am? he wondered. If it is, it's like banging your head against a brick wall, because it feels so good when you quit. He knocked on the door and entered without waiting for a response.

"I hope I am not disturbing you in your scientific endeavors, doctor," he quipped.

"Hi ya, Doug," Lorne greeted cheerfully. "Good to see you."

"I thought I'd better deliver my last shipment this year," Doug explained as he handed Lorne a small cardboard box. "Mostly discarded test tubes, but also the sodium hydroxide which you recently requisitioned."

"Thanks a mint," Lorne said as he put the box on the crowded workbench. "You deserve a Christmas bonus. What about a king-size bottle of nail polish remover? It's one of my latest products."

"Gee, man, that's damn decent of you, but I don't wish to take advantage of your generosity. Besides, I haven't used nail polish since I was a kid and wrote a dirty word with it on a neighbor's car."

"I hope you don't mind if I carry on while we chew the fat."

"As if my objection would make a particle of difference," Doug laughed, "but I do appreciate your courtesy."

Lorne transferred some brown soft soap to a three-gallon crock while stirring vigorously.

"What kind of a ghastly concoction are you conjuring up now?"

"I'm dissolving soap in methyl alcohol," Lorne explained as he studied the thickening liquid. "It's the base for one of my dry-cleaning chemicals. See all those jugs near the desk?" Doug nodded.

"That's twenty-four gallons of Terrysol which I sold inside a single week."

"Twenty-four gallons of what?"

"Terrysol. It's a brand name I made up for one of my products."

"You don't say," Doug observed with a trace of cynicism in his voice. "Any Marcussol around?"

"Hey, that doesn't sound too bad."

"Forget it. I refuse to let my name be used for commercial purposes. If you were making something more attractive than that batch of diarrhea, say a top-notch aphrodisiac, I might be more cooperative. By the way, how is Terry?"

"Gorgeous as ever," Lorne replied, still stirring energetically. And almost hypnotized by the miniature whirlpool in the slightly foaming solution, he added: "I want to marry her."

Doug, always fast with his comments, this time seemed tongue-tied.

Lorne looked up smilingly. "Well, where's the witty remark?" he asked.

"I've got to choose my words carefully," Doug replied. "This sounds serious."

"It is," Lorne agreed. "What do you say?"

"I say 'don't'."

"Well, I asked for that one," Lorne thought aloud as he pulled himself erect. "I love her, Doug. I really do. Our personalities click. I'm sure we were made for each other."

"Boy, you've got it bad," Doug said sympathetically, shaking his head for emphasis.

"I've never felt better in my life."

"Lorne, you need that girl like a moose needs a hat rack. Maybe in the sack she's without peer, maybe she's a hell of a good conversationalist as well. I know she's a terrific dancer, but marriage-never!"

"If I didn't know you better, I'd think you're jealous," Lorne said. "Don't tell me you've got no use for her, because I know better."

"I can think of at least one use," Doug smiled, "but that's not the point. If you like the girl, if she satisfies you, and I hasten to add that I don't mean just sexually, that's great, but marriage would only spoil it all."

Lorne raised his hands in mock despair and said: "I beg you to spare me the Dungeon lecture. I am completely familiar with your views on matrimony. To you marriage is nothing but a gift-wrapped booby trap."

"A perfect epitome. It's like boxing. It's a lot more fun for a spectator than for a participant. On a date the circumstances are quite different than in marriage. You try your damnedest to impress each other, but after you've sacrificed your freedom on the altar, the picture quickly loses its color. The newness wears off, instead of trying to impress each other, you take each other for granted. Soon the chores outnumber the charms and drudgery takes the place of romance. The satisfaction of conquest deteriorates into the misery of captivity. Love withers in marriage."

"Pardon me."

Both Doug and Lorne were startled by the unexpected voice. At the door stood a neatly dressed man, a brief case in his hand.

"I'm looking for Vincent's Custom Chemicals," the bespectacled visitor announced.

"You've found it," Lorne said, observing the man with foreboding.

"I am Charles Preston," the man said without a speck of enthusiasm, "inspector for the city license department."

There was a brief silence as Preston surveyed the chaos of the garage's interior.

"Are you the owner of this, er, enterprise?" "I am," Lorne confessed.

"According to our files you have no license to operate any form of business, including that of manufacturing, Mr. Vincent," the inspector stated with bureaucratic formality. "Why haven't you seen to that?"

"Why?" Lorne echoed, trying hard to set a world speed record for instant answers. "I didn't think I required one in my case. You see, it's not a business in the usual sense of the word. It's sort of a part time effort, more experimental than anything else. Besides, I'm not making a living out of it."

"Have you at any time sold any of your experimental products?" "Yes, I have," Lorne admitted, glancing at Doug.

"Then you are in business," Preston said authoritatively.

"The extent of your transactions has no bearing on your obligation to be properly licensed."

"I didn't know that."

"Well, now that you do, are you prepared to make an application for the required manufacturer's license?"

"Why, sure. How much is it?"

"How many employees do you have?"

"None. This is a one-man operation."

"In that case the fee will be fifteen dollars."

"That's reasonable enough," Lorne volunteered, visibly relieved it did not cost more than that.

"There's one other thing, Mr. Vincent," the inspector continued imperturbably. "You can't carry on your business here. This area is zoned 'residential' and your type of operation is allowed only in industrially-zoned areas."

"In that case there's little point in applying for a license until I have found the proper premises," Lorne said with a sigh.

"That's up to you," Preston said with feigned congeniality. Reverting to his former firmness, he warned:

"I trust you understand that further production or sales before the issuance of the required license will subject you to immediate legal action by our department."

"I understand," Lorne said with the servility of a castigated schoolboy.

"I must also advise you to vacate this building as soon as possible, because your chemicals constitute a fire hazard incompatible with fire regulations."

"Anything else, Mr. Preston?" Lorne suddenly erupted, his voice breaking under the strain of frustration. He no longer could--or for that matter desired to--conceal his contempt for the cynical attitude of the civil servant.

"No, that pretty well covers it," Preston replied calmly. And turning toward the door, he said: "Good-by, Mr. Vincent. Good-by, sir."

"As I was saying," Doug commented after the inspector had left, "you've got enough to worry about without wedding bells."

"Don't rub it in," Lorne said as he stared dejectedly at the shiny array of jugs on the floor.

"I don't blame you for feeling rotten," Doug said sympathetically, "but you may as well face the facts. The next joker to drop in will probably represent Ottawa. 'My name is Joe Blow, federal sales tax. I understand you've been manufacturing a bit without paying the government its legitimate share. A mere oversight, I'm sure, but the government is rather touchy in such matters. I'll quote you the percentages....'"

"You're a big help," Lorne commented as he sat down on a drum of methyl hydrate.

"I'm sorry, Lorne. I am just trying to get across to you that it takes money to make money and you haven't got any."

"Skip the obvious."

"All right, but does it change the picture? Call the whole thing off, Lorne, while you can still save your skin."

"The power of negative thinking," Lorne remarked drily. "Where do you think the world would be today if man had always followed the road of least resistance?"

"Pessimism is one thing, realism is something else again. I'm trying to be realistic right now. There is no profit in chasing rainbows.

Why don't you get yourself a job in some lab? I bet you'd make three times as much as you do now."

"I want to stand on my own feet. I'm not interested in any form of serfdom."

"Would you rather be your own slave?"

"Yes, because I don't know another master I'd rather work for. You know, for a few moments I was actually discouraged, but now I'm surer than ever that nothing and nobody is going to stop me. Tough breaks are nothing new to me. Instead of hindering me, adversity inspires me. *Per Ezclua ad astra:* Through adversity to the stars. How true. I realize you don't believe in my plans and I'm not sure Terry does, but the most important thing is that I believe in them. Self-confidence is the greatest asset in any endeavor."

"You're quite a guy, Lorne," Doug surrendered smilingly. "I've never seen anyone like you. God, how I hope you'll prove me wrong. You sure as hell deserve it."

VII

The fly alighted from the bare bone disappointedly. It briefly studied a used tea bag and a nearby potato that was green with mold, but it was unable to discern anything that could still its gnawing hunger. The creature weakly spread its wings and described a two-coil spiral above the refuse that had spilled from a garbage can which a scavenging dog had toppled earlier in the day.

Now it flew hopefully to the kitchen window of the old house the garbage can belonged to, but a strange translucent barrier stopped it from entering. Drowsily it staggered to the far end of the windowsill where it was welcomed by the bright sunlight that warmed the paintless, weather-beaten wood.

The fly did not know why its limbs felt leaden, why its movements were uncertain: it just sensed something was amiss. It was a warm afternoon and in the sun the temperature was just above the seventy degree mark. It was like spring, only it wasn't. It was November and only two nights ago, the mercury had plummeted below the freezing point, coating the streets with a treacherous film of ice following a light drizzle. But now a warm Pacific wind breathed pleasantly across Vancouver.

The fly had been aroused from its winter slumber a few hours ago when the warm sun rays reactivated its tiny body with new energy.

Reluctant at first, it later left the safety of its hide-out in the cement crevice of a warehouse wall.

Bewildered by the countless vibrations the traffic in the street produced around it, the fly moved about on the sunny section of the sill until a sudden air current enticed it to again try its wings and continue its haphazard journey. But the insect quickly lost altitude as it flew by Max's Second Hand Store and it was dangerously close to the sidewalk as it passed Marie's Lunch. Then, totally unexpectedly, it was pulled back by the suction of an opening door and a moment later found itself inside the small coffee shop, a thousand wonderful odors welcoming it.

The Pyrex coffee pots bubbled gaily on a hot plate. A colossal woman of around fifty wobbled to the percolating brew and lifted one of the glass pots with her pudgy hand. After she had filled a green mug, she returned to the counter and smilingly announced: "This one is on the house."

The customer slowly raised his head, his eyes vaguely aware of the faded apron that hung loosely below the woman's imposing bosom.

"Thanks, Marie," he said softly as he returned her smile in miniature. Then his eyes, forced back deep into their sockets by time and agony, returned to the bare surface of the counter. Marie Chamois observed him with pity glistening in her eyes.

A grey tweed coat, worn and torn by years of wear, carelessly covered the hulk of the middle-aged man. His hollow cheeks were covered by the stubble of a two-day-old beard. His dark hair was long and unkempt. The coarse lines which life had indelibly etched into the pitted skin of his face, gave him a fossiliferous countenance.

"What d'ya got planned for Sunday?" Marie asked her lone customer as she lit a hand-rolled cigarette.

"I haven't planned anything," he said dismally. "I'm in no shape to do any planning. According to the prison doctor I'm damn lucky to even be around."

"Oh, I don't think you've got anything some good home cooking can't cure," Marie said cheerfully.

The man smiled wanly. "You're quite the gal," he said appreciatively.

"How about having dinner with me?" she asked as she tapped the ash off her cigarette onto a cracked saucer. "You're too good to me," he said boyishly.

"Nonsense. Six o'clock?"

"Okay," he said. Then he added: "Barring unforeseen circumstances."

Marie shook her head sympathetically. "I will accept no excuses, you understand now. Even if you should manage to find your boy, you can come together, you know."

"You don't understand," he said, almost curtly. "My son believes I'm dead. I never want him to think otherwise. I just want to know how he's making out for himself. If he is all right. If I can just have one good look at him, I can die peacefully."

"Jake Vincent, you're impossible," Marie exclaimed, "and morbid to boot."

"Well, I'll be damned," Jake said suddenly. "Look at that. A fly in November. Have you ever seen anything like it?"

"I guess the weather has him fooled," Marie said as she slowly moved to the segment of apple pie the insect was exploring. Then with incredible skill and speed for a woman of her age and build, her hand shot out with lethal precision and caught the fly. Inserting her thumb into her fleshy fist she crushed the fly amid some crumbs of pie crust, then lifted the lid of the wood stove and brushed the contents of her hand into the fire. The brief hiss that followed escaped her ear.

"That's what I mean," Jake commented. "Here one moment and gone the next."

"It's only a fly, Jake," Marie said disparagingly.

Jake swallowed the last of his coffee, put down the mug and explored Marie's friendly round face with his probing eyes. He was convinced that the core of the woman was no different than the surface. She obviously had never probed the mysteries of life.

"Marie," he said finally, "I bet the average fly leads a more useful existence than the average human being."

Shortly afterward Jake sauntered along Powell Street on his way to Victory Square where the destitute and the forsaken met and passed the day in the company of a regular platoon of pigeons.

During his one-month stay in Vancouver, he had pretty well kept to himself, uttering little more than a grunt when someone tried to strike up a conversation. Marie was the only exception to his policy of silence.

After twelve long years of prison life, freedom seemed more like a burden than a privilege to Jake. Only the possibility of seeing Lorne kept the embers of hope aglow in his tormented soul.

He carefully spread his old coat on the grass and lay down on it. He closed his eyes, welcoming the sun's warmth with a wan smile. Suddenly he found himself standing again in the warden's office, his suitcase hanging leadenly in his perspiring hand.

"If anyone deserves parole, it's you, Jake," the chief keeper had said warmly. "You've been a model prisoner."

Silently Jake had accepted the firm handshake. Outside the office his sister had welcomed him with a big smile, the tears streaking her make-up. How strangely wonderful her kiss had felt on his cheek! He had realized he had forgotten what a woman's lips felt like. How much else had he forgotten about the outside world?

Eileen had driven him to Edmonton, begging him to come home with her. "Since Lorne left us, Boris has become a different man," she had said in a bid to erase his aversion towards her husband. "He wants to help you find Lorne. Honestly."

But Jake had stubbornly rejected the idea. He had also turned down her offer of financial help, knowing its real source.

"I've got enough money to get by on," he had said with typical Vincent pride. "I only hope I've got enough time as well."

A race against time...and odds. There was only one clue in the mystery of Lorne's whereabouts, but it was an important one. Every Christmas following his departure from the Dobrynchuk residence four years ago, Lorne had sent presents to both his aunt and uncle. The parcels had borne no return address, but the postmark in each case had been Vancouver. The accompanying notes had been cordial in composition, but vague in detail. "I often think of you. I am doing fine. Hope you have a wonderful Christmas." That sort of thing.

Considering Canada is the world's second largest country, it was no small measure of luck that the search was at least restricted to the relatively small slice of real estate occupied by the nation's third largest city.

A light breeze caressed Jake's face and he smelled the salt of the Pacific. Drowsily he tried to plan his next move. He had already consulted the various directories, dropped in at the missing persons bureau, phoned the city's few laboratories and the university, but all to no avail. He also made it a point to study the countless faces of the downtown crowds, though he realized that the chance of thus finding Lorne was extremely small. Still, he knew that if Fate should allow him to cross his son's path this way, he would be prepared for it. Eileen had given him a photograph of Lorne that had been taken at the time of his high school graduation and Jake was convinced he would have no difficulty in recognizing his son. He yawned unabashedly. God was he tired!

People had told him that it was the change of climate that caused his sleepiness, that it would soon wear off, but Jake could not help remembering what the prison doctor had told him just before his release. "That ticker of yours may give you trouble, Jake," old doc McLean had said. "Avoid excitement and strain. Don't push yourself too much." The doctor had not mentioned the alternative. Jake knew without having it spelled out for him. He was walking on the edge of eternity right now. Remembering the lot of the fly, he felt a chill creep up his spine. Time was running out while the odds against a successful conclusion of his search seemed to multiply at a distressing rate. What could he do next? What guarantee did he really have that Lorne was still in Vancouver? Couldn't he have moved God knows where to since last Christmas? Even life in prison had never seemed this hopeless.

He finally fled from despair into sleep. A few moments later he found himself chopping wood on his Inglewood farm, sweating profusely in the crusty snow. The music of Martha's violin reached his ears. The bucked poplar split and splintered obligingly under his swinging axe. He inhaled the invigorating air gratefully as he paused for a moment, watching the smoke rise peacefully from the chimney toward the cloudless sky. Suddenly a familiar voice startled him. He turned quickly around and discovered Batford kissing his wife near the barn. Axe in hand, Jake ran to them. "Don't get upset, darling," she said calmly. "He means no harm." He stared at her aghast, suddenly realizing that it was not Martha, but Joan, his first wife.

"Where is Lorne?" Jake asked angrily.

Batford grinned sardonically. "He's gone," he said. "You're lying, you goddamn bastard," Jake exploded. "Lorne would never leave me."

"He didn't," Joan said simply. "You left HIM."

"No," Jake cried hoarsely, "no, you mustn't say that." Before he could vent his fury with violence the pair faded out of sight and Jake found himself back in his cell. The game of make-believe repeated itself for the thousandth time. Lying on his cot he feasted his ears on the sound of some children playing outside, pretending one of the happy voices to be his son's.

"Lorne!" Jake shouted. "Lorne!"

Someone shook him roughly by the shoulders. Slowly he returned to reality, thinking at first he recognized the voice of Jack Strachan, his cell mate.

"All right, snap out of it," the voice said authoritatively. "Come on."

Jake saw the uniform, but it was not brown like the prison guards wore: it was dark blue - police! He noticed the crowd that had gathered around him.

"What a sight for children," he heard a woman say with unbridled disgust.

"On your feet," the constable urged, trying to lift Jake.

"Vancouver is full of them," another anonymous voice announced. "It makes a person wonder where they get the money to get drunk."

The last word made him jump up with surprising agility. "I'm not drunk," he protested. "I just had a little nap. Is that against the law?"

"You were talking in your sleep," the policeman said good naturedly, "and not too sensibly, I might add. Now just go home peacefully and everything will be all right."

Jake walked away, his coat flung carelessly over his arm, the mocking voices dying behind him.

"Home," it echoed in his throbbing head: "Home!" He remembered the drafty attic room on Powell Street, the naked light bulb that hung precariously at the end of the frayed electrical cord near his bed. Home. Air conditioning with a northerly wind, running water with a good rain. His cell had been more comfortable, but at three bucks a week what can one expect? The Waldorf Astoria's bridal suite?

"I think the shutter speeds are out," the young man said gravely. "Do you think it can be fixed?"

Malcolm Nithdale looked at the empty sardine can, then at his son. "I'll see what I can do, David," he said calmly.

"I didn't think I would have any trouble. It's an expensive camera," David Nithdale said, his hand groping nervously in his coat pocket. "Look at these prints."

A handful of advertisements torn crudely out of a newspaper fluttered into Malcolm's lap.

"Please hold them by the edges," David cautioned. "I don't want any fingerprints on them."

"I'll be careful," Malcolm promised, staring absentmindedly at a chewing gum ad.

"Notice how they're all overexposed?" David asked.

"I see what you mean," Malcolm said sympathetically as he rose from his chair. "I'll take the camera to Zanler's first thing in the morning and see what they have to say about it."

"Zanier's?" David echoed, confusion creasing his forehead with a frown.

"Yes, your favorite camera shop, remember?"

Frustration suffused David's eyes with sudden tears. "I don't remember, dad," he blurted.

"That's all right, David," Malcolm said as he put his arm around his son's shaking shoulders. "We all forget things at times."

"I remember less and less," David sobbed. "What's happening to me?"

"You're just a little upset, that's all," Malcolm said, feeling utterly helpless.

A nurse walked toward them. "Come, David," she said pleasantly. "It's time for your afternoon lessons."

Malcolm watched his son follow the girl with the docility of a lamb. David did not look back. He would soon forget his father had visited him.

Outside things seemed better. It was a nice brisk day, the blue sky was sparsely spotted with small puffs of clouds and the nip in the wintry air was invigorating.

The layout of Essondale was not unlike that of a campus. The buildings were generously spaced apart and the lawns were maintained with meticulous care. The agony was well hidden.

Malcolm walked slowly toward the parking area, his thoughts dominated by the harrowing experience of the visit. About a year and a half ago Fate, in a moment of madness, had reduced David Nithdale from a bright university student to a human vegetable. Malcolm's only son and oldest child had entered the University of British Columbia at the age of sixteen with three scholarships for moral encouragement. His picture and record of scholastic achievements had appeared on the front page of the Vancouver Sun and he had participated in a CBC[1] panel discussion on the merits and dangers of nuclear power. He had also been a real camera bug and his unusual angle and lighting techniques had won him several prizes.

But the prospects of a promising future had exploded into nothingness when his car had been smashed into an unrecognizable mass of twisted steel and pulverized glass in a head-on collision with a large freight truck. The truck driver, who subsequently had been found guilty of driving without due care, had suffered only minor cuts and bruises, but David and his girlfriend had not been so lucky. Joan Meldor had been killed instantly and David had hovered

---

[1] * Canadian Broadcasting Corporation

between life and death for more than two weeks. Except for some irreparable cerebral damage, he had eventually made a complete physical recovery, but barring a miracle he would always remain mentally deficient.

"Nice day, sir." Malcolm looked up. A patient sitting beside a nurse on one of the park benches stared at him with a broad smile.

"Nice day," Malcolm muttered mechanically as he walked on. When he reached his car, he looked back at the buildings. Hell, he thought. Hell on earth.

Kim, his wife, did not know he was here. He never told her about these visits and she never asked. Kim had not seen David for nearly a year and neither had the girls. When Dr. Coventry, the psychiatrist, had explained the hopelessness of David's condition, they had accepted the verdict with the same finality a funeral dictates. Anything that might revive the sadness of the past had become taboo. His books, trophies and other personal belongings now rested carefully hidden in a trunk in the basement. His name was never mentioned at home, his past never discussed. Life seemed more bearable that way. Time heals all wounds, provided one does not pick at the scabs of oblivion.

And now as Malcolm entered his car, he began to doubt for the first time the wisdom of his visits to his son. He pushed his hands deep into his pockets, discovering the sardine can and the paper advertisements. Who benefited from these visits? Who even appreciated them? No one. And still he knew deep down that he would return again next week, maybe sooner. Why? It was not love that motivated him, for Malcolm loved no one - not even himself. It could not be hope either, for there was none. Neither was it pity, for Malcolm was incapable of compassion. No, the real reason for his regular visits was a form of masked egotism, because essentially it was part of himself that languished behind those brick walls.

With the thunderclap of tragedy, the past had superseded the future in importance, for regardless what the future might bring, it could never replace what the past had taken.

Malcolm abruptly ended his meditations and a few moments later he was headed towards Vancouver. At least things looked better at work. All sales were up over last year, including those of dry cleaning chemicals. It looked as though his prediction about the speedy end of his competitor had come true.

Wayne Scott had told him a month ago that the products of Vincent's Custom Chemicals were no longer available and the situation had not changed since.

That's the trouble with those fly-by-night operations, he mused complacently: a noisy birth and an early funeral.

"Driver, I have you know I make this trip at least twice a week and it has never cost me more than ninety cents," the elderly lady protested vigorously as her bony fingers dawdled above her purse.

"I'm sorry, madam, but the meter doesn't lie. As you can see it reads ninety-five cents and that's what it is," Lorne said patiently, holding the door of the cab open for his ornery customer.

"Very well," the woman said haughtily as she handed him a one-dollar bill, "that's the last time I've taken a Starlite taxi."

"That's your privilege," Lorne smiled, dropping a nickel change into her waiting hand.

A minute later he was mobile again.

"Twenty-seven cruising in six," Lorne reported.

"Okay, twenty-seven," the dispatcher's voice crackled over the two-way radio.

Lorne glanced at the fare sheet. It had been a good day. He turned his car onto Kingsway. It was almost four o'clock. In the next hour things would really get hopping.

He had been back on day shift for nearly a month now and he could not help remembering the look of surprise on the supervisor's face when he had asked him for the change of shift.

"You were on days three months ago," Bud Anderson had reminded him. "Then you asked to work nights."

"I know," Lorne had said, "but I like to spend my evenings with my girlfriend."

The explanation had sounded quite plausible and Bud had granted his request, but the real reason for his desire to work days was quite different.

He slowed down, pulled the car over to the curb and picked up the mike again. "Code five for twenty-seven," he said.

"Go ahead twenty-seven."

A code five covered anything from a race to the nearest John to a coffee break, but it did not include anything like Lorne had in mind. He walked around the car, opened the trunk and lifted out a cardboard box. After he slammed the trunk shut again, he walked to a nearby beauty parlor.

"Hi ya, Lorne," the receptionist greeted him.

"How are you, Corine," Lorne smiled. "Jim in?"

"No, but he left a cheque for you," Corine van Noorden said cheerfully.

"Good show," Lorne commented as he walked past her to the back of the shop. Her accent always amused him. Corine had recently arrived from Holland and although her English was generally well composed, her pronunciation betrayed her foreign extraction.

He merely nodded to acknowledge the glances cast at him by the hairdressers. In the storeroom he took four gallon-jugs out of the box and placed them on a shelf. Just think, he mused, I may well be the world's first shampoo bootlegger.

Since his request to work days had been granted, Lorne had made all his clandestine deliveries by taxi-- perhaps another world's first.

At the desk Corine handed him the cheque. "It's good shampoo," she complimented him with a genuine smile. "I use it all the time."

"Thank you," he said, looking at her rather boldly and discovering the charm of her face. She was not particularly pretty, but she had an honest countenance, her eyes not veiled by feminine mystique.

"Where did you learn to speak English so well?" he reciprocated.

"At school," she replied simply.

"Does everybody study English in Holland?"

"In high school, yes. French and German, too."

She visibly enjoyed the look of marvel that lit up his face.

"Do you find much difference between Dutch and English?" Lorne asked.

"Quite a bit."

"Say something in Dutch to me."

Corine blushed slightly. "Like what?"

"Well, something like 'how are you?'"

Hoe maakt U het?"

"Who mahkt uh it?" Lorne tried.

"Hey, that's pretty good," she laughed.

"I'll be back for my second lesson next month."

The radio crackled as he slid behind the wheel.

"Fare at Kingsway and Fraser."

Lorne grabbed the mike with lightning speed. "Twenty-seven almost there," he lied.

"All right, twenty-seven: she's all yours."

He stepped on the gas and the car surged forward. A guy's got to be fast, he reflected as he checked his rear-view mirror for cops. His speedometer hovered near the 45-mile mark, fifteen miles above the speed limit. Lorne knew the dispatcher would be watching the clock to see how long it would take before the fare was booked. If it would take too long he would know Lorne was not as close to the fare as he had indicated and that would spell trouble with a capital T. With competition as keen as it was, service had to be swift if a cab company wanted to stay in business.

Well, at least I've got rid again of my contraband merchandise today, Lorne thought happily. He still had not found a proper place to continue his business--legally.

So far, everything he had seen had either been unsuitable or too expensive.

He pulled over to the curb when he spotted the woman. "Ashley Hotel," she said as she entered.

A whiff of dime store perfume greeted Lorne's nostrils as he leaned forward to turn down the flag of the meter. Piloting the car onto Fraser Street, he glanced at her. He was not surprised. She was crowding forty, a fact she obviously and unsuccessfully tried to hide with a generous supply of cosmetics. Her plain, oval face was framed by a second-class mop of bleached hair.

"Keeping busy?" she inquired as she lit a cigarette. "Can't complain," Lorne replied noncommittally.

"Can't kick myself," she volunteered between puffs. "Been long with Starlite?"

"Just about a year."

"Jimmy Hale back yet?"

"No, he's still in hospital. He had an accident, you know."

She smiled contemptuously. "Some accident," she said, tapping her cigarette nervously above the dashboard's ash tray. "The cops beat the hell out of him."

"I understand Jim tried to sweep the street, using a policeman as a broom," Lorne said drily. "Apparently that's against the law."

"That goddamn cop asked for everything he got," she protested vehemently. "He accused Jimmy of being drunk on the job and Jimmy proved he wasn't."

Lorne stopped the car in front of the Hastings Street hotel. "Eighty five cents, please," he announced.

The woman pulled up her skirt, pulling a dollar bill from under the top of her stocking.

"That's a strange place to keep your money," Lorne remarked as he handed her the change.

"What's strange about it?" she asked, raising her eyebrows. "That's where I make it."

"Absorb the exquisite decor to fortify your memory," Terry said gaily as she handed Lorne a drink. "I want you to always remember this apartment, because I've spent the happiest moments of my life here."

"You make it sound as if it's a thing of the past," Lorne commented.

"By tomorrow it will be," Terry said with a touch of sadness in her voice. "I'm moving to Kitsilano first thing in the morning." She brought the drink to her lips and sipped just enough to moisten her tongue. "I quit my job at Narson's last week," she confessed. "So, since you can't eat the cake and have it, too, I'm gonna share an apartment with a girl friend of mine."

"Well, I understand there's quite a demand for stenographers in Vancouver, so it probably won't take you long to find something else," Lorne said.

"I'm in no hurry," Terry said cheerfully. "I'm sick and tired of sitting behind a desk all day."

"Would you prefer housework?" Lorne asked boldly.

Terry leaned back in her chair, crossing her legs daintily. "I've got a hunch that question is loaded," she said.

"You're right," Lorne said as he walked over to her and taking her hands in his, he continued: "I'll rephrase my question. Do you want to marry me, Terry?"

"Marry?" Terry echoed, finding herself at a temporary loss for words.

"Yeah," Lorne said, pained by the negative suggestion in her voice, "I know it's not exactly a new idea and rather conforming, but the fact remains that marriage has been the rage of the ages."

"I hate to say 'no', but I can't say 'yes'," Terry said as she stroked his hair. "It simply couldn't work."

"If you love me only a fraction as much as I love you, I'm sure it would be one of the best marriages on record. I love you, Terry. I love you very much."

"I love you, too, Lorne," she said smilingly, "but why spoil it all by marriage?"

"You sound like Doug," Lorne said bitterly. "Next you'll be handing me the can't-we-be-friends routine."

"How about another drink?" she asked, rising to her feet. "I can't think of a better antidote."

"Cheers," she said a moment later, after handing Lorne his glass.

"To nothing," Lorne toasted.

"Why nothing, Lorne?" Terry asked, hurt creeping into her eyes. "We have so many wonderful things to remember, darling, and I'm sure we can add many more."

She seated herself beside Lorne on the modern settee.

"The world's greatest love stories are all about people who were not married, at least not to each other," Terry said sympathetically. "It's true that often such courtships led to the altar, but the story always ends there, because it is at this point bliss is exchanged for boredom and routine takes the place of enchantment."

"You've given marriage more thought than I suspected," Lorne said, placing his half-empty glass on the table beside him. "Still, I think we could be very happy together."

"Oh, you sweet, wonderful dreamer," Terry said. "How can you be so clever in some ways and so, so...naive in others. I simply can't see myself as a married woman."

"Why not?"

"Well, for one thing I'm accustomed to more luxury than you could possibly afford. Let's be realistic, Lorne: love may be great on a honeymoon, but it's poor currency when you try to pay your bills with it. Look around you. Everything is the best. I've got more clothes than I know of and I want more. Maybe that sounds selfish, but I feel no need to apologize for it. I came into this world as poor as a church mouse, but it didn't take me long to figure out that the life of a pauper was not for me. When I was sixteen, my father had had a steady job for more than twenty years and the poor guy had nothing to show for it, except overdue bills, a worn-out wife and five kids perpetually clamoring for things he couldn't afford but bought anyway. So one morning I put my few worldly goods in a shopping bag and left home. I haven't seen any of them since."

Lorne put his arm around her shoulders. "You know, Terry, baby," he said. "We've got more in common than you think. My childhood wasn't exactly a bed of roses either. As for the future, I think we basically want the same things. I guess it all boils down to financial security. I'm working like hell to get there and I will. It's just a matter of time."

"Who cares about the future?!" Terry suddenly erupted. "What guarantee do we have there even is a future? It's the present that counts, Lorne, and the present is too precious to sacrifice for a future that may never come. I was told once that there are only two things in life that count more than everything else and that's oneself and now. Life is too short to waste on hoping that tomorrow will be better. Hope based on hope. It's the cruelest form of self-deception going."

She jumped up and walked over to the record player. A few seconds later the apartment was filled with the sensuous sound of a rumba. Terry started to dance, her hips moving bewitchingly to the Latin rhythm. "The night is young, darling," she cooed, "and so are we."

The sight of Terry's uninhibited gyrations had an intoxicating effect on Lorne. He walked over to her and for a few minutes managed to duplicate her movements, his muscles loosened by the captivating melody. But the proximity of her lush body melted the last vestiges of restraint in his soul. He pressed her close to him, covering her face and neck with a shower of kisses.

"I need you, baby," Lorne sighed, a surge of dizziness sweeping through his trembling body, his hands groping hungrily for the privacy of her flesh.

The pink bedroom was as tastefully furnished and decorated as the rest of the apartment, but Lorne had only eyes for Terry. Her lips parted obligingly as he pressed his mouth passionately on hers, her body gently undulating under his.

He knew now that nothing could stop him. Nothing did.

VIII

Christmas means different things to different people. To Harry Weldan it represented a feast of indulgence, an elusive flight from reality. It was a time he chose to forget the hardships of the past, the misery of the present. Poker and beer afforded him a chance of cheer in his cheerless world. For a few precious hours his thoughts did not concern his dying wife.

"You deal," Dick Denver said as he puffed a huge cloud of cigar smoke in Harry's direction.

Harry shuffled the cards expertly, wondering what kind of a hand he would end up with. It was good to be here, away from the stinking garbage cans, the sloshy potholes, the crawling van.

"I'll open for four bits," Jack Longworth announced stolidly. He was a big man who did not look his fifty-two autumns. Like Dick and Harry he worked for the city, only he was the driver of the truck they were obliged to follow with their inexhaustible supply of trash. The privilege of shelter is nothing to scoff at, particularly on rainy days, for showers are as common in Vancouver as feathers in a hennery.

"I call and up it fifty cents," Dick said, trying hard to look indifferent with three jacks staring at him.

"Jesus: a dollar!" Harry exclaimed. "I'll stay." For a moment it was so quiet, he could hear his companions breathe. "Cards?" he asked. "I'll take one," Jack said.

"Give me two," Dick said, hoping fervently for a full house. But the required pair failed to materialize and Dick suddenly remembered telling his wife to go easy on the grocery money. He already had lost close to twenty dollars. He thought of Loretta and the kids, his belated concern for their well-being barely perceptibly creasing his brow.

After Dick had fattened the pot with an additional fifty cents, Jack Longworth's face broke into a confident smile.

"Bluffing, eh?" he said teasingly.

"If you're so sure, why don't you call me?" Dick countered with an air of aloofness that was purely artificial.

"All right, I call," Jack said, putting three queens down.

"Well, they say you can't win them all," Dick sighed, "but I guess you can lose them all."

Harry Weldan silently congratulated himself, grateful he had pulled out in time. He had lost, too, but not nearly as much as Dick. Why is it, he wondered, that the guy who least needs it, always cleans the pot? Jack Longworth was a bachelor who had considerably more money than worries, a rather logical phenomenon, perhaps, but nonetheless a bit painful to observe for his colleagues who were forced to make ends meet under circumstances where the income-obligation ratio was very much the opposite of Jack's.

"What about a beer, Harry?" Jack asked after Dick had left.

"Bring me two," Harry said with an amiable dab of insolence, "it'll save you a trip later."

"How did you make out?" Jack asked as he swung the refrigerator door open.

"I think I just about broke even," Harry said with a yawn, stretching his legs under the table.

"Here's to better luck next time," Jack proposed as he handed Harry his bottles. "How's the wife?"

"Getting closer to the grave every day," Harry said, unhappy about the unexpected turn in the conversation. Then he took a big gulp of beer as if to wash the unpleasant thoughts away.

"Yeah, it's a son-of-a-bitch," Jack continued, "knowing there's no hope. I guess, she takes it pretty hard."

"That's the strange thing about it, but she don't," Harry said. "You know, she told me the other day that I suffer more than she does and I'm almost believing it."

"Well, maybe she's right. I've never seen a guy worry as much as you do. Don't do anyone any good worrying. Life goes on, Harry. A year from now it'll all seem like a bad dream."

"Yeah, I guess so" Harry agreed unconvincingly.

"Tell you what," Jack said spiritedly. "Let's really live it up. What do you say if we'd really have us a wild time?"

"Like what?"

"Like what?! Jack echoed. "Like a hot piece of tail, that's what. I know a couple of young babes that can make you forget anything. They're damn pretty and shapely as hell. Out of this world. What d'you say, Harry?"

"I say, what the hell are we waiting for?"

Corine van Noorden was awakened by a shout. It was Ricky, her sister's five-year-old son. He had apparently discovered Santa's gifts under the Christmas tree and now gave ample vent to his excitement. "Daddy, daddy!" He cried ebulliently as he ran towards the bedroom beside hers. "Look what Santa brought me." Corine got up and dressed quickly. It was her first Christmas in Canada. She had left Holland a little more than half a year ago to join her sister and start a new life away from the small nation that would always remind her of the horrors of war. When Canadian troops had liberated the city of Rijssen after several days of fierce fighting, she had been only twelve, her mind indelibly engraved with the consequences of Nazi tyranny. People had predicted she would soon forget the odious past, but Corine knew she would never forget how she had lost her father and young brother.

Back in 1945 when Mary had married Stan Naylor in one of the hundreds of colorless weddings then in vogue for allied soldiers and Dutch girls who wished to tie the nuptial knot, Corine had proudly accepted her role as sole supporter of her mother. She became an outstanding high school student and during holidays she earned enough to take the edge off their poverty. Once I've graduated, she thought hopefully, I can really be of help.

But barely a month before she had written her final exams, her mother had married Dirk Leeuwenhoek, the middle-aged neighborhood tobacconist whose wife had died when liberation from Nazi oppression had only been two days old. *Meneer* Leeuwenhoek was no stranger to Corrie, as she was then called. He had been a regular visitor to the van Noorden residence for many years and after her father's death had helped the family in many ways.

Still the news of his marrying her mother had been a staggering blow to Corine. She realized that with Dirk Leeuwenhoek moving in, her role would soon be reduced to the usefulness of a vermiform appendix. Time proved her right. Dirk Leeuwenhoek was always kind to her, but every time she looked at him, she saw her father stand behind him. The inevitable comparison was not in Leeuwenhoek's favor. Tolerance is a poor substitute for love. Corine regarded the whole marriage nothing short of a betrayal of her father whom she loved as much in death as she had in life.

In June 1952, the wedding bells still echoing painfully in her ears, Corrie received her high school diploma. But instead of graduating cum laude, as had generally been expected, she had made it only by the skin of her teeth. It did not matter to Corrie. For a while little did. Soon the house of her birth became too small and when she landed a job with a local bank, she took her first step toward independence by renting a small room. When the newness grew into routine, she realized the colorless nature of her existence and in that frame of mind she had written to Mary.

She had asked Mary for help in her efforts to start a new life and she had received it generously. Stan had filed the necessary papers to make her emigration possible and in April she had rejoined her sister with confidence and good cheer after a separation of six years.

"Can we run the train now?" Ricky pleaded as he admired the locomotive of the railway set.

"After breakfast, dear," Mary said. "Come on. Time to get washed up and dressed."

"Daddy is still shaving," Ricky tried to stall the issue.

"I was," Stan announced as he emerged from the bathroom. "On your way. Quick march."

After the traditional exchange of gifts, Corine left for church. From Harlow Street where they lived it was only a ten-minute walk to St. Andrews.

"That's one thing I like about working on Christmas," Lorne said as he tallied his fares in the Starlite dispatch office, "fourteen dollars and twenty cents in tips."

"You must have had the generous customers," Percy Jones, another cab driver, remarked dispiritedly. "I'm lucky if I've got two bucks."

It was half past six when Lorne left for home. He had worked ten hours and been on the move since he had wheeled his car onto the road. Now as he waited for the bus to take him to Lorenzo Street, he thought about his date with Terry and the things he planned to tell her between kisses.

He recalled happily how she had changed since they had had their argument a few weeks ago. The future could not look brighter. He had found a place near the waterfront where he could continue his business legitimately.

Nineteen fifty-three is going to be a great year, he thought confidently. Next week he would pick up his manufacturer's license at city hall and before mid-January he would deliver nearly two hundred dollars' worth of products.

Already he had more than eighty dollars in back orders alone. Dry cleaning chemicals and shampoos in particular were selling well. Starting next week his customers could order by phone. He shared an office with the proprietors of the building he was about to move into.

Orvil Hamilton, co-owner of the two-storey structure, operated a sheet metal business in the front section of the main floor, while his partner, Don Langford, used the entire second floor manufacturing lamps and rod iron furniture. Lorne had rented the rear portion of the main floor.

Unlike others he had contacted, Hamilton and Langford had not insisted on a lease. He would simply rent the premises on a month to month basis. The office staff would handle his telephone calls. It was an ideal set-up.

When Lorne came home, he quickly opened a tin of spaghetti and meat balls and transferred the contents into a frying pan. The metal coil of the hot plate quickly turned red and soon the reddish substance hissed and sizzled as Lorne diligently stirred it to prevent it from burning.

The meal was like any other meal he had eaten any other day in the past year. The room was as bare as it had been the day he had moved in nearly two years ago; Just a bed, a table plus two chairs, a dresser and the naked light bulb that hung desolately from the center of the ceiling.

But Lorne did not miss the pine scent of the Christmas trees that adorned most homes nor the colorful lights or the carol singing. He accepted Christmas like any other day, because it was like any other day - at least to him. It was that simple. Yet, this Christmas was different, because now there was Terry.

As he ate his meal he wondered if the perfume he had bought would please her. Ten dollars for the tiny flacon had seemed like a ridiculous price to pay, a sum he could ill afford, yet well spent if it would please her. But that he did not know. He could not predict her reaction, because he knew little about perfumes and even less about women.

"I think we're heading for a new record," Phyllis Brandon said cheerfully as she leaned back in the plush rocking chair, her legs folded beside her. "Just think, honey, we've got all night ahead of us and already we've got $200 bucks."

"And tax free," Terry commented without enthusiasm.

"You're so right. Mind passing me the brandy? Thanks." And pouring herself another drink, she continued: "No girl makes that kind of money pounding a typewriter."

Terry sat down and lit a cigarette. Blowing the smoke slowly toward the lamp stand beside her, she asked suddenly: "Tell me, Phyllis, have you ever been in love with a guy?"

Phyllis raised her eyebrows in contempt and snorted: "Of course not."

"Of course not?" Terry echoed. "Why 'of course'? Isn't 'not' bad enough?"

"Men are egotistical animals," Phyllis explained. "For two years you've rented your body to them, surely this simple fact of life hasn't escaped your attention."

"All men?"

"All men."

"Even your father?"

"Especially my father."

Terry poured herself a drink. "If all women thought like you the human race would soon be extinct."

"And the world would be a better place to live in," Phyllis complemented. Then she tipped her drink and placed the empty glass on the side table near her.

"You're talking nonsense now," Terry protested, visibly confused with the unexpected turn in the conversation.

"That's right, absolute nonsense, just like your idea to trade your most precious possession for a steady job as an underpaid Cinderella in a one-man show." Before Terry could comment, the telephone rang.

"Hello," Phyllis sang in her sweetest voice. Terry studied her closely. "Why sure I remember you. That's fine. Yes, she's here too. Bye, bye."

"A double deal?" Terry asked after Phyllis had hung up.

"Yes, and possibly an all-night session as well, at least as far as the dough is concerned. Remember Jack Longworth?"

"Oh, no," Terry sighed, "not that ugly bruiser again."

"Don't worry, baby," Phyllis said reassuringly, "I'll handle him. You can have his friend."

"Who is his friend?"

"I don't know. He didn't say."

"At any rate, I'll stall him this time. We've got lots of booze left."

"When will they be here?"

"About twenty minutes," Phyllis replied.

Terry mentally debated whether or not to tell Phyllis about her date with Lorne in about two hours' time. Naw, she reflected, there's no point in fanning the flames. I'll just shake the trick somehow and go.

"I'm gonna have a sandwich. Can I fix you one?" Phyllis asked from the kitchen.

"No, thanks. I think I'll just have a cup of coffee."

You know, it's a crazy thing. Longworth is a ruthless man in bed," Phyllis said matter-of-factly, as she opened a can of salmon, "but I prefer him to the pansy type any time."

"I bet the brute can swear an hour straight without repeating himself," Terry said as she poured the coffee.

"You know," Phyllis remarked, "I actually believe he gets a sexual kick out of using his vilest vocabulary in the presence of a woman." "I've no doubt he does," Terry said.

Just then there was a light knock at the door.

"It can't be them already," Phyllis said. "I haven't finished my sandwich yet."

Terry lifted the coffee to her waiting lips as she heard Phyllis open the door, and say: "You're early."

The thunderous roar of laughter that followed confirmed Terry's suspicion that Jack Longworth had arrived.

"When it comes to sex, it's never too early," Longworth bellowed. "My friend here and I are hard up as hell."

"We're ready for you," Phyllis smiled unabashed. Then she saw an expression of horror spread over the other man's face. Following his eyes she noticed Terry's figure frozen in the kitchen doorway.

97

"What's the matter, Harry?" Longworth asked in a puzzled voice. But Harry Weldan ignored the question and bolted for the door.

"I don't understand," the big man said apologetically.

"You know that guy?" Phyllis asked as she walked toward Terry.

"Know him?" Terry echoed, visibly stunned, "My own father?"

Jack Longworth studied the girl incredulously. What kind of a nuthouse is this anyway, he thought. He left half angry, half confused. It was his lousiest Christmas ever.

Later Phyllis pressed Terry close to her breast as they lay on Terry's bed. "Don't feel too badly, darling," Phyllis said consolingly. "My father raped me when I was only thirteen. Men are a selfish lot:

especially fathers."

Then she kissed Terry gently on the forehead. "The exceptions are on the surface only. Beneath they're all alike."

The long shadow of paternal sordidness had suddenly obliterated all faith Terry had so painstakingly gathered during her dates with Lorne.

"I know you're right," she sighed as she snuggled closely to Phyllis. "Even my tears have forsaken me."

"I love you, Terry," Phyllis whispered, feeling surer than ever that the girl in her arms would stray no more. And planting her kisses closer and closer to Terry's mouth, she moved on top of the girl, her fingers groping hungrily for the young flesh.

To Terry's surprise there was no hint of revulsion in her heart, no desire to escape the woman's advances. A strange, newly found calm captured her mind. An uncontrollable passion swept feverishly through her body, permeating her every feeling, activating her every muscle until the last vestiges of reason had been destroyed and perversion reigned unopposed.

"Tell me you love me," Phyllis panted, encouraged by the undulating movements of Terry's lithe body.

"I love you, Phyllis," Terry heard herself say through the fog of confusion that enveloped her in increasing density.

"That's good, baby, Oh, God, that's good," Phyllis moaned.

Part III

IX

"Mr. Farrington is out of town this week," the sweet voice said over the phone.

"Well, who's next in charge?" Lorne inquired, his voice betraying his annoyance.

"Mr. Brock, our branch manager."

"All right, put him on."

And a moment later: "Ted Brock here."

"This is Lorne Vincent of Vincent's Custom Chemicals. I put an order in for a drum of butyl alcohol ten days ago and I am still waiting. What's the score?"

"Our shipments from the East have been coming in late the last few weeks."

"When I first dropped in at your office, Mr. Farrington assured me that your company carries a large stock of the chemicals I am using. This is the second time I am forced to wait. Do you realize that I am losing money because I can't fill my orders?"

"I am very sorry."

"I can't bottle apologies," Lorne snapped. "If this happens again I will be forced to deal elsewhere. When can I expect my shipment and this time without qualifications?"

"You'll have it Saturday or Monday at the latest."

"You mean I have to wait four more days?"

"If we get it sooner, we'll waste no time in getting it to you. It's the best I can do."

It was hot and stuffy that day. Lorne rose from his chair and walked over to the window of his small office. Overlooking the water he watched a gillnetter return to the packing plant nearby, its hull heavy with fish, screeching sea gulls flying hopefully overhead.

It makes a guy wonder, Lorne thought, here you work like a bastard trying to get orders and then you can't fill them. The same thing had happened a month earlier with a shipment of jugs. But the delay had not hit him as hard then because he had bought some used ones and cleaned and filled them like in the old days.

The old days. Lorne snickered. So much had happened in a little more than six months. He could even accept the fact that Terry was no longer in Vancouver. For many weeks her absence had gnawed at his mind. His every action had been overshadowed by her abrupt departure.

He remembered how he had waited in the restaurant until closing time.

"Don't be blue," the young waitress had said. "It's Christmas - a time to be merry."

Silently he had risen and walked toward the door.

"Hey, you forgot something," the girl had said. It had been the bottle of perfume.

"It's no good to me. You take it," he had said before slipping into the dark night.

He had decided not to go to her apartment that night. But after several days had gone by, he had been unable to suppress his curiosity any longer.

On New Year's Eve, after asking permission to leave his cab, he entered the Belinda Apartments.

She must be home, he mused as he climbed the stairs, because the lights are on. Then he stopped dead in his tracks--it could just be Phyllis. Diffidently he knocked on the door. When it opened he looked with bewilderment at an elderly woman.

"Yes?"

"Is Terry in?"

"Terry?"

"Yes, Terry Weldan."

"You must have the wrong suite."

Lorne was about to protest when he noticed a pipe-smoking man appear behind her.

"Probably one of the tenants before we moved in, Clara," he suggested. Then directing his voice to Lorne:

"We only moved in yesterday."

"Maybe Mr. Boulton, the caretaker, can tell you where she moved to," the woman said, "he lives downstairs in suite number four."

The hall of the main floor was filled with the sound of merrymaking. One of the doors was open and Lorne saw a glimpse of a man hoisting a woman off the ground and promptly dropping her when she emptied a glass over his head. Still confused by the news he had just learned from the couple upstairs, he knocked at the caretaker's door. He was greeted by a loud burst of laughter followed by shuffling feet.

A small girl opened the door and smiled shyly at Lorne.

"Is Mr. Boulton in?" Lorne asked.

The girl dashed into the partying crowd, leaving the door open. A few moments later a man in his forties, wearing a party hat, holding a glass in one hand and a gaily colored horn in the other, appeared. Cocking his head to one side, he inquired: "What's your problem? Out of ice cubes like the others?"

"I'd like to know Where Terry Weldan moved to."

The man suddenly pulled his head erect and scrutinized Lorne with a mix of interest and suspicion.

"So would a lot of people, including myself," Dick Boulton said. "She and her friend still owe me a month's rent." He emptied the glass in one gulp. "You're one of her, err, friends?"

"Sort of," Lorne replied noncommittally.

Boulton smirked knowingly. "A friend, a client, a trick, call them what you like, they all came for the same thing."

"You're her third friend tonight," he volunteered, "but I guess she must have some enemies as well, because both she and Phyllis left rather hastily on Boxing Day."

"Maybe they'll be back," Lorne said unconvincingly. "That's what I thought until Phyllis phoned me later that day." "Phoned you?" Lorne chimed, suddenly all ears.

"Yes, she said she phoned from the airport to tell me that I could rent the apartment right away, because they wouldn't be back. I guess the cops got wise to them. Maybe they got behind on their payoff."

"What do you mean?" Lorne asked, his eyes narrowing with hostility.

"'Well, peddling your ass ain't exactly legal…"

Lorne's fist flashed toward Boulton's face, but the caretaker parried it deftly, his glass shattering into a thousand pieces and the party horn landing in the midst of it.

"Listen, punk," Boulton breathed heavily as he held Lorne pinned against the wall. "Those two babes paid me five hundred bucks a month for that apartment and you don't make that kind of dough in the Salvation Army."

"Terry worked as a stenographer until a few weeks ago," Lorne protested feebly.

Boulton released his grip. "How old are you kid?" he asked derogatorily.

"What's that got to do with it?"

"Well, you look old enough to know better," the caretaker said, his voice calm again. "I have laid them both, so I am not just guessing. Cost me almost half a month rent. Want to come in and have a drink?"

"No, I'd better be going. Thanks anyway and I'm sorry I made a fool of myself."

"That's quite all right. Men have done crazier things for the sake of a woman." Boulton casually swept the glass fragments toward the wall with his foot, then picked up the horn. "Don't lose any sleep over her," he suggested good-naturedly. "There are lots of others."

At first Lorne had gallantly attacked the veracity of Boulton's assertions, but the more alternative reasons for Terry's affluence he managed to dream up, the surer he became that the caretaker had to be right. The subsequent phase of his disillusionment covered the inventions of excuses for her questionable choice of field of endeavor, but though his mind was both prolific and proficient in the execution of that task, it did little to placate his hurt ego. Finally, after a full week of soul-searching he lulled himself into believing that the generosity with which Terry had dispensed her physical favors did not alter his love for her. After all, he, too, had used her for the gratification of his own selfish desires, although his intimacies had been on the house' so to speak.

But this conclusion left the major riddle in mid-air: why had she left? Lorne was convinced that Terry loved him though obviously not as intensely as he loved her, and consequently he could not understand why her abrupt departure had come about without a warning let alone an explanation. Her disappearance was both puzzling and annoying. Frankly, Lorne felt both stupid and hurt for having misjudged her so profoundly.

Now it was summer and time had dulled the pain, yet no day passed that he did not think of her and he knew that he would never stop loving her.

Business-wise things were quite different. On the anvil of faith he had forged his dreams into realities. His daring enterprise was now legitimate and his profits had doubled in the past four months. He had more than seventy steady customers and paid off nearly half of a one thousand dollar bank loan.

But he had also reached the point where he had to buy some form of transportation. Up to now he had traveled by bus and on foot to call on his customers, a fact he had always tried to hide. Most of his deliveries were made through a cartage company, but many of his deliveries he clandestinely shipped in person by using his cab during slack hours.

These methods were money-saving but time-consuming and he realized he could increase his sales only if he could make all his calls and deliveries by car or truck.

"Ready for a cup of coffee?"

Lorne whirled around. It was Orvil Hamilton, the sheet metal plant owner.

"I was daydreaming," Lorne said apologetically. Then he fell in step beside him.

"Cambie and Forty-first and step on it."

Lorne glanced at the young man as he pulled away from the curb. From Vancouver's West End the trip would take at least half an hour. It was five thirty and everybody was in a big rush to get home.

"Cigarette?"

"No, thanks," Lorne said.

"I phoned three different cabs and you were the first to arrive," the fare confessed.

"You must be in a hurry," Lorne commented.

"Wouldn't you be if you came home and found your wife and everything you own missing, gone?"

"Jesus," Lorne said sympathetically.

"You're married?"

"No."

"Take my advice. Don't lose your head like I did or you may lose a lot more than that."

"Phew, that was close," Lorne remarked as he barely managed to squeeze between a moving bus and a parked car.

"I've been hooked five years. Like a fool I worked every bloody day and three times a week an extra shift so we could live in an apartment we really couldn't afford."

"She didn't work?"

"You're kidding? That's not lady-like, don't you know?" He angrily pulled on his cigarette, ignoring the falling ashes. "Last week I lost my job. Lack of efficiency they said. Balls! Lack of sleep it was, but I guess they go together. A friend of mine had the same thing happen to him. I mean his wife knocking off like that. Yessir, just phoned some moving outfit and put the whole caboodle in storage. I told my wife. She just laughed. That was a couple of months ago. Now she has pulled the same stunt. She's probably bragging to her parents about how smart she is."

"That's where you're going?"

"Yeah. And if she's there I'll break her goddamned neck."

"You're still in love with her, aren't you?" Lorne asked daringly.

The man studied him quizzically. "Are you crazy?"

"You're not rushing to her because of the missing furniture. It's her you care about."

"Yeah, maybe you're right. It's a strange thing when you consider how thin the line is between love and hate."

Lorne smiled. "Still want to go and see her?" he asked.

"Why sure." And pausing to reflect for a moment, he said: "Maybe I can talk some sense into her. What d'you say?"

"I am not saying anything. I've probably said too much already."

Later after he had dropped off his distraught fare Lorne drove to a service station on nearby Main Street. As he stepped out of the car and opened the trunk, he failed to see a black car stop across the street.

"Hi there, Jerry," Lorne greeted the young operator.

"What are you bringing us today, Lorne?" Jerry Allen asked, as he put down his grease gun.

"One gallon of windshield cleaner, one gallon of liquid soap and a bill."

"What's the damage?" Jerry smiled as he walked over to the cash register.

"Seven twenty-five including taxes, Jerry."

"I'm really pleased with that cleaner, Lorne," Jerry said as he handed him the money. "Works like a charm."

"I'm happy to hear that," Lorne said appreciatively.

When he returned to the cab, Lorne saw someone sitting in it. Opening the door he saw no customer but Bud Quirko, the company supervisor.

"What're you doing, Lorne?" Quirko asked with a wan smile. "Making some dough on the side at the company's expense?"

"1 just made a delivery, what's wrong with that?" Lorne bluffed.

"Nothing, absolutely nothing," Quirko grinned, "unless, of course, you forgot to book the call."

"All right. Quit playing cat and mouse. What do you want me to do: fall on my knees and beg forgiveness?"

"Naw, why humble yourself. I understand you want to be a big businessman."

So he knows, Lorne inferred.

"Well, there's nothing wrong with that, Vincent, except one thing: big shots don't drive cabs--they ride in them." And moving toward Lorne: "Come on, get in on the other side, I'm driving you to headquarters where you can pay us what you're owing and I bet that's a lot more than you've got in your pocket right now."

"Well, just then Cinderella appeared, all dirty with soot, and looking like a terrible mess in her ragged clothes."

"Didn't the prince recognize her?" Ricky Naylor asked impatiently.

"You bet," Corine van Noorden smiled. "Who is that?" the handsome prince asked. 'Oh, she's just the maid,' the sisters replied. But the prince ordered her to try on the slipper and when it fit, he threw his arms around her and said: "I don't know what's happened to you, darling, since I last saw you, but we can soon change that. "Will you marry me?" Well, who wouldn't? So she said 'yes' and her sisters were really browned off. I mean jealous."

"Good for them," Ricky said warmly. "They were no good anyway, were they, Corine?"

"That's for sure," Corine agreed. "Well, now it's time to go to sleep. Good night."

"Good night."

She bent over the little crib and tucked in the blanket around Ricky's three-month old sister Debra and left.

Once in the living room, Corine picked up the Vancouver Sun. The headline read: Korean Armistice Imminent.

When will people learn that war creates always more problems than it solves? She wondered.

A moment later she jumped up with a start when the front doorbell rang.

"Lorne!" she exclaimed when she opened the door. Then concern creeping into her voice: "Aren't you working tonight?"

"I got canned."

"Canned?"

"Yeah, fired."

"Oh no. Come in."

"I was gonna ask you if you wanted to go for a walk."

"I'd love to, but I can't. I'm baby-sitting. Stan and Mary went to a movie."

Lorne followed her into the living room. Since she had first visited his lab three months ago, he had visited her now and then and on one occasion he had taken her to a movie. That was after she had helped him wash and fill jugs and jars for three days in a row. This was the first time he felt he needed to talk to her.

"What do you plan to do now?" she asked as she seated herself opposite him.

"I don't know, Corine. I really don't know. I thought perhaps by talking to you I might find a solution."

She blushed slightly. It was the biggest compliment he had paid her so far.

"Why were you fired?" she asked, tucking her skirt over her knees.

"I was caught delivering some stuff to one of my customers with my company cab."

Corine nodded understandingly. "Maybe it's a good thing," she said.

"Good?" Lorne echoed, "It's a disaster?"

"Now you can devote all your time to your business," she explained. "Isn't that what you wanted all along?"

"Sure, but it's too soon."

"That doesn't sound like you at all, Lorne," Corine said. "You can sell far more and we both know it."

"That's right, but I need some form of transportation to make my calls and deliveries and I can't buy it because I owe money already and I don't want to get any further into debt."

Corine smiled mysteriously. "Come on," she said, "I've got something to show you."

Lorne followed her obediently through the kitchen into the backyard.

"Would that solve your problems?" she asked pointing at a 1948 Studebaker.

"It's yours?" he asked incredulously.

"Bought it last Saturday," Corine said proudly as she opened the door and invited him to slip in behind the steering wheel.

"It's a beauty," Lorne said as his fingers checked the controls.

"You haven't answered my question yet," Corine reminded him. "You can have it five days a week as long as I can use it weekends."

"That would be great," Lorne thought aloud, "but why would you do this?"

Because I love you, she thought, but she said simply: "Because you need it more than I do."

How could she tell him that he meant the world to her, that she needed him a thousand times more than he needed her car? How could she admit that she had bought the car with only three hundred dollars down and only him in mind?

Later when she handed him a cup of coffee, Dutch style, little extract and plenty of milk, she startled him again.

"I've been thinking how you can boost your shampoo sales," she started. "Several times our customers have asked where they can buy it and, of course, we had to tell them they can't. How about packing it, say in eight and sixteen ounce bottles and printing the beauty salon's name in big letters on a fancy label and in small letters at the bottom. You could print: Manufactured by Vincent's Custom Chemicals, Vancouver."

"Sounds terrific. I wonder how it would go over."

"I can think of at least one customer," Corine smiled. "Paul Lucas?" Lorne guessed.

Yes. He thought it would prove to be a good seller and he asked me to mention it to you."

"I'm glad you did. You can tell your boss that I'm already working on it."

"How about another cup?"

"I'd love to," Lorne said as he watched her walk to the kitchen, her narrow hips slightly swaying, her slim figure looking almost boyish in the plaid skirt and white cotton blouse. If only she were Terry, he thought.

X

"They hanged him," Elsie Beldan announced happily from behind the News Herald.

Fred Beldan strained his ears to hear more, but his wife did not elaborate. "Hanged who, Elsie?" he asked with a touch of servility in his voice.

"Why, John Christie, of course, you dope. Who else?"

In self-defence he swiftly devocalized himself by stuffing a whole boiled egg into his gaping mouth.

"Seven poor, defenceless women he murdered," she said as she lowered the paper, exposing the massive collection of hardware that cluttered her coiffure.

To Fred the words 'women' and 'defenceless' were purely antonymous, especially at breakfast time. To avoid her icy stare he looked at the toaster, wondering if his life could be restored to its former color if she, too, were stuffed behind some wall. He dropped the idea a moment later, knowing he could never do it--he did not know the first thing about masonry.

After washing down the ground egg with the remainder of his coffee, he rose to his feet and closed his eyes in distaste as he quickly kissed his wife on the cheek before leaving the kitchen. This feigned gesture of affection was the sole remnant of an old and brief love affair that had gone sour before he had had a chance to wash the confetti out of his hair. The tones of the wedding march still ringing in his ears, Elsie had confided that her trip to the altar had entirely been inspired by the money his father had left him a few months earlier.

The acrid revelation had triggered his life-long ambition to make realities more palatable. First by seeking rescue in alcohol, and when that method had been denied him by his doctor, by working long hours. But his current association with a young girl had proved to be the best heart balm. Sylvia Sterling fitted in his life like the missing piece of a complicated jigsaw puzzle: it made it whole.

She was pretty, passionate and understanding--the embodied opposite of his wife. To Fred she was a precious jewel, but like all gems, she cost money, and plenty of it.

To deceive Elsie on money matters was an arduous task. The only things she enjoyed reading were his ledgers and bank statements. For a while his dry cleaning business had borne the extra load without major difficulties, but as Sylvia's demands grew, the financial health of Lindhurst Cleaners had deteriorated to a dangerous point.

Lately even Sylvia's 'understanding' had proved below par and on one occasion she had called him a miser, although she had later apologized for it.

When he arrived at his shop, three of his five employees were already waiting. Five minutes later the premises buzzed with the usual sounds of hissing steam, gurgling liquids and rolling carts.

Business was slack in July when most women and children wear washable clothing and men leave their coats and jackets at home.

It was shortly after ten that morning when he was told that a gentleman at the counter wished to see him. A moment later Fred found himself shaking the hand of Malcolm Nithdale.

"I understand you're no longer using some of our products," Malcolm started, trying to smile forgivingly.

"You mean Prestine and Boratex?" Fred asked with feigned innocence.

"Precisely."

"I don't like competition any more than you do, Mr. Nithdale," Fred said apologetically, "but if you can buy something for nearly half price without any difference in quality, wouldn't you?"

Malcolm raised an eyebrow in contempt. Before he could utter a word a young woman announced her arrival: "Hi, Fred. Got my evening gown ready?"

"All set to go, Marion," Fred said. And returning a few moments later with the dress: "You'll knock them over big in that outfit."

"That's the idea," Marion laughed as she handed him a ten-dollar bill, "Well, have fun," Fred said as he gave her the change. Malcolm quickly appraised the girl's legs as she brushed past him, and then turned to Fred again. "I would appreciate it if we could continue our conversation in privacy," he said curtly.

"Why, sure," Fred agreed. "Let's go to my office."

After closing the door of the stuffy cubicle, Malcolm offered his prey a cigarette, then lit one himself. Blowing the blue smoke almost straight to the ceiling, he said: "I'll come right to the point, Fred. You owe us nearly two thousand dollars right now and our records show that your last payment was made three months ago. The contract by which you agreed to pay the outstanding balance in full expired last week. My question is a simple one: what do you intend to do about it?"

Fred stuck his index and middle finger in between his collar and neck, jerking his head backward, but he felt no more comfortable for it. Visions of the new press, primarily responsible for the high amount, his wife and Sylvia flashed incongruously through his mind as the temperature seemed to soar.

"Business is very slow," he began feebly.

"I'm not interested in your economic evaluations," Malcolm intercepted. "Can you settle the account?"

Fred felt his clothes stick to his sweating skin. He knew he could not even pay two hundred dollars, let alone two thousand. If Nithdale took it to a lawyer, Elsie would find out about the debt, and, God forbid, a whole score of other things.

"How about an extension, Mr. Nithdale, say until Christmas?" he tried.

"You're asking me a favor after telling me that you buy your merchandise elsewhere," Malcolm reminded him, and he thought this guy is scared shitless. He's got to cooperate.

"I'll tell you what," Malcolm continued, "I'll give you an additional six months to pay your account and provide you with an opportunity to show your appreciation. Those chemicals you're buying from Vincent's, have they given you any kind of trouble?"

Fred shook his head, his face a picture of surprise mixed with fear.

"I want you to spot say half a dozen garments with his chemicals after mixing them with some bleach. Then phone Vincent and show him the discoloration and ask him to compensate you for the damage. If he refuses threaten him with a lawsuit. That's all there's to it."

"But I can't use my customers' clothes for a deal like that. It'll ruin my reputation," Fred objected, ignoring the iniquity of the proposal.

"Of course not. That's why you should use your own clothes," Malcolm explained, rising to his feet. "Phone me the results. You have till next week."

Malcolm slipped complacently behind the wheel of his car. Seconds later he was on his way back to the office. He had never met Lorne Vincent, but he did have a fairly clear idea about his personality. Malcolm was convinced Lorne would not pay a cent for the damage and deny his responsibility for it, but a lawsuit was a bird of a different feather. He would have no choice but to appear in court and face the loss of time, suffer adverse publicity and the expense of a lawyer. Even if he would win, Fentex Industrial Supplies could always appeal the court's decision, so that in the end, win or lose, Lorne Vincent would be financially ruined.

Malcolm felt sure the case would never reach the appeal stage because Lorne could not possibly afford protracted court proceedings.

Yet, at times uncertainty gnawed at his mind. Malcolm already had been forced to concede that his young rival was a hell of a lot smarter than he had expected. Fentex had hardly a customer left in Greater Vancouver as far as Prestine and Boratex were concerned.

But the loss of these sales mattered little since Fentex served all of Western Canada from Vancouver. Moreover, the main transactions were still dry cleaning equipment - not chemicals.

But Malcolm had been long enough in business to know that it would only be a matter of time before this competition would spread eastward. In addition there lurked the even less desirable prospect of Lorne acquiring his own dry cleaning equipment line in which case his competition would no longer prove a mere nuisance, but become a direct threat to the very existence of Fentex in western Canada.

Consequently an effective extermination program had to be embarked upon and Malcolm planned to waste no time in launching it. Even if his present scheme should fail, a possibility he considered to be highly unlikely, he had several other plans in store to achieve the same end.

Jake Vincent deftly quartered the wet rag and cleared the counter's worn surface of the crumbs and coffee stains that the last customers had left as a memento to their visit. He rinsed the rag in the lukewarm water that stood gray and sudless in the sink. He glanced wearily at the wall clock. It was Valley Dairy Time and ten minutes to eleven. Marie would soon be home.

Each Monday for the past two months he had run the small cafe single-handedly to give Marie more time for herself. Usually she spent the day shopping, but sometimes--like today--she traveled by bus to Seattle to visit her daughter. This arrangement gave Jake a sense of purpose, a welcome diversion and an excellent opportunity to show his gratitude to Marie for the kindness she had shown him since their chance meeting a year earlier.

Marie's warm heart and patient ear had cushioned the shocks of frustration which he had experienced in his search for his son. Her genuine interest in his plight had never ceased to baffle him. She stood like a mighty beacon in his dark world of adversity and disillusionment and helped him greatly in steering clear of the treacherous reefs of despair that lurked ominously in the shallowness of his existence.

The confidence he had so patiently built up during those long prison years had all but dissipated as step by step his hopes had been snuffed out by the dead ends of his leads. He pulled the rubber stopper out of the sink and watched the birth of a miniature whirlpool, the lead bowels beneath burping in protest. He had advertised under. Information Wanted, he had checked every directory he had been able to lay his hands on and most painful of all he had checked with the Missing Persons Bureau where a burly cop had told him that the police had better things to do than organize reunions for jailbirds and their offspring. A flicker of hope had grown into a blaze of expectation when he had found the name Lorne Vincent in the latest telephone directory, but it had died when his son's namesake turned out to be a wizened veteran of the Boer War who apparently had moved to Vancouver from Manitoba to spend his last days in a climate benign to old age.

Just when he had seriously begun to consider the possibility that Lorne might have left the city, he had received a letter from his sister that the customary Christmas gifts had again been received from Lorne with the postmark unmistakably spelling Vancouver as in previous years.

Jake was just putting away some mugs, when the door opened and Marie entered.

"Any coffee left for a weary traveler?" she greeted him cheerfully.

"Coming up, madam," Jake smiled.

XI

Corine van Noorden was brushing her long auburn hair when the telephone rang in the living room.

She rushed from the bathroom through the hall to the jangling device, almost tripping over her own feet. Lifting the receiver she closed her eyes, expecting to hear Lorne's voice, but there was only silence.

"Hello," Corine said, still wondering if Lorne was playing a practical joke on her.

"Hello," a voice on the other end of the line replied. "Is Stan Naylor in?"

"No, I'm sorry, he isn't," Corine said, wondering why the voice sounded so muffled.

"What about Mrs. Naylor?"

"No, she is out, too."

"When do you expect them back?"

"Between ten and eleven." And she volunteered. "They're at a housewarming party."

"Fine. I'll try later."

"Is there a message?" Corine asked automatically, but the line went dead before she had uttered the last syllable of her question.

She slowly walked back to the bathroom. Maybe one of Stan's customers, she inferred as she re-applied the brush with long strokes to her hair. She glanced at her watch: it was ten past eight. Lorne had not dropped in since he had picked up the car Sunday night, although he had phoned Tuesday to say that business was booming. Now it was Friday and since their agreement called for her use of the car during the weekend, she had counted on seeing him tonight.

She tried to ban the doubt from her mind that Mary had planted there. "You can't buy a good husband, Corine," her sister had said when Corine had told her about the car offer. "He'll soon take it for granted. The more you try to do for a guy, the more he expects of you. Just play the old game of hard to get. It's as old as Eve, but it seldom fails."

Stan wisely had remained noncommittal and Corine had ignored her sister's advice, confident that the future would prove Mary wrong.

Lorne is different, she thought, as she briefly inspected her coiffure. She was about to enter the living room when the doorbell rang. That must be him now, she thought hopefully. But when she opened the door she stared into the grinning faces of three young toughs.

Before she could utter a word the tallest of the trio stepped forward. "Hello, baby. We wuz wondering if you felt like a little fun." Corine stepped back, aware of the alcohol on the youth's breath.

"Yeah, how's about it, honey?" the second one said closing the door behind him.

Oh, please God help me, Corine prayed silently. Then her eyes widened with horror when she noticed one of them had a knife.

Kicking and screaming with fear and fury she managed to free herself briefly, but the thugs quickly overpowered her.

"I thought she was going to be an easy lay," the second intruder protested.

"Shut up," the tall one growled. Then he suddenly lifted her off the floor and despite her kicking, managed to carry her into Stan's and Mary's bedroom where he threw her on the bed. When Corine tried to get back on her feet, he quickly pushed her back and warned ominously: "Don't force me to hurt you. I don't want to, but if you don't quit fighting you're gonna get it."

Then suddenly he threw himself on her and like a beast of prey, tore the clothing off her body, seemingly unaware of Corine's fingernails drawing blood from his face. "You bitch," he blurted in an avalanche of obscenities. Corine felt her limbs grow numb as the room spun into darkness.

"She's all yours, Ken," he said shortly afterwards. "I'll go and get Tom."

When the third youth entered the disheveled room, Ken was still standing beside the bed, staring as if hypnotized by the still figure.

"What's the matter, Ken?" Tom asked. "Don't you know a good piece when you see one?"

"I think Ted killed her," Ken stated flatly.

"Naw, she's just passed out and you're chicken," Tom said. And getting on the bed: "Watch me pump some life into her."

When Ken left the room he almost bumped into Ricky Naylor.

"Who are you?" Ricky asked suspiciously.

"I'm your sister's boyfriend and you should be in bed." "You are not my sister's boyfriend," Ricky protested.

"Well, that's too bad, get to bed anyway or I'll give you a damn good licking."

"I don't like you," Ricky cried as he ran to his room.

"What the hell is going on?" Ted yelled from the front door.

"The kid woke up. I sent him back to bed," Ken replied subserviently.

"The broad is bleeding pretty bad," Tom announced from the hall.

"Let's beat it." Ted suggested.

"We can't leave her like that," Ken objected." She might bleed to death."

"What the hell do you want to do? Hang around till the cops come?" Ted snapped.

Half an hour later Lorne parked Corine's car in the backyard and walked to the back door. When he found it locked, he went around to the front of the house.

Finding the door open and the lights on, he walked in, and saw Ricky near the master bedroom.

"Auntie Corine is hurt," the boy cried.

Lorne dashed into the room, horrified by the spectacle of violence. Bending over the limp body, he felt for her pulse and asked: "What happened Ricky?"

"Some strange men came and hurt auntie Corine," he sobbed. "Is she dead?"

"No, she's okay," Lorne said. Then he rushed to the living room and made several phone calls.

Ten minutes later the house was filled with policemen, a doctor, ambulance men, uninvited neighbors and a stray dog.

"We'd better get her to the hospital fast," the doctor ordered as he pulled himself erect. And turning to one of the cops: "This is my third rape case this month. What's going on? You fellows too busy writing parking tickets?" The young constable ignored the snide remark and turned to one of the bystanders.

"Come on, go home," he urged as the ambulance men carried the stretcher to the waiting ambulance.

A light drizzle briefly awakened Corine. Opening her eyes momentarily she noticed the curious faces then she succumbed again to the arms of Morpheus. Just as the ambulance sped away, its siren starting its first low pitched howl, a car pulled screechingly to a stop at the curb. Two men, one carrying a camera, dashed out. Lorne was about to close the door when they entered. "You're a relation of the girl?" "No, just a friend," Lorne replied, almost blinded by a flash bulb.

"Boyfriend?" The man persisted.

Remembering the scene and Corine's kindness to him, Lorne nodded, obviously irritated by the questioning.

"Your name?"

"You haven't told me yours yet," Lorne said, watching the men scribble details in great haste.

"Ron Jeffley of the Herald."

The door opened again and two more men walked in.

"Right here, Lieutenant," the constable greeted them.

"Clear the house," the lieutenant said curtly to his partner.

"So if you hadn't run out of gas, you'd probably been here an hour earlier." the reporter thought aloud.

"That's right," Lorne agreed." And the whole thing might not have happened," Ron said cheerfully, grateful for the mandatory angle of newspaper writing.

"Ready, Ron?" the photographer asked.

"Yeah, I guess the rest we can get from the cop shop and the hospital. Thanks Mr. Vincent."

"You're Mr. Vincent?"

"That's right."

I am Sgt. Bowden. Lt. McPherson would like to speak to you." Lorne found the lieutenant in the master bedroom, Ricky sitting wide-eyed on his knee.

"Okay, you go back to bed now," the policeman said, rising from his squatting position. "Thanks for your help."

"Will you get the bad men?" Ricky asked fervently. "You bet," the detective predicted jovially. Then turning to Lorne: "How long have you known the girl?"

"I met her about a year ago."

"Ever had relations with her?"

Lorne looked aghast at his interrogator.

"Well, have you?"

"No," Lorne said firmly.

"Then you wouldn't know whether she was a virgin, would you?"

"No, I wouldn't," Lorne replied, feeling the blood angrily rush to his face,

"I'm sorry, but we've got to consider all angles."

The telephone rang and Sgt. Bowden walked into the living room to answer it.

"Where does she work?"

"It's for you, Bob," Sgt Bowden interjected. "Doctor Carey at the hospital."

Lorne was straining his ears to hear the conversation when a shrill cry from the front door made him whirl around.

It was Mary. "My God, what has happened!" she cried. "Where are Ricky and Debbie?"

"They're in bed, they're fine," Lorne said. "It's Corine, she's in hospital."

"Corine, in hospital?" It was Stan, who had entered the house through the back door after parking his car in the garage.

"Yeah," Lorne explained somberly. She was raped."

"No, no;" Mary suddenly cried hysterically. "Not my baby, not my sweet baby sister."

"Please get hold of yourself, Mrs. Naylor," Lt. Mc Pherson urged. "Your sister is going to be all right. I just talked to the doctor. I've got a few questions I'd like to ask."

"A Mr. Beldan called yesterday afternoon," Florence Sommers said as Lorne was about to pass the switchboard of Hamilton Sheet Metal. "He asked you to call him right away."

"Thanks Flo. Anything else?"

"No, Lorne, that's all."

It was only a few minutes after eight when Lorne planned to fill a few back orders, then visit Corine in the hospital. On the advice of Stan he had kept the car.

He was just typing some invoices on his rented typewriter when the phone rang.

"Hello, Lorne here"

"Glad I caught you," Doug Marcus said.

"Welcome home. When did you get back from Europe?"

"Last week. Had a ball. Those women there, wow, that's hard on a man. I'm glad to be back in good old sedate Anglo Saxon Canada where the blood doesn't flow quite that fast. But tell me, what's this I read here about you being involved in a rape case?"

"It's a long story..."

"I bet," Doug interrupted. "I must say I like your alibi. Didn't even know you had a car."

"I haven't. It's hers. But really Doug, there's nothing funny about the whole affair. In fact, if you had seen her the way I found her last night, I'm sure you'd be as eager as I am to work the bastards over but good."

"Yeah, I guess so. It's sure too bad, but that's the price society must pay for refusing to legalize prostitution. They sure have us beat on the other side of the big puddle, Lorne. You can buy sex there as easy as candy here. All the hookers are subject to rigid medical control and as a result the incidence of VD is very low and rape is rare."

"We've got to get together pretty soon," Lorne said, not interested in the legal aspects of prostitution at that time of the morning. "It's a must," Doug agreed. "How about tonight?" "I'd rather make it tomorrow," Lorne said.

"Suits me fine. What time?"

"Say, about seven thirty?"

"Swell. I've got lots to tell you. Also have got some startling pictures that'll make your hair rise and God knows what else."

I'd better phone Fred now, Lorne thought after he had hung up. Probably ran out of Terrysol again.

Dialing the number Corine's bruised face and violated body again appeared before him. Doug sure didn't show much concern he thought.

"Good morning, Lindhurst Cleaners."

"Is Fred there, please?"

"Just a moment."

"Hello?"

"Lorne Vincent here, Fred."

"Oh, yes, Lorne. I've read the paper so I know you've got enough problems as it is, but I'd like you to come over this morning anyway and discuss some trouble I've had with one of your products."

"Which one?" Lorne snapped, concern creeping into his voice.

"Can't think of the name just now."

"Terrysol?"

"Yeah, that's it. The last batch of it seems hard on certain dyes."

"Did you use it in the recommended manner, mixed with steam?"

"Listen Lorne, I'm busy as hell. You come over and I'll show you what it has done to some of the clothes."

"All right, Fred. See you in about an hour."

It doesn't make sense, Lorne thought, as he carried his deliveries to the car. It doesn't make sense at all.

Half an hour later Lorne examined suits, dresses, skirts and a coat of which the dye had faded in various places. Regaining his composure after the initial shock brought about by the first complaint he had ever received about his products, Lorne said without looking up: "Tell me, Fred, if the stuff gave you trouble, why didn't you stop after it first happened? I count here nine pieces."

"It, it didn't show until later," Fred stammered.

Lorne bent over and picked up a gallon jar. "Is this it?"

"Yeah, that's the container we've been using."

Lorne quickly produced a small vial and poured some of the contents into it. "None of the other customers have complained although they've all received the same product, but I'll take a sample anyway just to be on the safe side."

"What do I do in the meantime? I figure I've got to pay several hundred dollars in compensation."

"Listen, Fred," Lorne said, surprised at his own impatience. "I'll know after I analyse this sample whether or not I am responsible. If I am, I'll meet all liabilities, but to be blunt about it I don't think I'm gonna find anything wrong with my product, because the story you've just told me simply doesn't ring true." And walking toward the door. "I'll phone you the results tonight."

After he had delivered his merchandise to his customers, three of which were dry cleaners, Lorne felt even more certain that he was not at fault. No one else had complained. But if Fred had fabricated the story, what could be his motive? Suing was rapidly becoming a lucrative pastime in North America, but one still needed at least a credible story to cash in on the big bonanza.

Maybe I've got nothing to worry about, Lorne thought as he entered the Vancouver General Hospital, but still I don't like it. And Fred: he had always seemed such a likable sort of fellow....

Lorne counted the doors as he walked through the long corridors. When he found the door of Corine's private room, it opened just as he was about to turn the knob. The man who stepped out into the hall was a stocky individual with short-cropped gray hair, a stethoscope dangling around his neck and an impressive array of pens in the top pocket of his immaculate white smock.

"You must be Lorne Vincent," he said in a subdued voice as he closed the door gently behind him.

"I am," Lorne confessed. "How is she?"

"Come," he said pleasantly. "I am Dr. Carey and I'd like to have a talk with you before you see her. We can use the office down the hall."

Must be more serious than I thought, Lorne inferred as he fell in step beside him, the whispering uniforms of the passing nurses seemingly accentuating the significance of the doctor's request. After entering a small, simply furnished room, Dr. Carey lit a cigarette, blowing out the match with the smoke of his first puff which he adroitly expelled through his nostrils.

"Sit down, Lorne," he said as he seated himself behind a desk cluttered with a mass of paper.

"Before you visit Corine you must realize that her most serious injuries are psychological--not physical. Physically she will be her former self again in a matter of weeks. Her psychological recovery on the other hand may take months, perhaps years. To what degree the incident will influence her personality is impossible to predict, but there is no doubt that it will leave a permanent mental scar. I want you to understand this, for the girl you're about to visit is not the same one you used to know. I don't know what she means to you, but I do know you mean a great deal to her. In surgery she kept repeating your name over and over and your name alone. If you want to help her, I'm sure you can do more for her than the world's best psychiatrists. No one has yet invented a pill to substitute love."

After Lorne had entered Corine's room he quickly grasped the value of Dr. Carey's preparatory words.

"Hello, Corine," he greeted softly.

"Hi, Lorne," she said without turning her head towards him.

Looking at her in awkward silence he wondered if her face was really as pale as it seemed or whether the sheets and pillow made her look that way. Seldom lost for words, he now groped for something to say.

"Stan told me you won't have to stay here long," he finally said clumsily.

When Corine didn't speak, he felt ill at ease and uncomfortably stirred on the metal chair beside her bed. Talking about the previous night seemed like a grotesque and hazardous undertaking to him, yet ignoring the very reason she was here seemed equally absurd.

"Have the cops talked to you yet?" he asked diffidently.

"They were here this morning," Corine said, staring blankly ahead of her. Then she added bitterly: "I doubt if they could find those animals if they were sharing their room."

Lorne, who was not too impressed himself by the record of the Vancouver police, said in gentle protest: "Maybe they know more than they let on."

"You know, Lorne, I actually think it would be better if they never found them."

"You can't mean that."

"I do," she said stubbornly and turning for the first time to him, she added: "What good would it really do? There would be a trial, unless they'd plead guilty, which according to Lt. McPherson is extremely unlikely. Then the whole sordid thing would be described and plucked apart in public. I would suffer more than they would. In the end at best they'd be sent to prison. Tell me, what good would that do me?"

"You've got to punish them."

"Punish them?" Corine echoed with a contemptuous smile. "A few years free room and board? What difference would it make, Lorne? Who would benefit? No one. Least of all me."

"Well, if they catch them and put them behind bars, at least they won't be able to do to some other innocent girl what they've done to you," Lorne countered, sensing the utter futility of his words.

Averting his eyes, Corine said as if thinking aloud: "Whatever the police plan to do, they'd better do it fast, because I don't intend to stay around very long."

"What do you mean?" Lorne blurted, his voice betraying the sudden concern he felt in his heart.

"I'm going back to Holland," Corine explained matter-of-factly.

Lorne instantly reprimanded himself silently for considering the possible inconvenience of losing her car. Then he said: "That wouldn't solve anything, Corine."

"Oh, Lorne," she said almost sympathetically. "Don't you understand? How can I stay here, knowing I may meet them again, God only knows where or when. How can I go back to Stan and Mary when the house will always remind me of what happened?"

Lorne realized her line of reasoning had led him into a verbal dead end. Recalling Dr. Carey's warning, he countered: "Corine, you must change the things you can and accept everything else..."

"'God grant me grace and endurance to bear cheerfully what I cannot change,'" Corine interrupted, "'Courage to fight for what I can help to change and wisdom to know the difference.' It's the motto of Alcoholics Anonymous. Lucas has it in his office. A reminder of his boozing days."

"The saying applies to all of us, not just alcoholics," Lorne continued. "I've had my share of misfortune, but you can't set the clock back. You left Holland to build a future here. You've done remarkably well considering you have only been here one year..." "A year and a half," she corrected.

"You speak the language fluently, you've got a good job, and you mean a lot to me." And when he saw the beginning of an appreciative smile color her cheeks he added: "You know, you're the first person who has ever taken a real and unselfish interest in my business affairs. I think together we could make a real team."

"You really mean that, Lorne?" Corine asked, her eyes set aglow by the spark of hope ignited by his words.

Lorne took her hand. "Darling," he said surprised at his use of the endearment, "I never meant anything more in my life."

I'm lying he thought, but if what I say makes her happy, why shouldn't I? Doesn't the end justify the means?

XII

"Anyway, I managed to get out before her husband returned," Doug Marcus concluded his account of his amorous exploits in Europe. And emptying his glass of scotch he glanced at Lorne who seemed less impressed than Doug had hoped.

"Sounds like a screwed up holiday to me," Lorne quipped.

"Particularly the tail end of it," Doug laughed. "How about another drink, Lorne?"

"All right, as long as you're not so stingy with the mixer. The last one nearly burned my guts out."

"I realize I have been selfish by bombarding you with all my stories, but I simply had to," Doug said as he handed Lorne his glass. "You see, I relive all those gorgeous moments while I recount them to you. Unfortunately, my parents fail to appreciate the finer things in life. They think beauty and ecstasy are found only in the works of people like Mozart and Renoir. This leads constantly to misunderstandings. For instance, when they speak of French architecture they think of the Pantheon and Notre Dame while my thoughts automatically turn to the curves and forms designed by Nature rather than by man."

"Your problem fills my heart with compassion," Lorne said mockingly.

"Seriously, Lorne, apart from a different outlook on sex, Europe has us beat in many other ways. You don't realize how ultraconservative we Canadians really are, until you visit Paris, London, Rome. Alcoholic beverages are freely obtainable in any quantity, yet they have fewer drunks than we have. Prostitution is generally condoned and as a result there isn't the high incidence of sexual offences that we have here. And although the standard of living is considerably lower than ours, people are definitely more cheerful. They are well versed in the art of living."

"Maybe those are additional reasons why Corine wants to go back," Lorne thought aloud.

"You're kidding. She really wants to go back to Holland?" "Yeah, why is that so hard to believe? A moment ago you were praising that part of the world, remember?"

"I know, but the strange thing is that most immigrants don't want to go back. You know, the grass always looks greener on the other side of the fence."

"With Corine it is different. It has nothing to do with economics or the easy access to booze: it is fear. The possibility of her meeting those bastards again is more than she can take."

"You make it sound so definite. Isn't it more likely that she will never see them again?"

"Not the way she sees it. She firmly believes that the cops will never catch up with them."

"Well, let her go."

"I don't want to."

"Why not?"

"I know this sounds stupid, but I really don't know."

"Maybe you're in love with her."

"No, that's not it, I mean, I'm not. I like her, mind you, but it's nothing more than just that."

"Well, how are you gonna stop her?"

"I know there's only one way."

"Which is?"

"By marrying her."

"That would be an act of madness."

"I know what you think of marriage."

"What I think of it is of no consequence. It's what you think of it that counts and frankly I don't think you really know."

"Of course, I don't: I've never been married before."

"Do you have to swallow sulphuric acid to know it's rather hard on the stomach? Most marriages are brought about by a desire to satisfy one's sexual cravings, but passion is like gasoline--it makes a hot fire but it doesn't last long.

Pity is even a weaker basis for matrimony, and that applies to you, doesn't it Lorne? You feel sorry for her."

"Yes, I do. What's worse, I feel sort of responsible for her trouble. If I had been on time that night, it could never have happened."

Doug shook his head. "Pity is a strange thing," he said, "feeling sorry for others usually develops into feeling sorry for oneself. Take my mother. When she met my father, she pitied him first, married him later and today, after a quarter century of imaginary self-sacrifice, she never misses a chance to let the world know how much better off she would have been if she had never seen him. You see, father as a young man, had both the ambition and brains to become a first-class surgeon, but he lacked money. That's where mother came in. She paid his way through university and financed a good portion of his post-graduate studies. He was nothing to look at, but always grateful and kind. With his looks, I guess he had no choice. They married shortly after he had completed his internship."

Doug silently refilled his glass and glanced out the window.

"Their honeymoon was brief but effective: when my father returned to his books, my mother prepared for my arrival. As it turned out, motherhood proved as disheartening to her as marriage had. My father furnished increasing evidence over the years that his true love was surgery and not my mother, and I gradually developed into an epitome of everything she had been taught to loathe: free thinking, free loading and free loving. Yet, if you were to ask them, they'd swear that their marriage is a success. They confuse the fact that they can still stomach each other with compatibility."

Doug and Lorne were startled by a knock on the door. It was Lynda the Marcus' maid.

"Mrs. Marcus just called to say that she will not be in until late tonight. Will you have supper here?"

"No, I'll eat up town, Lynda," Doug smiled. "Why don't you take the night off?"

"Thank you," she said, vanishing as abruptly as she had appeared.

"Nice girl," Doug remarked after she had closed the door. "Good lay too."

Lorne smiled understandingly. "Say, why don't we have supper together?"

"Sounds like your best suggestion today."

"I hope you are as well versed in business matters as you seem to be in sex."

"A good lawyer is well versed in everything," Doug said as he opened the door for Lorne. "What's your problem?"

"The threat of a lawsuit," Lorne said simply.

The rain slashed with increasing velocity and vehemence against the slanted attic window. Occasionally a bolt of lightning would light up the room, revealing the peaceful silhouette of a man on a narrow cot. Then the thunder would shake the window and rattle the china in the cupboard of the small room, but Jake Vincent remained unaware of Nature's spectacular manifestations.

A few hours earlier he had left Marie, his stomach warm with the supper she had prepared for him. He had departed under the pretext of having to write some letters, but the real reason had been the growing despondency that threatened to conquer the last vestiges of his will to live, pushing him to the very edge of the abyss of despair.

He had rushed up the two stairways, his heart pounding audibly in protest. Panting he had reached his bed on the point of collapse, a smile of satisfaction playing around his thinning lips. He knew that such exertion would result in swift transition from the stark spectre of reality to the soothing world of unconsciousness.

Now he had succumbed to a deep slumber, his chest rising and falling less erratically than it had a while ago.

He was unaware of the water that dripped from the ceiling onto the bare plank floor, unaware that even in sleep reality would overtake him.

Marie, her kerchief and coat drenched with rain, opened the door when her knocking remained unanswered. Now as a puddle of water formed around her shoes, a newspaper clutched tightly in her hand, she shook Jake by the shoulder.

"Wake up, Jake," she pleaded almost frantically. "Your son, Lorne: I think we've found him."

Slowly Jake returned to reality. At first he grumbled in protest to the rude awakening, cursing his tormentor, but when he saw Marie's face in the eerie light of another bolt of lightning he grasped the importance of his awakening.

"What's the matter, Marie?" he yawned, as he raised himself on his elbow.

"It's Lorne," Marie said excitedly, her flushed cheeks drying the shrinking droplets that rolled haltingly down her face. "Where's the damn light switch?" she asked impatiently.

"Wait, I'll get it," Jake said as he rose to his feet. A moment later a bare bulb that hung suspended from one of the rafters burst into light.

"Here," Marie announced proudly as she handed him the folded paper. "Picture and all."

"Oh, my God," Jake stammered, tears suddenly burning in his eyes, "oh, my God, this IS Lorne."

Then he sat down, weeping uncontrollably. Marie quickly took the small flask from her coat pocket and filled the first glass she could find.

"Here," she said motherly, "to celebrate and calm your nerves."

Jake lifted the glass with trembling fingers to his lips and poured the Scotch down his gullet without pausing. Then he dried his eyes with the back of his hand, removing the blur from the photograph and the dancing headline above it:

> CLAIMS LAWSUIT IS BANKRUPTCY ATTEMPT
>
> Lorne Vincent, 23-year-old manager of Vincent's Custom Chemicals, said in Vancouver county court today that a lawsuit Wby the manager of a Vancouver dry-cleaning store is an attempt by a US firm to force him out of business. Vincent is sued by Lindhurst Cleaners, for having sold chemicals and equipment that allegedly caused extensive damage to merchandise and store premises. The outspoken young businessman, who handles his own defence, declined to identify the U.S. firm.

The news item after dealing at length with technical evidence, ended with:

> Vincent later commented: "I'm confident about the outcome of the case - it's the timing that gripes me. I plan to get married next week and I am not looking forward to spending my honeymoon in court."

"I noticed it after finishing the dishes," Marie explained. "At first I thought nothing of it, but when I saw the name 'Lorne Vincent, I took a good look at the picture and suddenly I knew it was him. He's you all over, Jake."

"A businessman," Jake mumbled, shaking his head. "My son a businessman." Suddenly he laughed hysterically. "Just think, Marie, for years I worried he might end up a bum like me," he said, shrugging his shoulders in helpless wonder.

With a lawsuit like that he still may, Marie thought, but she said: "Now your worries are over. What are you gonna do?"

"I don't know yet," Jake said pensively. "It's all so sudden, so hard to believe."

"Well, you'd better get over to the house in the morning so we can see what you look like in Charley's suit. I haven't seen him for fifteen years, so I guess it's quite safe if you borrow his clothes to go to church in."

"Church?" Jake echoed sheepishly.

"Yes, where else do you think he's gonna get married?" Marie said cheerfully. And taking the newspaper from his hands she continued: "Look its right here in the classifieds."

Jake read the announcement solemnly, then he exclaimed: "Wednesday?! Why, that's the day after tomorrow."

Jake admired himself in the mirror. It seemed as if his reflection was a retouched photo taken many years ago.

"Clothes make the man," Marie said admiringly. "Now are you sure you won't have a bite to eat before you go?"

"I couldn't swallow anything thicker than water," Jake replied as he adjusted his tie for the third time. The suit had been too big, but Marie had sewn well into the night until her husband's suit fitted Jake as if it had been custom-tailored for him.

Jake had asked Marie several times to close the shop and accompany him to the church, but she had stubbornly refused.

"Honey," she had said, "this is one time you should be alone with your emotions. Maybe sometime the four of us can have a get-together here.'"

"You know that'll never be," Jake had interrupted her almost angrily. "I never want him to know that I'm still alive. I have done very little for him in the past; I can do even less for him now. No, he must never know."

When Jake arrived at the church he was the only one there and he began to wonder if there had been some mistake and the wedding had been scheduled for a different time or at another church. For a moment he considered the idea of walking to a nearby restaurant for a cup of coffee, but he quickly abandoned the thought in fear of missing the arrival of his son. As he paced up and down in front of the old building, his thoughts returned to the countless hours he had spent on his narrow cot in his prison cell. The times when the lights had been turned off and sleep had not come. The silence broken only when one of the guards had made the rounds, his footsteps always ringing hollowly on the steel catwalks.

What's the use of living he had cried in silent agony, his hands tugging rebelliously at his drab prison apparel. What is just about my being here? Hearing the happy voices of playing children nearby, remembering, always remembering, my own son. Is justice served by my stay here until death releases me? Or even if I should survive, how much more hostile will the world outside await me than it did when I was born into it?

But the questions had always remained unanswered. So he had tossed and turned, hoping frantically that sleep would open the gate to the wonderful void of unconsciousness. Now the senselessness made sense. Now the wasted years suddenly gained meaning. The moment he had grown to regard as nothing but wishful thinking now was about to become reality:

He would see Lorne, his son. He would see the matured embodiment of his love for Martha. Now he could rest assured that she would continue to live through their son.

Gradually people appeared from nowhere, entering the church, babbling amiably, their faces reflecting the excitement of the pending ceremony.

But none of the arrivals looked even remotely like Lorne. When eleven o'clock was only minutes away, Jake in near-desperation asked an elderly man if this was the Vincent wedding.

When the man said it was, he smiled curiously as if mocking Jake's ignorance.

"I haven't seen neither the bride nor the groom," Jake protested.

"They are already inside," the man confided.

"But," Jake added, "I've stood here for the past hour and I haven't seen either one of them."

"Of course not," the man said as he started to climb the stone steps, "the bridal couple always enters the church through the side entrance into the minister's chambers."

Finally Jake, too, entered the church, seating himself in an empty rear pew as if afraid someone might recognize him.

He felt tense with excitement as he saw the backs of the young couple, no longer doubting the young man was in fact his son. The ceremony seemed to take forever. In feigned reverence Jake simulated the congregation: moving his lips silently when they sang the hymns, narrowing his eyes when they prayed.

But finally the big moment he had waited for so long, arrived And with the traditional tones of the Wedding March emanating from the organ, Lorne and Corine came smiling toward him down the centre aisle. As his son walked by him within touching distance, tears quickly blurred the happy image, for although Jake had wanted it no other way, the fact that Lorne was no more aware of him than he was of the paintings on the wall was an excruciating experience.

It took everything Jake had to stop himself from shouting his son's name. He felt the blood throb angrily in his temples, sudden perspiration fusing his clothes to his trembling body. Then, as his brain grew numb, his mind lost touch with mundane realities. Hazily Jake felt himself being sucked into a whirlpool of nothingness, Death beckoning at the bottom of the abysmal spiral. A woman shrieked in sheer abhorrence as two men rushed toward him, but Jake's limp body was already beyond help.

Autumn winds had all but defoliated the trees, covering the moist earth with countless leaves which now cushioned the steps of the young couple. And high above the October sun shone with impotent splendor, its rays no longer tanning.

Migratory birds prepared for their southward trek, forming kaleidoscopic clusters in the cloudless sky, while on terra firma the underbrush rustled with activity as rodents darted to and from their habitats swelling their winter food supply.

The wind had adjourned to add to the peacefulness of the day. Its task was completed, for with the leaves removed the danger of snow breaking the branches posed no longer a serious threat. Only the evergreens stood unchanged.

When they reached the crest of a rock bluff, they paused and looked at the log cabin below, smoke spiraling almost perpendicularly above the primitive rusted chimney.

He put his arm around her slender waist and leaned his head against hers. "I was born in a log house," he said *sotto voce*.

She raised her eyes to his, her lips giving birth to a tender smile. "I love you very much, Lorne," she said in a small voice.

"You know, sweetheart," he said pensively, "it feels great being here. Nature is so different from city life. I mean, everything is so wonderfully genuine: no phoney cordialities, no hidden clauses, no misleading advertising. Take that rabbit we saw a while ago. There wasn't a grain of pretense in its movements."

"That's what our marriage must be like," Corine commented. "We must always be ourselves and never pretend to be otherwise."

"Yes, baby - always."

"Will you always be true to me, Lorne?" she asked, her eyes clinging to his trustingly.

"You know I will."

"Yes," she said serenely, "of course, I do; but it's so nice to hear you say it."

"I never want anyone but you, baby, because you've given me everything a woman can possibly give." Then, as if to accentuate his words, he embraced her and watched her close her eyes as he kissed her. A few moments later they strolled on, hand in hand and--for a while-without speaking, for their thoughts were too intimate to be put into words. Was it really only yesterday that they had been married? Corine smiled. It seemed so much longer than a day. Late last night they had arrived at the cabin and this morning they had awoken to the golden magnificence of the autumn landscape.

Lorne glanced at her, his heart aflutter with the ecstasy of her presence: he was no longer alone. His thoughts also turned to the night before. How she had fallen asleep in his arms after no more than a few kisses had been given in honor of Eros. He had spent much of the night awake, remembering Dr. Carey's words of caution. "Leave the initiative to her at first," he had said. "Any suggestion of force may remind her of the brutality she experienced last summer."

"What are those black things hanging in the trees?" she startled him.

"Those are mushrooms the squirrels have put there to dry," Lorne explained. "They'll all be gone when spring rolls around."

She pressed his hand to show her love. They stopped again and this time their kisses triggered the passion that had remained latent until now.

"Oh, Lorne," Corine whispered, "I need you, darling. I need you very much."

"Come," Lorne said between kisses, "let's return to the cabin..."

"No, darling," she sighed, "I want you to make love to me right here." And so at the foot of a huge ponderosa pine they consummated their marriage.

"Impossible. My father died in the war," he had said. But they had not listened. "It's all a mistake, I'm telling you. You've got the wrong Lorne Vincent." But then the door had opened again and his aunt Eileen had joined the strange woman with the French name and old wounds had been ruthlessly reopened. Corine standing silently at his side, he had finally protested: "If this is true, and God forbid, then you lied to me when I was still a small child."

At that point the tears had exploded in Eileen Dobrynchuk's eyes and she had clasped her hands around his. "That's how your father wanted it," she sobbed, "that's how he wanted it, Lorne."

Now he sat between the strange woman and his aunt while the taxi snaked its way through the afternoon traffic and as his aunt revealed the sad truth, he merely asked 'why?'--over and over again. When he was at last alone in the dimly lit room, his hands shifting uneasily at the edge of the coffin, he accepted the terrible truth as he stared at the still face of his father.

Memories, presumed dead long ago, now were resurrected in painful detail: the countless times his father had read to him while he was in bed - Huckleberry Finn, Tom Sawyer and later David Copperfield. How they had together tackled his homework, his father always stressing the value of education. Lorne also remembered the many times they had gone to the river and romped in the grass or swam in the cool water. But most fondly he recalled his father telling him about his mother. How cheerful and strong she had been despite her blindness, how abundant her love and rare her complaints. Although he had never known her, Lorne knew it was she who had given him his perseverance and self-confidence.

As he escaped from this phantasmagoria, his eyes returned to his father's face and he realized in silent shame how little he had thought of him since their separation. In the end Lorne was forced to admit that he had borne a grudge against his father for leaving him as a child. And now, with Aunt Eileen's revelation that he had spent twelve years in prison for defending his son's honor, Lorne felt the terrible injustice pierce his soul like a scalloped knife. "How can life be so cruel?" Lorne mumbled as tears burned in his eyes. "How can life be so terribly unjust?"

When the utter futility of his visit finally dawned on him, he bent cautiously over the casket and kissed his father gently on the forehead. And studying the wrinkled face for the last time, he whispered: "I'll always love you, Dad: both of you."

Then he pulled himself erect, wiped his eyes dry with his handkerchief and re-entered the waiting room.

Eileen Dobrynchuk and Marie Charmois were awaiting him solemn-faced on a bright blue settee that had obviously never been intended for a funeral parlor.

"We have to decide whether to have the funeral here or in Edmonton," Aunt Eileen said soberly. Lorne looked at her and at the woman whose name he had failed to memorize when she had been introduced to him earlier that day. Then he said calmly: "My father will rest in Inglewood - right beside my mother." Eileen Dobrynchuk noticed a coldness in Lorne's eyes she had never seen there before. Unable to speak, she merely nodded in agreement. The other woman placed her pudgy hand on Lorne's arm. "He was a fine man," she said sympathetically. "You can always be proud of him."

The funeral took place two days later after Jake's grave had been hewn in the frozen ground beside Martha's the previous day and the earth lay in chunks around the gaping hole. An Inglewood minister who had never known Jake spoke a brief eulogy and reminded his small audience of life ephemeral and death eternal.

After the coffin had been lowered, the bits of earth sounded harshly on the lid as the mourners said their symbolic farewells.

And so they left: Lorne, Corine, Marie, Eileen and the minister, each with their own thoughts trying to understand what can't be understood, for Death knows no alternative. The four of them tried in vain to find the homestead where Lorne had been born and Martha had died, but even the rough foundation of the farmhouse had vanished. In the afternoon Lorne took Corine to the spot where he had launched the news making rocket, while Eileen Dobrynchuk and Marie Charmois reminisced about the man each had known so differently. The Dobrynchuk estate was much the same as Lorne had left it. Even the key for the door at the rear portion of the brick wall was still in its old place.

"You can't set the clock back," Lorne thought aloud as he gazed across the Saskatchewan River, but sometimes it's set back for you. Corine pressed his hand in silent sympathy.

Yes, outwardly little had changed. The people he had shared the mansion with had changed. They had aged, left or died. Harry Wenzel, the gardener, was dead. So was Tom, the Dobrynchuk's philandering cat. Cora the maid had married and now lived in Ontario and Ilse Hoffmeister, a young woman fresh from Germany had replaced her. Melvin, the butler, looked even more aristocratic than Lorne remembered him, with gray on the temples and his alert eyes framed by glasses. Even Boris Dobrynchuk had not escaped the effects of time.

His objectives in life had not changed, but his approach in business matters had mellowed somewhat. After supper he invited Lorne to join him in his study.

"It's good," he started, "to see you're followingk in my footsteps." "Well, not exactly," Lorne protested.

"Not exactly maybe," Boris agreed, "but in business just the same. I read about you in the paper. You're doingk fine." And after pausing for a few moments while he lit a cigar, he proved his usual thoroughness: "Dun and Bradstreet agree."

"1 didn't realize they even knew about me," Lorne said, visibly pleased that the international credit investigating firm had taken notice of his existence.

"Still you could do better if you had more capital and I am willingk to provide it. I was thinkingk of twenty-five thousand."

Lorne smiled. "I appreciate your offer of help, but I think I can manage on my own."

"Nonsense. Double nonsense*" Boris erupted. "I am not tryingk to help. You know me better than that. I think you've got something good goingk and I like to invest in your set-up."

"I'll bear it in mind," Lorne said noncommittally.

"We could discuss the terms in detail tomorrow," Boris went on.

"No, I'm afraid not. I'll be leaving for Vancouver first thing in the morning," Lorne said firmly, and with a touch of cynicism he added: "Today is the last day of my honeymoon."

Part IV

XIII

The German military truck slowed down to negotiate the turn onto Herenstraat, its load of loosely piled loaves of bread tumbling chaotically forward. Hendrik van Noorden had waited for this moment for the past hour and a half. He dashed to the truck as fast as his fifteen year-old legs could carry him. A moment later he hoisted himself onto the truck's tailgate.

Corine watched in awe. It was a new game they had been playing only a few days. She knew the bread was deliciously crusty - fresh from the bakery and still warm. In a few minutes she and Hendrik would sink their teeth into it and still their gnawing hunger. Compared to the tulip bulbs and potato peelings they were fed at home, plain ordinary bread was a gourmet's delight.

She watched Hendrik crawl out of the truck, his threadbare jacket bulging with at least one loaf. Then, just as his feet touched the street, the rat-tat-tat of a submachine gun suddenly tore through the relative quiet of the street and Hendrik's bullet-riddled body fell onto the pavement. A German soldier rushed toward him, the murderous weapon still smoking in his hands. He roughly turned the lifeless body over with his hobnailed boot, glancing at the glassy eyes and the growing pool of blood that colored the stolen bread which now lay eternally outside Hendrik's reach.

Corine screamed at the top of her lungs as she looked at the alarm clock. It was just past two o'clock. Now it came back to her: this was Canada 1958, not hunger-stricken Holland 1944. It was fourteen years, a husband and two children later. Time stands still in dreams only. She looked at Lorne, a tender smile faintly visible around her lips. "I'm sorry I woke you, honey," she said. Then the nightmare came back to her and a frown erased the smile.

"The war again?" Lorne asked.

She nodded. It was nothing new. During the five years they had been married it had happened many times. The cold-blooded murder of her brother had been etched sharply onto her memory. Even the terrifying sound of the submachine gun had lost none of its gruesome clarity.

The nightmare, borrowed from life itself, came back whenever the pressures of her existence overtaxed her nerves. Corine lifted her face seeking comfort in Lorne's eyes. "Lorne," she said softly, "this time it was different. The soldier's face: it was HIS."

Lorne pressed her head against his chest. He understood. 'His', 'him' and 'he'- pronounced with dread-inspired accentuation--always referred to the first of the ruffians who had raped her. It was a euphemism they both knew only too well.

"It was only a dream, sweetheart," Lorne said as he stroked her hair.

"I'm so afraid," she confessed in a small voice. "I think it means I will meet HIM again."

"Dreams are fantasies inspired by fear or ..." He almost inadvertently added 'wishful thinking', but he checked himself just in time. Generalizations can be dangerous, he inferred. And smiling at her, he said: "We've got every reason to be happy. Just think how much progress we've made. Total production has doubled in the past six months and we now supply more than seventy percent of all dry cleaners in Vancouver." He stopped when he realized he was not addressing a shareholders meeting, but his wife. Still, how else could he cheer up Corine? What else was encouraging?

Kathy, their two-year-old daughter, had been rushed to hospital only the night before with a bad case of pneumonia. He remembered the sleepless nights they had spent at her bedside, witnessing the mismatched battle of a child trying to escape the clutches of Death, hearing the panic-inspiring gasps for air of their own flesh and blood. How do you talk that into oblivion? He also had to circumvent the avalanche of problems that had accompanied the construction of his one hundred-thousand-dollar plant in nearby Richmond. Most formidable were the extra costs he had not counted on and the withdrawal of financial support he HAD counted on.

"Everything is going to work out just fine," he heard himself say. But as he spoke to her in reassuring terms, he could not help wondering how he would feel in her position.

Corine envied his optimistic attitude. Lorne never seemed to worry. His philosophy was the epitome of simplicity: 'when it's time to work, you work. When it's time to sleep, why, you sleep. What else?' Lorne considered worrying a waste of time. "You can't solve a problem by worrying about it," he had often said. Worrying only complicates matters.' But Corine knew she was different and always would be. "Daddy, I'm thirsty." It was Larry in the adjoining bedroom.

"Okay, Sport, I'll get you some water," Lorne said as he swung his legs onto the floor.

"I want to get it myself," the four-year-old boy protested.

"All right, Mr. Independent," Lorne chuckled, grateful for Corine's smile, "but don't drain the tap."

They heard the pitter patter of his bare feet as he walked to the bathroom, then the generous burst of water as he let it cool before quenching his thirst. A few moments later he was back in bed and silence returned to the house.

Lorne fondly recalled the ecstasy of the beginning of his honeymoon. How deliriously happy he and Corine had been when on the third day she had started her period: Larry was truly theirs!

"Would you like me to get you some water, too?" Lorne asked, barely suppressing an urge to yawn.

"No thanks, darling."

A few minutes later Lorne was sound asleep again, while Corine fought to stay awake, afraid the nightmare would return. But it is not easy to stay awake in the dark with fatigue numbing the senses and a soft mattress cushioning one's weary body. So Corine quietly left her bed and went to the living room, plunging it into a flood of light with the flick of a switch. As she sat on the five-year-old sofa, her legs neatly folded beside her, her thoughts involuntarily trailed back to the days of the war that had changed her forever.

Pappa van Noorden had never been the same. His wife, Aagke, had cried big tears for about a week, breaking Mary's record by a little better than six days, but then she had gotten over it and lived very much as though Hendrik had never been. Mary, or Maria as she was then called, had been too preoccupied with the mysteries of boys to spend too much time wondering about something she could neither change nor ever hope to understand. Corrie had shed fewer tears than either her mother or her sister, but her reticence whenever the subject of Hendrik's death was brought up, was mistakenly regarded as indifference. The truth was that she kept her grief to herself. Her father was the family's only extrovert. Jan van Noorden now fully understood the meaning of having to live in fear of terror. The fact had been ruthlessly driven home by his son's death.

He had loathed the German occupation from the time the Teutonic barbarians had ended the democratic Dutch government in four short days of blood-soaked terror, but he had never actively opposed their presence. He had simply continued to ply his trade as a shoemaker in his small shop on Rembrandt Straat, in the end substituting leather soles with wood and compressed paper. He had politely declined all invitations to join the underground resistance forces, believing participation to be more risky than it was worth. "We kill one German and they kill twenty of us. How can you win a war that way?" he had argued.

But the brutal murder of his son had changed his attitude. Now he was no longer concerned with risks: it was revenge he sought. He would never forget how the Germans had demonstrated their authority by leaving Hendrik's body on the spot where he had died as a ruthless two day reminder of who was boss.

For nearly half a year, until a few days before the Allies replaced Nazi tyranny with freedom, Jan van Noorden was one of the most daring members of the Dutch underground. His greatest triumph was the derailment of a military transport train near Amersfoort. When the soldiers crawled out of the wreckage, leaving their dead and dying comrades to the leaping flames that soon enveloped the splintered carriages; he awaited them in the dark of the night--alone. He had ignored the pleas of his friends to flee the scene and chosen to stay behind to pay a sacred debt. His body trembled as his Sten gun burped death. He laughed unashamed as his enemies fell in mortal agony before him. "This is for Hendrik and that's for Hendrik," he had shouted.

Two months later he joined his son. He and three other members of the underground had successfully blown up a small bridge when a lone German plane spotted them and strafed the quartet with enough bullets to kill a platoon. Only Piet Brinhuis, though gravely wounded, had lived to tell the story.

Corine lit a cigarette with the butt of another and rested her throbbing head against the back of the sofa. She had spent many nights like this, catching up on her sleep during the day when nightmares for some unknown reason did not trouble her. She planned to do the same thing today after taking Larry to her sister where he could play with Ricky and Debbie.

She slowly got up and walked to the adjoining hallway. Briskly she dialed the number of the Vancouver General Hospital.

"Children's ward, please," she asked, surprised at the tremor in her voice. And a moment later: "Could I talk to the supervisor, please?"

"Speaking."

"Oh," she said, a bit startled. "This is Mrs. Vincent. Could you please tell me how Kathy is?"

"She's much better, Mrs. Vincent," the nurse said sympathetically. "She has responded very favorably to the oxygen and her breathing is almost back to normal."

"Oh, thank you," Corine sighed in gratitude. "I'm sorry to have bothered you, but I can't help worrying about her."

"That's quite all right, Mrs. Vincent. I understand."

As Corine returned to the living room, she glanced at her watch. It was almost four o'clock. She seated herself in the room's solitary easychair, stretched her legs and lit another cigarette. Watching the smoke spiral to the ceiling, her mind soon again surrendered to the vast backlog of her memories.

Life is so strange, she thought. If mother hadn't married Leeuwenhoek, I would never have met Lorne and without Lorne I would never have had Kathy and Larry. What would have happened if I had stayed in Holland? She wondered. But she realized she would never know the answer. When a choice is made, the alternatives, with few exceptions, remain eternal mysteries.

She loved Lorne as she knew she could love no one else and she took secret pride in the fact that her intuition had not betrayed her. Lorne was both a good husband and a good father. He never missed an opportunity to let them know how much they mean to him.

Yes, they had two wonderful children, different as day and night, but two wonderful children just the same. Larry had popped into the world with grace and precision, weighing in at nine pounds and five ounces. Apart from an occasional cold, he had never been sick. Yet, his young body was already scarred like a veteran soldier of fortune. The scars were the inevitable result of his acrobatic behavior in and around the house.

To Larry life was just one big fascinating experiment. Like playing submarine in the bathtub when no one was looking. His latest record was making three complete longitudinal revolutions under water before coming up for a breathing spell.

He was ignored during the common street brawls for the neighborhood kids had learned that Larry simply could not be defeated. Larry was no fighter, but he was remarkably fast, although he never used his speed to run away from a fight. He merely used his agility as a form of defense. He could jump and duck with ballet precision and former antagonists had always been forced to give up sooner or later by sheer exhaustion and frustration.

Speed fascinated Larry and he had an impressive trophy in the form of a three-inch scar on the back of his head as proof of his velocity addiction. He had acquired the trophy last winter at the end of a swift descent down Fraser Street on his sleigh. He had slipped under a parked car, an exhaust pipe bracket carving the permanent memento.

Corine smiled when she recalled how proud Larry had been of the bandage headgear he had worn on leaving the hospital.

Kathy's history was quite different. She had been an incubator baby and barely survived the agonizing difficulties of her breach birth. At two months her skin had erupted in a mean rash, puzzling examining doctors and frightening her parents. But six weeks later the condition had disappeared as mysteriously as it had started: swiftly and without apparent cause.

Dr. Grenberry, the pediatrician, had facetiously complained that the sudden disappearance of the rash had robbed him of a chance to make medical history with a treatise on the strange malady.

At the age of eight months Kathy had had bronchitis and on her first birthday she blew out the sole candle on her cake with bulging cheeks festively spotted by the measles.

Thank God, she's going to be all right, Corine thought as she closed her eyes. She folded her hands in pious gratitude, but it was a short prayer for as she groped for words to express her thankfulness, sleep took possession of her.

Outside the world slowly awoke as dawn sneaked across the horizon and erased the stars from the cloudless sky: it promised to be a beautiful August day.

Lorne woke up when his searching hand discovered the emptiness beside him. He got up quickly and silently stole into the living room where he found

Corine seemingly enjoying a peaceful slumber. His watch told him it was a quarter past six. Time to get cracking, he mused as he walked to the bathroom. It's gonna be busy as hell today.

Half an hour later he was on his way to the old plant at Vancouver's waterfront. The promise of another sweltering day hung unmistakably in the air. The summer of 1958 already was one of the longest and hottest in the province's history. The newspapers were filled with reports about the hundreds of forest fires that raged throughout the province, destroying millions of dollars' worth of timber, British Columbia's principal source of income.

When Lorne swung his faithful Studebaker into the parking lot behind the building, he was surprised to find Wayne Scott's car already there. Lorne entered the building through the rear door and found Wayne working feverishly in the shipping section.

"Morning, Wayne," he greeted, "Beat me to it this morning, eh?"

"Yeah," Wayne replied as he continued to pack jugs into cardboard boxes. "This stuff for Prince George has got to be out of here before nine."

"I'll give you a hand," Lorne said as he took off his jacket.

Wayne had worked for him for three years now and Lorne had never regretted his decision to hire him. He remembered that fateful day in the spring of 1955 as clearly as yesterday. It had rained cats and dogs that afternoon when Wayne had dropped in. Lorne had liked him instantly.

Corine had just phoned to say Larry was going to have a playmate according to the doctor, when there was a knock at the door-less entrance of Lorne's small office.

"Lorne Vincent?"

"That's me," Lorne said as he studied his visitor closely. Salesman, about thirty and married, he inferred.

"I am Wayne Scott."

Lorne accepted his handshake. "What can I do for you?" he asked, wondering why the man had not mentioned what company he represented.

"Mr. Vincent," Wayne started, "I have been instructed to find a way to put you out of business."

"You've entered a crowded field of endeavor," Lorne commented stoically. "Would it be too much to ask by what means you plan to accomplish this?"

"The most powerful instrument the world has ever known:

money," Wayne explained simply. "I've sized the place up on my way to you..."

"And now you're sizing me up," Lorne interrupted.

"Correct. Would you care to try for the $64 question?"

"Yes, what's your conclusion?"

"My conclusion," Wayne said with a confident smile, "is that you will not sell your enterprise for anything near the amount I am authorized to offer."

"Try me," Lorne said, his curiosity aroused.

"Twelve thousand."

Lorne erupted into a spasm of laughter. "Who in the world dreamed that one up?" he asked boisterously.

"The western division manager of Fentex Industrial Supplies." "Oh, no, not Nithdale again," Lorne blurted in disgust.

"No, not Mr. Nithdale," Wayne said, pronouncing the name with obvious contempt. "The idea was concocted by his successor, Waldon Jefferson."

"Well, you tell Mr. Jefferson to go to hell with his idea."

"I can't think of anything I'd rather do," Wayne said cheerfully, "but I prefer to reserve the remark until the day of my resignation."

"And when will that be?"

"With your cooperation it could be today."

"Where do I come in?" Lorne asked interestedly.

"Mr. Vincent, right now your sales are limited to the Greater Vancouver area. You could double your sales by covering the rest of the province as well. I know the trade and I know the people. Give me ten per cent and I'll start tomorrow. I guarantee you'll have most of Fentex's customers before the end of this year."

Lorne hesitated. It could be a trap. "What's in it for you?" he asked.

"A sound future," Wayne replied with palpable frankness. I've witnessed the terrific progress you've made in only two short years and. I'm confident this progress will continue and accelerate. Besides, I'm sure I can get along a hell of a lot better with you than with Jefferson and his ilk."

Lorne rose to his feet and extended his hand. "Okay, it's a deal," he said.

Six months later Orvil Hamilton moved his sheet metal business to nearby Burnaby and Vincent Custom Chemicals immediately filled the vacuum, occupying the entire main floor of the building.

Now as Lorne prepared the Prince George order for shipment, he realized more than ever how much he was indebted to Wayne. Joe Tiflin, the shipper, was a hard worker, but he was also extremely punctual, starting at eight sharp and quitting at five on the dot.

There was not enough work for an extra man and not enough money to pay Joe overtime, so Wayne and Lorne often pitched in wherever help was needed to keep things rolling.

The work load had sharply increased lately and the effect was beginning to show on his employees. Tempers were short and smiles were rare nowadays and the worst was still to come. The current lease would expire at the end of October and the new plant would not be ready for production until a month later--at the earliest. So everyone had to work at top capacity to build a large enough stock to tide them over during the interim period.

When the shipment had been completed, Lorne said: "I'd like to talk to you before you go, Wayne."

"Okay, Lorne, I'll see you in a few minutes. There are a couple of things I wanted to discuss anyway."

Lorne had just begun to clean up his cluttered desk, when Wayne walked in.

"Well," Lorne started, "1 may as well come right to the point. One of our financial supporters has withdrawn his offer of ten grand. I hate to tell you this, but since we can't afford any more delays, I've decided to scrap the soap production program - at least for the time being."

Lorne saw the hurt creep into Wayne's eyes. The idea to manufacture soap had been his brain child. Wayne had spent endless hours calculating the cost of such a scheme. He had made countless inquiries about the necessary equipment. In short: he had thought of everything--except this.

"I thought all the pledges were on paper," Wayne said reflectively.

"They are."

"Then he can't back down. He's committed. Ask Doug."

"I did," Lorne said, sorry he had to pull the last straw of hope out of Wayne's reach. "You see, the agreement also specifies October 31 as the starting date of production. We'll be damn lucky if we can move in by that time. Installation of equipment will take at least another month."

In the silence that followed, Lorne recalled the night Wayne had dropped in at the house to reveal his daring plan which now was about to be shelved.

"Do you know how much a pound of soap powder costs?" he had started.

"Haven't got a clue," Lorne admitted. "How much does a pound of soap cost, Corine?"

"I don't know about a pound, but I pay eighty-seven cents for a box."

"See," Wayne commented triumphantly, "you don't know. Few people do. But do you know WHY you don't know?"

"I guess, I don't pay enough attention to details when it comes to groceries," Lorne confessed laughingly.

"You're not even warm," Wayne shot back. And turning to Corine: "have you got a box of soap I can borrow for a minute?"

After she had handed it to him, Wayne accusingly pointed at some fine print. It read: 2 lbs. 7 ozs. And in wax pencil below it: 87 cts.

"How many housewives do you think can figure that one out?" he asked.

"And please note where this important bit of information is printed: right on the flap you cut out to pour the stuff. Clever, isn't it? In addition the manufacturers always provide generous amounts of air space above their products. You'll never see a box that's filled to the top. But to come to the crux of the matter, the current retail price for soap powder ranges between thirty and fifty cents per pound, depending on the gimmicks they use to market the stuff. You know, miniature towels, china or what have you. Now I've done a lot of figuring and I'm convinced that we can undersell any brand by at least thirty per cent and still make a handsome profit."

They had talked until deep in the night and Lorne had finally agreed to give it a try. That had been nearly a year ago.

"You can't do it," Wayne had said abruptly. "You simply can't do it. If we don't go ahead now, someone else will."

Lorne looked up, visibly startled. It was stupid, but he had not thought of that. Their plans to manufacture soap had long ceased to be a secret.

"Think of the potential market," Wayne continued: "Hotels, laundries, restaurants, institutions and eventually the retail trade."

"I know, I know," Lorne said with a touch of frustration, "but where do we get the money from?"

"I can raise half. If you can get the balance, we're sailing."

"Five g's each," Lorne thought aloud. "I think I can manage that somehow."

"You had me worried there for a minute," Wayne smiled.

"It still won't be easy, but with your help it will at least be possible," Lorne said appreciatively.

"I'm sure you'll have your money back inside two years, plus interest, of course." And reaching for the phone: "I'll give Doug a call right now to make it official."

"Before you do that I would like to make another suggestion," Wayne intercepted. "Instead of interest on my dough, how about a share of the profits?"

"How much of a share?" Lorne inquired cautiously.

"Five per cent of my total sales."

"That would bring your commission up to fifteen per cent," Lorne said in disbelief.

"That's right," Wayne said calmly.

"Well," Lorne said, sarcasm creeping into his voice, "maybe I've got the other figure wrong. Did you say five thousand or fifty thousand?"

"You know what I said," Wayne snapped, "and you don't have to accept my offer, but before making your decision you may also wish to consider my other investment..."

"Other investment?" Lorne echoed.

"Yeah. Or have you forgotten that I've spent the last three years making new customers for you. I'm sure you'll agree that my sales represent considerably more than ten per cent of your current profits."

Lorne bit his lip. Wayne is right, he thought, but that doesn't make his idea any more palatable. Then, after a few tense moments of utter silence, he rose from his chair.

"Okay, partner," he said, extending his hand. "It's a deal."

XIV

Waldon Jefferson looked every bit a gentleman and if he wanted to, he could even act the part. But sometimes he carelessly became himself and thus revealed the hard core under the smooth veneer of aged pretense.

"What did you tell him?" he asked.

"1 simply told him the deal was off," Darwin Fletcher replied matter-of-factly. And he volunteered: "he asked me why and I told him. So, he said he was sorry, and that was it."

"Sorry?!" Jefferson roared with laughter. "That, that's the understatement of the year."

Fletcher studied his visitor with a look of insouciance. He failed to see what could possibly be so funny about his withdrawal of the ten thousand dollars he had promised to Lorne Vincent. Fletcher had learned a few things during the twenty years he had been in business and he had a chain of dry cleaning stores to prove he had learned the right things. He had withdrawn his offer simply because Jefferson had shown him a way to make more money with less risk if he did. His lawyer had discovered a convenient loophole to get out of his obligation without the danger of any adverse legal consequences. So, he had changed his mind --profitably. "He's gonna be a hell of a lot sorrier before I'm through pulling the strings," Jefferson continued gaily.

"I think you're making a serious mistake, Waldon," Fletcher said calmly. "I know Lorne quite well and he's a lot smarter than you seem to think."

The jovial expression vanished instantly from Jefferson's face. "Your admiration for him certainly did not impede your decision to switch allegiance," he charged incisively.

"Your naiveté surprises me," Fletcher said contemptuously. What do I care, he thought. I don't like the bastard anyway. "My decision to take you up on your offer was motivated by greed, not loyalty. I don't give a damn what will happen to either you or Lorne Vincent so long as it does not affect me adversely. In business you can't be honest and successful both." And his eyes burning into Jefferson's: "Surely, that's no news to you."

Jefferson was about to speak when Fletcher continued: "I asked you to come here to remind you of the terms of our contract - not to discuss business ethics." He opened the top drawer of his desk and produced a copy of a sales contract. "It says here," Fletcher continued impassively, "that Fentex Industrial Supplies agrees to sell and install specified items of dry cleaning equipment on or before September 30 of this year to Ralston Drycleaners. Do you wish me to go into the details?"

Jefferson could feel the veins on his temples twitch in anger. Details, the son-of-a-bitch had the nerve to ask. Details. How could he forget? Had he not committed himself to sell him nearly twenty thousand dollars' worth of equipment at cost, a saving to Fletcher of more than six grand?

"What are you getting at?" he snapped, undiluted hatred glowing in his eyes.

"Oh, nothing in particular," Fletcher replied nonchalantly, beginning to enjoy the conversation, "except to say that the fall is always a busy time for us and I will be in no position to postpone the delivery date of the contract."

"Well, you've got nothing to worry about," Jefferson said confidently. "The deadline is still more than six weeks away."

"So it is," Fletcher smiled mysteriously. "So it is."

A few minutes later Jefferson swung his car into the heavy traffic of Main. Street. I wonder what the hell he's got up his sleeve, he thought. Most of the equipment he wants we have in stock and the rest we can get from Seattle inside a couple of days. Still Fletcher's words carried ominous overtones. I'm not going to take any chances, Jefferson resolved firmly. He remembered what had happened to Malcolm Nithdale: a job at head office where ass-kissing and suck-holing were mandatory to stay afloat. The price of failure was a smarting one: you were reduced to a nobody and reminded every time it was necessary to get you back in line. Second chances were rare at Fentex.

No, he was going to be a success here. His sales would increase just as soon as he had torpedoed that Vincent character and that wouldn't be long now. In the meantime he would continue to step up his sales program in Saskatchewan and Alberta. Already the sales in those provinces had reached the point where they off-set his losses in British Columbia.

Still he knew that time was running out, that many of his fellow executives eyed his struggle with the interest of vultures watching a doomed man take his last steps. He had been in Vancouver for three years now and thus far had been unable to stop his young opponent's progress. Lately, the only times he had been able to sell any chemicals at all in British Columbia was when Lorne Vincent was temporarily out of stock. The crumbs in other words. If it had not been for the company's dry cleaning equipment, Fentex would have been belly-up in this part of the world two years ago. Yet, things looked better now than they had for a long time and ironically enough he was indebted for that to no one else but Lorne Vincent, for it was he who had volunteered to stick his head through a sixty-thousand dollar noose. All he, Jefferson, had to do was to spring the trap door and the mortgage would do the rest. It seemed a safe bet that his deal with Fletcher would do the trick, because the withdrawal of the ten thousand dollar pledge came at a time when Vincent could least afford it. And, of course, there was the windfall information that Vincent would lose at least a month's production which could well constitute the coup de grace.

With some of the confident buoyancy he had felt earlier in the day, Jefferson marched into his office.

"Are you enjoying yourself, Helen?" He greeted the switchboard operator. Helen Patrick just smiled. She knew no answer was expected.

"Sylvia, will you please get Mr. Tomkins in Seattle on the line?" he asked just before slipping into his private sanctuary. He seated himself behind his desk and scribbled some questions for the pending telephone conversation on a piece of paper. No, sir, he wasn't going to take any chances with Fletcher. The bastard probably was hoping to reap additional benefits from a breach of contract.

The phone rang. "I've got Mr. Tonikins on the line now, sir," Sylvia McPherson announced in her usual sweet voice.

"Thank you, Sylvia." And a moment later: "Hello, Harold. How the hell are you?"

"Sweating. It's hotter than Hades down here and the goddamned air-conditioning conked out on top of it all. What's on your mind?"

"How many model P-120 presses do you carry in stock?"

"None."

"None?" Jefferson repeated sheepishly, a surge of perspiration exploding through his skin. "Don't tell me it has been scrapped like the 518 and the 464."

"No, it hasn't and I'm sure it won't be for quite a few years. Hot little Number that P-12."

Jefferson breathed easier. "Well, I guess I'd better order direct from New York."

"Wouldn't do you any good," Tomkins said cheerfully. "They're out, too, and so are the other branches."

"What's the score?" Jefferson asked, panic recapturing his mind.

"You mean you don't know?" Tomkins asked incredulously.

"I wouldn't be asking you if I did," he said testily.

"Well, the foundry that casts the frames for the P-12's has been crippled by a strike for the past two months. Sneldon is confident a settlement is imminent, but even if the strike ended today, we'd have to wait at least six weeks before we could fill any orders."

Ted Sneldon was Fentex's sales manager at head office. "What about Tilby compressors and Kregton tumblers?" Jefferson asked as he mopped his brow with a handkerchief.

"No problem."

"Well, you'd better send me two of each before it is."

"Will do."

"Thanks Harold. We'll be seeing you."

"You bet. And next time you hop over, take your wife along. Harriette would be delighted."

Jefferson pressed a buzzer before the receiver hit the cradle. Sylvia appeared promptly.

"Get me Mr. Sneldon in New York," he said curtly. "If you can't get him at the office, try his home. It's past four there now. "A few minutes later Jefferson talked across the continent.

"I'm sorry to trouble you, Mr. Sneldon," he started obsequiously, "but it is imperative that I get a P-12 press here before the end of September."

"Waldon Jefferson, do you mean to tell me you interrupt our board meeting to ask me for something you damn well know I haven't got?" Sneldon snarled.

Jefferson swore under his breath. Here I am fifty-four years old and I get told off like a goddamned school kid, he thought, but he explained respectfully: "I promised to supply one before September 30 to one of the largest dry cleaning chains. It is part of a deal that will probably spell the end of Vincent's Custom Chemicals."

"Now listen here," Sneldon continued in the same derogatory vein, "I am not responsible for your promises: you are! I suggest you honor your commitments and refrain from gambling with Fentex's reputation or be prepared to suffer the consequences."

Before Jefferson could utter another word, the connection died in his ear. The humiliating action triggered an avalanche of obscenities that would impress the toughest hoodlum and brought Sylvia storming into his office.

"You called, sir?" she inquired prosaically.

"No, I didn't," he snapped, his face beet-red with rage. The girl left even quicker than she had come in.

He stared morosely at the abstract drawing he had produced during his conversation with Sneldon. The erratic lines had all but covered the notes he had made during his call to Tomkins. Fletcher knew, he inferred bitterly. The son-of-a-bitch had known all along....

He walked over to the window overlooking Burrard Inlet. The mountains stood out in sharp relief against the azure background. A tugboat struggled to sea against the incoming tide. His fury subsiding a bit, he began to wonder how Fletcher could have known about the P-12 situation before he had found out himself. Even more alarming was the question what Fletcher expected to gain from this predicament.

Looking up he noticed several sea gulls. One of them described a graceful U-turn and with true marksmanship dropped a squirt of excrement which in the next instant painted an elongated white streak on the window. I wish I could do that, he mused. I'd fly to New York right now.

Lorne held the flask against the light, tilting it for a moment to study the viscosity of the liquid. The colorless fluid, retarded by its thickness, retreated slowly from the concave surface. Lorne smiled confidently.

"What magic elixir have you concocted now?"

Lorne whirled around. It was Stan Naylor, his brother-in-law.

"I've just prepared a sodium lauryl sulfate solution," Lorne explained, "or in plain English: a detergent. How many drums would you like?"

"I'm a soap man myself," Stan said facetiously. "But seriously, Lorne, are you thinking of making detergents, too?"

"You said it. Production will start as soon as we'll get the soap program running smoothly."

Stan sat down, his hands resting on a thin brief case in his lap. "In that case," he said, "you'd better tell me a thing or two. I know soaps aren't detergents and detergents aren't soaps, but what exactly is the difference?"

Lorne returned the flask to a small tripod and leaned back against his workbench. "Well," he started, "detergents are actually wetting agents. They're also described as soapless soaps, which is a rather nonsensical term, but it does help identify the substance's properties in the popular mind. The principal advantage of a detergent over a soap is that it does not precipitate calcium or magnesium ions so that it can be used equally effective in either soft or hard water. This quality prevents the formation of a ring in a washtub, for example."

"Thanks for the chemistry lesson, professor," Stan grinned. "And now, if we may briefly turn to the equally fascinating world of economics, I like to show you the road to greater financial health."

"Shoot," Lorne said simply. He liked Stan, both as a brother-in-law and as his accountant. Stan had looked after his books for five years now and during that period made numerous money-saving suggestions. Stan had quit his job two years ago and started out on his own with more guts than contacts, but he had made a go of it, and a good go at that. Someday, Lorne was convinced, Stan would work for him exclusively. "I think we can get three thousand bucks, maybe more." "Who's the philanthropist?" Lorne asked laughingly.

"No philanthropist," Stan said, "just some unknowing customers and suppliers. The idea is to get longer terms from your suppliers and more cash sales from your customers. So far you've paid your accounts payable well within the time limit, while showing too much leniency to your debtors. You can actually increase your working capital by taking full advantage of your suppliers' terms and at the same time encourage cash sales by offering a small discount, say two per cent. Cash sales also simplify the bookkeeping end of it and cut costs, because you don't have to send out as many bills and reminders. In short, the money will roll in faster than it leaves and that gives you a chance to use it before passing it on."

"Stan, you're a genius," Lorne smiled appreciatively. "I'm a bit short of medals right at the moment, otherwise I'd pin one on your lapel."

"If you can look after the sales end of it with Wayne, I'll take care of the suppliers," Stan said happily.

"What time have you got?" Lorne asked, glancing at his watch.

"Quarter to three."

"Jesus, my watch must have stopped!" Lorne exclaimed as he took off his lab coat and flung it on a chair. "I've got to be at Lemton Distributors at three. That doesn't leave me a hell of a lot of time," "About fifteen minutes, I'd say off hand," Stan volunteered.

"Tell Esther I won't be back until after four," Lorne said before dashing out of the lab. Esther Price was his receptionist and secretary.

Lorne kept the speedometer needle as close to thirty as traffic conditions allowed him. He was in high spirits. Kathy had returned home from hospital and seemed her former self again and more than a week had passed since Larry had acquired his latest bruise. As for business: things couldn't be better. Doug had negotiated a deal with the contractor that meant a saving of five thousand dollars and served as compensation for the plant's late completion date. This, together with Wayne's five g's, easily offset the loss of Fletcher's financial support.

Lorne swung his car onto Water Street and gratefully watched a truck pull out of one of Vancouver's coveted parking spots. He deftly manoeuvred his car into the vacated space and inserted a nickel into the parking meter. Across the street he saw the four-storey brick building he was looking for. A huge sign on mezzanine level spelled in red letters: LEMTON DISTRIBUTORS LTD., flanked by brand names the company handled.

Lorne dashed across the street and then calmly mounted the worn basalt steps which led to the main entrance of the antiquated building. Entering the business premises he was welcomed by the familiar staccato of busy typewriters.

The interior was as modernistic as the outside was dilapidated. It seemed incredible this actually was the same building. Lorne's attention was drawn to an attractive girl who walked towards him with a sexy smile.

"May I help you?" she asked with a sweet voice that was in complete harmony with her tantalizing figure.

"I have an appointment with Mr. Blackmoor," Lorne explained with the monotone common to hypnotized persons.

He looked her straight into the eyes, but she did not lower them. This baby knows the score, Lorne thought. "Your name, please?" she asked.

"Lorne Vincent."

She walked seductively to the nearest phone. Lorne watched her lift the receiver, press a button and hang up again. Then she returned to him, obviously aware of his admiring glances.

"Mr. Blackmoor is busy at the moment," she said. "Perhaps you'd like to sit down. He won't be long."

From his chair Lorne noticed a clock on a pillar in the center of the office. It was five past three. Scanning the layout, he noticed two men sitting behind desks directly in front of a brightly lit office that was separated from the rest of the floor by a low brick wall topped to the ceiling by corrugated matted glass. On the door neat black lettering spelled: C.E. Blackmoor. And directly beneath 'President.'

The men, both in their mid-thirties, were busily paging through catalogues and made notes. The rest of the employees were all girls, ranging in age between eighteen and thirty. They were all strikingly attractive, although the receptionist was undoubtedly the prettiest of the lot.

With a staff like that it is no wonder Lemton does a terrific amount of business, Lorne thought. The gals probably get a screen test before they're hired.

When his eyes had grown accustomed to the stimulative surroundings, his thoughts returned to the phone call he had received the day before and which had led to his presence here now. It had been shortly after ten in the morning when the phone had rung impatiently on his desk while he had been finalizing some business in the john. When he had at last gotten around to answering the jangling device, a booming voice had announced that Cecil Blackmoor wanted to see him.

"I've got a business proposition that will be of mutual benefit to us," Blackmoor had prophesied. "Three o'clock tomorrow afternoon at my office. All right?"

"I think..."

"Good show," Blackmoor had cut him short. "We'll be seeing you then."

Cecil Blackmoor, more intimately known as Big Ceis, was well known in Vancouver business circles. He was hard as nails and shrewd as the devil himself. His only weakness, if one can call it that, was his insatiable appetite for pretty women. A common rumor persisted that he had acquired his initial capital as a pimp, but this nasty bit of gossip may have been inspired by envy which was rather prevalent among less successful businessmen. At any rate, the fact remained that Big Ceis had forged a small retail store on Cordova Street into a Canada-wide wholesale firm inside twenty years.

Lorne was startled by the voice of the pretty receptionist. "Mr. Blackmoor is ready to see you now," she said.

Lorne followed her through the aisle between the desks, his eyes feasting on her swaying hips. She knocked on the glass-paneled door and without waiting for an answer, opened it.

"Mr. Vincent, Mr. Blackmoor," she announced cheerfully.

Cecil Blackmoor rose from his chair and extended his hand. "Glad you made it," he greeted jovially. "Sit down."

Lorne obediently sank into a huge leather chair, his hand still tingling from the vise-like handshake it had been subjected to. Big Ceis was a broad-shouldered, bald-headed six-foot-five giant whose weight defying agility made him look at least a decade younger than his fifty two autumns.

"You've got a very attractive staff," Lorne complimented.

"I'm a born aesthete," Blackmoor explained smilingly. "I really appreciate beauty, especially when it moves on high heels." Then his smile vanished and an earnest expression took its place, erasing the small facial wrinkles that had briefly appeared around his eyes and mouth. "But let's get to the point. I've got a complete report on your business and I don't mind admitting that I am impressed. You remind me of the horse no one bet on and then won the race. In fact, I know some people who were convinced you never even would be in the running. Of course, the contest isn't over yet, but in business it never is. The main thing is, to use another equestrian term, you're now firmly in the saddle. Last week, as you may know, I toured your new plant in Richmond. Harry Collins said you'd okayed it."

Collins was the contractor. Lorne remembered now that Harry had asked permission to show a friend around in the plant. Lorne had not objected, he had only been surprised that Harry had found it necessary to ask his okay. Now he understood.

"To make a long story short, I think you could handle our packing contracts."

Big Ceis produced a silver cigarette case and offered a cigarette to Lorne before taking one himself. A small replica of a reclining woman proved to be an unusual table lighter: pressing one of the oversize breasts, one of her slender legs flipped up and a small flame appeared above a tiny orifice in her pubis.

"Some of the products I have in mind are shampoo, spot removers and, once you get rolling, packages of soap powder." He handed Lorne a sheet of paper and continued: "Here's a list of the items, complete with the necessary specifications. We will, at least for the time being, supply the containers which will all carry the Lemton label. Each separate order will be for at least one thousand dollars and you'll have two weeks for delivery. How soon can you give me a cost estimate?"

He doesn't even doubt I am interested, Lorne thought. The power of positive thinking. "Provided I'll get the proper cooperation from my suppliers, I can have it on your desk in about a week," he replied cautiously. "As a matter of curiosity, who provides these products now?"

"We've got two firms back east and one right here in Vancouver," Blackmoor replied. Then he volunteered: "The local company's prices are too high and the ones back east pose a transportation time problem. I want to expand this part of my business and I'm sure you can play an important part in this expansion."

"I appreciate your confidence," Lorne responded.

"It's well deserved, Lorne. I know you started from scratch like I did. Your accomplishments in this day and age of cut-throat competition are almost miraculous." Blackmoor rose from his swivel-chair, signifying the end of the meeting. He walked around his desk to Lorne, now also standing, and added:

"Don't be too greedy in figuring out your prices, but don't cut your profits either just to get the contract. I'm sure we can arrive at a deal that will prove beneficial to both of us."

Moments later Lorne was on his way back to the old plant. Quite a guy, Big Ceis, he thought. Quite a guy.

XV

"For the last time, Corine, I'm not going to put my blue suit on," Lorne said testily. "If he wants to see fancy clothes he can go to the downtown haberdashers."

Corine returned to her dishes in the sink, hiding the beginning of tears now glistening in her eyes. Mechanically she started to wash a dinner plate her hands had discovered in the cooled-off, sudsless water. What has happened to us? She wondered. Why can't I suggest anything anymore without getting an argument?

Since the opening of the new plant half a year ago, Lorne had suffered from progressive spiritual sclerosis. His attitude towards her, and to a lesser degree toward Larry and Kathy, had become painfully curt. Corine's hope that he would become his former considerate self again once the initial and inevitable wrinkles were taken out of the production program had evaporated several months ago. For six dreadfully long months he had worked from early in the morning until late every evening, save Sundays. This murderous pace had produced magnificent results businesswise, but it had also rubbed his nerves raw. He had grown short-tempered and extremely irritable. But the effects were not only psychological: physically, too, he had suffered. Since the opening ceremony, the laughter, the cocktails, the best wishes... he had lost more than twenty pounds and his face had assumed an ominous pallor. And now, as the price for obsessive dedication, he sat in the living room like a haunted stranger, impatiently awaiting the visit he had so reluctantly agreed to.

Lorne had aged six years in those six months, but he still refused to slow down. Corine had humbled herself by begging and shamed herself by erupting in anger during her countless pleas for sanity, but all her efforts had been in vain.

"You can't expect success to fall into your lap while you're sitting on your ass," he had retorted. "You've got to fight, fight, fight."

In final desperation she had turned to the minister of her church and explained that Lorne's version of success threatened to tear their marriage to shreds. Rev. Girard had readily agreed to tonight's visit. Lorne had just as readily termed the whole idea absurd. "If you're so interested in helping me, why don't you give us a hand at the plant?" he had asked sarcastically. But his fatigue, so often the catalyst in their marital disputes, that night had served as Corine's ally. Too tired to argue, and recognizing it as the only shortcut to bed, he had finally given his consent. Appreciative of her victory, Corine nevertheless was filled with apprehension about the pending encounter. Among the numerous problems that beset Lorne, religion was conspicuously absent. He had been to church only once: the day he got married.

Corine felt very tense and she was convinced she could burst into tears at any moment. When the telephone suddenly rang with unusual harshness on the wall behind her, the glass she was drying slipped from her hands and crashed into a thousand fragments at her feet.

Lorne appeared at the scene with the speed of an apparition. He tore the receiver off the hook as Corine gathered the pieces of glass, her vision blurred by the tears that now raced uncontrollably down her cheeks.

"Speaking. Just hold on for a moment, Wally." And placing his hand over the mouthpiece, Lorne angrily turned to Corine: "For Christ's sake will you stop your snottering. I've got Walter Crosley on the line. What do you want him to think?" Corine left hurriedly, but before she managed to reach the bedroom, the bell chimed in the hallway. Oh, my God, she thought, that must be him now. She quickly retraced her steps and dried her eyes with her apron. It's a good thing I put the kids to bed before doing the dishes, she mused.

"Good evening, reverend," she greeted as she ushered the minister in. And taking his coat and hat, she whispered in an apologetic tone: "Please excuse my husband's appearance. He just came home and didn't have time to change his clothes."

"I understand," Rev. Girard smiled benignly as he followed her to the living room. Lorne, apparently unaware of the minister's arrival, continued his phone conversation fortissimo. "How can anybody be so goddamned stupid?" he inquired belligerently. "Of course, you should have fired him. You've got to get rid of the weeds." Then, after a brief pause: "Sure, I appreciate it, Wally. Just don't forget that orders got to be dealt with on a priority basis. That means Alberta comes first."

A moment later he slammed the receiver home and walked into the room. If he was surprised to see the minister, his face certainly did not show it.

"Well, how are you, Lorne?" Rev. Girard greeted, offering his hand.

"Great, just great," Lorne replied, accepting the handshake.

Corine could not believe her eyes: Lorne was actually smiling.

"While we're on our feet," Lorne continued cheerfully, "let me announce another major development in the continued progress of Vincent Custom Chemicals: I've just received word that our sales territory now includes Saskatchewan as well. Just think, that leaves only Manitoba before we can tackle the real challenge: Ontario. Can you imagine western industrial products being sold in Eastern Canada? That's gonna be an awfully bitter pill for the Bay Street boys to swallow."

"My congratulations, Lorne," Rev. Girard said obligingly. "Where is all this going to end?"

At the cemetery, Corine thought, but she said hastily: "That's wonderful, honey. The way you talked to Mr. Crosley, I thought something dreadful had happened."

"Oh, that," Lorne said with a suggestion of embarrassment. "Well, actually he is a good guy. He just can't make decisions. That's the trouble nowadays: humanity is slowly becoming nothing more than a vegetable patch. People simply don't know how to think for themselves anymore. They've got to be thought for. Spectators have always outnumbered actors, but today the number of people who dare to act at all has become so small that individualism is about to share the fate of the brontosaurus."

"I'm afraid you're right, Lorne," the minister commented, "but that's the price man must pay for organized society."

"Let's sit down," Corine suggested, wondering how she could steer the conversation onto a more domestic plane.

"Does Mr. Crosley now have to look after both Alberta and Saskatchewan, Lorne?" she asked sweetly after they were seated.

"Well, for the time being: yes. Of course, as soon as the sales volume warrants it, we'll have to open up a branch in Regina or Saskatoon."

It sounds like you're a pretty busy man," the clergyman remarked with feigned innocence.

"Busy as hell, reverend, if you'll pardon the expression, and I understand you're here to try to talk me out of it."

"I admire your frankness," the minister said laughingly. "And I admit you're right."

"I'd better check the children," Corine said as she rose to her feet. Leaving the room she could not help thinking of a hawk circling high above its prey only in this case it was difficult to predict who would turn out to be the victim.

At least he isn't the stuffy type, Lorne thought as he studied the minister.

"I may as well level with you," Girard confided condescendingly. "I'm here for a selfish reason. You see, since I am partly responsible for your marriage, I've an interest in preserving it."

"Our marriage is in no danger of dissolution," Lorne parried angrily.

The minister smiled forgivingly. "When the pressure is high small problems tend to become big problems. I'm sure you agree that the pressure has increased considerably since the opening of your new plant."

"That's inevitable."

"To a degree: yes. But pressure is a funny thing, it can drive an engine and it can blow it to pieces. A safety valve spells the difference. In human affairs it's known as recreational relaxation. I don't want to sound corny, but a balanced diet of work and play is still a key factor in every success story."

"Success also exacts sacrifices," Lorne countered. "I know I've been only a part-time husband and a part-time father lately, but I have no choice. I'm building up a business without financial reserves to take care of mistakes, and believe me that's a full time job."

"Lorne, I'm not suggesting that you stop, I merely would like to see you slow down a bit. It doesn't pay to sacrifice the present for a better future. Believe me, your most important investment is right here at home. It's a happy family that pays the highest dividends."

They were startled by Corine's return. "Would you care for some coffee?" she asked.

"Excellent idea," the reverend said appreciatively. "After talking so much with your husband, my vocal cords will benefit from some lubrication."

"I hope you don't mind doctoring it yourself," she said apologetically as she placed the loaded tray in front of them.

"Mine needs no medication. I take it straight," the minister said, reaching for one of the steaming cups.

Lorne helped himself to generous servings of both cream and sugar, and then leaned back in his chair. Not a bad job, he thought as he brought the cup to his lips. As long as you have the gift of the gab, you're in business. Still he saw no reason for envy. Must be depressive at times, he reflected. It's no fun always having to listen to someone else's problems. And returning the cup to the table, he resolved: I won't burden him with my troubles.

"I understand you don't believe in God," Rev. Girard interrupted his thoughts.

So there is the real reason for the visit, Lorne inferred. Give those guys a toe-hold and before you can say cuckoo, you're in shackles.

"Let's put it this way," Lorne said calmly, "I don't believe God believes in me."

Well, it's original if nothing else, the cleric thought, planning his strategy. "Why is that?"

"Because during the thirty-odd years I've been in this part of the dust bin I've found no evidence to the contrary."

Rev. Girard seemed puzzled. "Tell me," he said, "if you have no faith in God and His marvelous plan of salvation, how do you fill the vacuum?"

Corine watched her husband in silent apprehension, remembering the many times she, too, had assailed his agnostic convictions.

"It's simple," Lorne replied, "I believe in myself."

"Self-confidence is a great thing," the minister agreed, "but it isn't faith, at least not in the Christian sense. Faith is more, much more. It is the recognition of God as the sole and absolute ruler of the entire universe. It is the unconditional and unqualified acceptance of God as the almighty and infallible Architect of all Creation--and that includes you."

Look, Ma: no pulpit, Lorne thought derisively. But he said: "As a businessman I naturally endorse the free enterprise system, but that does not deter me from subscribing to Lenin's postulation that religion is the opium of the people. Religion has always been a powerful tool of the strong to suppress the masses, a devious method to ensure affluence for the few at the expense of all others. No, I'm afraid I've no admiration for so called Christianity, not even now that the club has been replaced by the pie in the sky. In fact, I think even Christ would be disgusted if he were on earth today, for goodness inspired by fear or the promise of reward is not goodness but speculative hypocrisy."

Corine dejectedly lowered her eyes, feeling both guilty and uncomfortable as the sponsor of this duel in polemics.

"A true Christian believes in the infallibility of Christ - not in the infallibility of His flock," Rev. Girard explained patiently. "You see, though Christ is divine, Christians are only human. They have made mistakes and they are still making mistakes. You must realize that Christians are followers of Christ: not His equals. Still, history leaves no doubt that without Christian unity, Europe would have been overrun by barbarians and the great cultural heritage as we know it today, would never have been."

"That may be so, but it doesn't alter the fact that religion exists, and has survived the Age of Reason, primarily because it can neither be proven nor disproved," Lorne said, stubbornly refusing to digress. What an argument, he thought: to make mistakes is only human. Hell, there are about three billion people farting around on this earth to prove that theory! "Life without God may seem senseless," he continued, "but to accept the dogma that life is God-given, God-guided and God-taken is absurd. Surely God did not create the whole universe just to see how people behave on a planet that is less than a speck of dust in comparison to the vast expanse of outer space. At any rate, the whole experiment would be needless since God is supposed to be omniscient and thus has advance knowledge of the outcome. And while we're on the subject, how can you possibly believe God is all merciful if at the same time you believe that He metes out eternal punishment for temporary sin?"

"That's a loaded question. If I were to answer it, I would accept its premise and I don't. The truth is God does not mete out eternal punishment for temporary sin. Jesus Christ died on the cross to atone for our sins. If we repent and accept Christ as our Savior, we shall not be punished. God sends no man to hell; only man himself can do that. If a person knows what is right, but persists doing wrong, only then will he suffer the wrath of God. As far as your questioning of God's purpose is concerned, it has been said there are three roads leading to Him: the road of love, the road of faith and the road of logic. The road of logic is probably the most difficult, for logic is a calculated science which may be stimulating for the mind, but is without nourishment for the heart. Still it is, in my view, the most conclusive means by which we can irrefutably prove God's existence."

"You mean you can prove the existence of God through logic?" Lorne inquired skeptically.

"Yes."

Lorne leaned back in his chair with a touch of arrogance. "That I've got to hear," he said, confident the minister's visit was about to be concluded by a hurried farewell.

"To reject the existence of God," the reverend began, "is to regard everything, from minute atoms to vast solar systems, as the result of an accident, for without God there can, of course, be no planning. Either the universe and all that's in it is created or it is not. That's logic, isn't it?"

"Yes," Lorne agreed. Give a guy enough rope and sooner or later he'll hang himself, he thought. And glancing at his watch, he mentally added: I hope it's sooner.

"Very well," Rev. Girard continued with buoyant optimism, "let's look at a painting for a few moments. Rembrandt's Night Watch, for example. Ignoring its artistic merits, let's instead analyze it scientifically. The results might be something like ninety-seven grams of burnt sienna, seventy-two grams of ochre, or to generalize a bit and be less specific: twelve pounds and five ounces of pigment, a couple of pints of linseed oil and a few rolls of canvas. In short, instead of studying the life-like figures of the Dutch notables, their colorful costumes, their earnest faces, their swords and lances, we concern ourselves strictly with the painting's chemical composition. Now the point is, does this quantitative analysis enable us to reproduce this masterpiece? Of course not, because the most important ingredient is missing: the artist! We also have a pretty fair idea about the composition of the human body, but we can't make copies of ourselves for the same reason: the artist is missing. And in this case the artist is God."

"You've got a point there," Lorne conceded respectfully. "Still, accepting the existence of God does not simplify the riddles of life: if anything it complicates them. It does not, for example, explain man's role on earth."

"You're right, but that's another story as the saying goes. The story of Christianity."

"The saddest story ever told," Lorne remarked drily. "An incredible tale of savagery and inconsistencies, written in blood and blurred by tears.

From the Old Testament with its endless descriptions of persecution, plunder and revenge right through until today when we complain about the high cost of storing surplus food in Canada while two-thirds of the world's population is starving. And how do you propose to explain the fact that the citadel of Christianity, Rome, is also the capital of a country which boasts the largest communist party this side of the Iron Curtain? Poor advertising, don't you agree? And speaking of poor advertising, Latin America and Spain and Portugal which colonized and exploited it, represent parts of the world where Catholicism has its firmest grasp and where by some strange coincidence is also the greatest poverty, illiteracy and human misery in the entire western hemisphere."

"I am not a Catholic," Rev. Girard said simply.

"No, you're not a Catholic," Lorne said bitterly, "but your church still sprouted from the same seed. The Protestants had their own witch burnings, didn't they? Only a fool would consider the record of Christianity an enviable one. You know, it makes me puke when I hear some prelate deplore the lack of freedom that prevails under a dictatorial regime. Does Rome really expect us to forget what happened when it had absolute control? For centuries the popes ruled with iron fists, and while millions of people perished at the stake or in the Church's dungeons, they had the gall to call themselves infallible. Christian theocracy was the world's worst form of dictatorship. It thwarted science, condemned reason, ridiculed mercy and retarded social justice for more than a thousand years. Christianity has been spread, not by or for the love of Christ, but as a pretext to invade and exploit other nations. Now don't get me wrong. I'm not criticizing the teachings of Christ, I'm just saying that they've never been put into effect on a large scale. They have been more abused than used, in other words. Even Hitler's soldiers had 'God with us' stamped on the buckles of their belts."

"Christianity has had its share of difficulties," the harassed minister conceded, "but where would the world be today without it?" "That's a good question," Lorne snapped.

"All our laws are based on Christian principles. Without these there would be chaos."

"How much more chaotic can things get?" Lorne countered. "Though church membership is apparently soaring upward, so is crime, divorce and what have you. Now I don't go to church, but I don't rob banks either. Why don't I rob banks? Well, it's not because I can't use the money nor is it because it says in the Bible -Thou shalt not steal- and least of all it's because I'm scared I may end up in jail. No, I don't stage hold-ups because I realize that you can't build a better world by stealing, that in the long run there is more profit in giving. In other words, I realize that by harming others, you harm yourself also. Similarly I can best serve my own interests by serving others. So in the final analysis my attitude is based on reason inspired by egoism, the survival instinct if you like."

"I would like to go on," the reverend said pleasantly, but I have two more visits to make." And rising from his chair: "I enjoyed our talk. Perhaps we can have another go at it some other time."

"Perhaps we can," Lorne said without enthusiasm as he led the way to the hall.

When the minister had left, Corine asked gently: "Have you learned anything, darling?"

"Not really," Lorne said, sitting down again. "If anything, he merely confirmed my views."

"Don't you think he's nice though?"

"As a person, yes. As a preacher he's no different than the rest. What gets me is that all those characters think they're right and everyone with a different belief is automatically wrong."

"Oh, Lorne," Corine said, close to despair, "why do I even try?"

"I don't know, baby. I really don't know. I would like to please you, but I guess religion just isn't my cup of tea. Maybe my childhood is responsible for that. I learned at an early age that if you want something, you don't pray for it: you work for it."

"Have you ever prayed, Lorne?" she asked, her eyes reflecting a flicker of hope.

"No."

"Then how can you belittle the value of praying?"

"Because I think it's the cruelest form of self-deceit ever invented by man."

Tears threatened to explode in her eyes, but somehow she managed to keep them at bay.

"Let me give you an example. If a guy is about to kick the bucket, his loved ones offer prayers for his recovery. If he does recover, it's praise to the Lord, but if he dies people will say: 'it was God's will.' Just like that. Heads: you lose and tail: I win. What a game. When a child cries at the grave of his mother, the faithful will say: 'God wanted your mummy, Bobby, Now wipe your tears, 'cause Mummy is looking at you from Heaven. She's happy with the Lord,' Now I find it a trifle hard to believe that a mother can be happy when she has been separated from her child through death. And assuming for a moment that your beliefs actually have foundation, don't you think the child needed his mother a lot more than God does?"

The Lord giveth and He taketh," Corine quoted from her catechism. "We're here to serve God and be judged by Him - not vice versa, Lorne."

"You haven't answered my question yet,"

"I don't think man was meant to know all the answers," she said diffidently. "Only God knows everything."

"That's a poor argument. Don't you ever have doubts?" "No. I have faith and once you've got faith there's no room for doubt."

"Well, I've got plenty of doubts about religion and frankly, faith or no faith, I don't see how anyone can be without doubt when even Jesus in His agony on the cross said: 'My God, my God, why hast thou forsaken me?'"

The following morning Lorne arrived at the plant half an hour later than usual. He had eaten his breakfast without trying to break previous speed records, he had talked to Corine about the children and only briefly paged through the morning paper and he had even remembered to kiss her good-by before climbing behind the wheel.

Now he sat opposite Wayne Scott in his large and comfortable office.

"Wayne, how would you like to spend more time with your family?"

"If this is a joke, it's in bad taste," Wayne observed. He was away from home five, often six days a week, seriously dulling the romantic lustre of his marriage. He knew Betty and the children had suffered considerably by his regular and long periods of absence. "What's the deal?" he asked.

"I want you to look after my sales. I simply can't handle local sales, run the plant, continue my research and be a responsible father and husband to boot."

"I was wondering when you would see the light," Wayne said happily. "But who's gonna look after my territory?"

"We'll have to find someone," Lorne replied simply. "As soon as we've got someone suitable, you can break him in."

"Best birthday present I've ever had," Wayne commented appreciatively.

"Don't tell me..."

"Yes, today is the day. Thirty-seven."

"I'll take you out for coffee," Lorne proffered.

"Your generosity is overwhelming," Wayne said drily. "But tell me, when do we start the search for my successor?"

"Know anybody off-hand?"

"Depends on what you plan to offer."

"Ten per cent plus expenses and medical coverage. I was thinking of running an ad in the Sun this Saturday." "I've got a hunch that won't be necessary."

"So much the better," Lorne said. "Incidentally, I want you to keep looking after the Lower Mainland. I'll take care of Lemton until things are running smoothly."

"Do you think we can actually start delivery of our detergents next week?"

"Definitely. Bulk sales only, of course. Esther is mimeographing the pricelists today. I've hired four extra men to help take care of the production end of it. It's getting to be a fantastic year, Wayne. Sales to Big Ceis alone have soared past the ten thousand-dollar mark. The way things are developing, our dry cleaning chemicals may soon be only a sideline. If the detergents will go over as big as our soap has, we will really go places."

There was a knock at the door.

"Come in."

It was Ted Melville, the foreman. "We're out of amyl acetate," he announced glumly.

"I ordered a drum last week," Lorne said. "Did you check with Joe?" Joe Tiflin was the shipper who also handled supplies. "I did," Melville said lamely. "Nothing has come in yet."

"Just leave it to me, Ted. I'll look after it. What were you working at?"

"Trelinex. We're getting low on it."

"Have those used quart bottles been cleaned yet?"

"Yes, we put them on the drying rack last night."

"Swell, you can start filling them then with methanol. The door had barely been shut when Lorne picked up the phone and briskly dialed the familiar number, his face suddenly flushed with anger.

"Good morning, Feltham and Carrfield," the switchboard operator sang in his ear.

"Mr. Dennison, please."

"Roy Dennison here."

"Lorne Vincent speaking..."

"Oh, yes, Lorne. How are you this morning?"

"How the hell d'ya expect me to be?" Lorne snapped. "That drum of amyl acetate that was supposed to be here last Friday at the latest still isn't here today."

"I 'm sorry, but we're right out of stock."

"It's a bit late for that piece of info, don't you agree?"

"I thought..."

"Now listen here, Roy," Lorne erupted, "don't hand me that thinking routine. You obviously did not think or you would have known last week that you didn't have the stuff. You could have told me then instead of promising delivery of apparently non-existent stock." "Please, Lorne, let's be reasonable," Dennison pleaded.

"Reasonable?" Lorne exploded. "Are you people reasonable? I can't fill my orders because of your inefficiency. I'm sick and tired of phony pledges. I can't afford them. But I tell you this, Roy, if I haven't got that drum this afternoon, you won't have me as a customer tomorrow."

And without waiting for Dennison's reaction Lorne slapped the receiver home. Turning to Wayne, he said: "You know, if I should fail in business it will be because of my suppliers' unreliability. Any resemblance between what people say and what people do is becoming increasingly coincidental."

"Can't you overcome this problem by building up your own stock?" Wayne asked defensively.

"Can't afford it. Besides, you simply can't figure out your needs ahead of time. Every week is different."

"Does this sort of thing happen often?"

"All the time, Wayne, and it's getting worse. Either you don't get the stuff on time or else they ship something you never even ordered. It just about drives me nuts. And big companies are often worse than the smaller outfits. Organized confusion they call it. Only the other day I got a letter from one of the biggest laboratory supplies dealers. It acknowledged receipt of my inquiry about prices and specifications on constant temperature baths. And you know what they sent me? Prices and brochures on fractional distillation equipment! Doesn't that make you wonder how the hell they even manage to stay in business?"

"Our success is probably largely due to the fact that we are the exact opposite," Wayne suggested. "We bend backwards to please our customers."

"I read once that service is like a lubricant without which the Mercurian wheels soon grind to a halt. I guess that's true for small and growing businesses which face keen competition, but the big companies aren't affected by competition in the same way. They usually handle the best known products and are protected by exclusive franchise agreements. A buyer either has to gamble with an unknown product or take the crap the giants dish out so generously with the merchandise they sell you."

"What are you gonna do if Feltham and Carrfield doesn't come through this afternoon?" Wayne changed the subject.

"I'll phone Canadian Chemicals. They'll either supply me direct or refer me to a more reliable dealer."

"Well, I'd better be going," Wayne said as he got up.

"Not until we've had coffee," Lorne said laughingly. "After spending the last half hour lecturing on the iniquity of broken promises, I can't very well go back on my word now."

By mid-afternoon that day the amyl acetate arrived. Lorne grinned inwardly. It pays to get tough, he mused. If you don't, you'll soon get trampled under.

After discussing the revised production schedule with Ted, it suddenly occurred to him that he had not seen Doug for nearly a month. Doug usually dropped in at the house on weekends to chat about a thousand and one things and play with the children, but lately he had shown up less and less.

Doug had blamed the spring assizes and Lorne, being up to his neck in work himself, had given the matter no further thought until now. A visit by his best friend was always a welcome experience. They often reminisced about the days when Doug had smuggled laboratory equipment and chemicals out of the university to support Lorne's modest research. Another popular topic concerned Doug's triumphs and tribulations in court. Doug elaborated about his amorous exploits only when he and Lorne were alone and those stories were no less fascinating. Lorne's standard topic dealt, of course, with his business experiences. Somehow four weeks had slipped by without any communication between them and Lorne suddenly felt guilty of negligence. He dialed the number from memory.

"Morley, Graham and Patton."

"Mr. Marcus, please."

"Mr. Marcus is not in," the law firm's receptionist said. Then, after an apparent moment of hesitation, she inquired: "Are you Mr. Vincent?" "Yes, I am," Lorne confessed.

"I thought I recognized your voice," she said in a tone of suppressed enthusiasm. "I'm sorry to be the one to tell you, but Mr. Marcus is in hospital."

Lorne felt a spasm of nausea. "Which one?" he heard himself ask in a voice he did not recognize.

"St. Luke's."

After he had hung up he stared dejectedly ahead. St. Luke's. That made sense for it was at that hospital that Doug's father was chief surgeon. Quickly the questions the news had prompted began to multiply in his mind. Why had Doug not told him? How long had he been there? Most importantly: why was he there?

XVI

Lorne felt as if a lump of lead fell into the pit of his stomach when he entered Doug's room. For a moment doubt of recognition tore through his brain. The emaciated human shape, propped up in the out of place looking white hospital bed, bore painfully little resemblance to the robust body that had once belonged to Doug Marcus. The eyes, which had sparkled with laughter so often in the past, now looked forlorn and grotesque in their enlarged sockets. The skull revealed its form with ominous clarity through the pallid skin. Veins, like dark knotted cords, stood out in stark relief on his thin hands, the parchment-like flesh clashing lugubriously with the immaculate whiteness of the sheet beneath it.

"Good to see you, Lorne," he said in a voice that had retained most of its vitality. "Welcome to my plush tomb. The body has perished, but the mind lingers on."

"Why didn't you tell me?" Lorne asked humbly, unable to match Doug's macabre sense of humor.

"I've been too damn busy feeling sorry for myself. But after due deliberation in the abyss of despair, I've changed my attitude and instead of worrying about when it will end, I now try to enjoy life while it lasts." "I'm so sorry..."

"No, no, no," Doug interrupted. "I want cheer: not sadness. You can't imagine how wonderful it is to see someone without a shot of morphine in his hands."

"I didn't know until I called your office about an hour ago," Lorne said apologetically.

There's no need to ask him what has happened, Lorne reflected. If the hospital sends you home in that condition - it can only be one thing.

"I caved in at the office the day after I last saw you and Corine." With visible exertion Doug managed to move himself into a straighter sitting position. "I learned belatedly that when it comes to your health, you should never push your luck. They opened me up, took one look inside and closed me up again. Father told me the verdict: a matter of weeks, three months at the most. He was very professional about it. 'The results of the operation are not encouraging,' he started. Just like that. I am a patient, you see. The fact that I also happen to be his son is merely a coincidence. I've got excellent care, very efficient nurses, but he fails to see that even an abortive attempt to act more like a father and less like a doctor would mean a million times more to me than all his precious medical know-how. And mother, she cries every time she sees me. She loves shedding tears and God knows she can mass-produce them. But she hasn't missed a single meeting of her lodge. But that would be asking a lot, wouldn't it? How she loves to parade with those other useless dames in long garbs and with fancy titles. All men and women who delude themselves into believing that they're the cat's meow because they call one another exalted this and most worshipful that are so goddamned despicable to me that it just about makes me puke. I guess I sound bitter, but it takes a bit of adjustment to accept the fact that your own parents treat you as a stranger - even in the end." Lorne felt a chill creep up his spine.

"It's strange," Doug continued, "how five weeks can look like five years. It seems so long ago since I last played with Kathy and Larry. It seems like centuries since I felt carefree and happy. Still, I have learned more in the past few weeks than in all the years before. I now look at life like an observer since I'm no longer an active participant. I realize that the things I've always taken for granted really mean the most, while matters I used to consider so bloody important are relatively insignificant. Actually, I haven't felt good since early last fall, but I convinced myself that I was just tired. I told myself you can't build up a practice by staying home and I overlooked the fact that you can't do it either when you're dead. You know, the irony of it all is that I was just on the verge of making something of my life. I took my work seriously and I had found satisfaction in accepting the challenge law provides. Hind sight is great, of course, but if I had had a medical check-up half a year ago, chances are they might have been able to remove the tumor and my prospects today would probably have been a lot better. Do you mind if I continue to chew your ear off?"

"No, not at all," Lorne said. He was glad Doug could find words to express himself. It was a lot more than HE could do. What is there to talk about when hope isn't part of it? What can you say when you know that despair will make a mockery of your words?

"Perhaps some of the things I'm bringing up will prove of value to you later. Maybe you will find a useful application for my philosophical conclusions. I know I won't. I can see now that most of our problems in this life are the direct result of our refusal to come to grips with reality. People go through life with a cloak of artificialness wrapped around them. The neon lights, padded breasts, thermostatically controlled heat, they're all part of it. We foolishly seek security in a world that never knew it and we try to make sense out of a senseless existence. We worry about the frost killing our early flowers and we are heartbroken when our favorite hockey team loses a game, but few people's sleep is disturbed by the fact that nuclear annihilation is a growing threat twenty four hours a day. We propagate at a criminal rate and in exchange for a few minutes of pleasure bring innocent children into a world that's rotten to the core and knows no certainty but death. We insist on kidding ourselves and even facelift our funeral homes to perpetuate this cruel hoax. We make our caskets as attractive as possible with a soft lining the dead will never feel and we furnish and decorate our mortuaries in much the same manner as we do our better offices. We use euphemisms for everything that has an unpleasant resonance. People no longer die: they pass away. Nobody is crazy, but we do have our share of mentally disturbed people. The war department is now the Department of Defense. And so on ad nauseam. But Death is as much a fact of life as Red China, whether we recognize it or not. It's only a matter of time and since time is so relative, it makes essentially little difference when your time is up, because if a man has been a failure for forty years, he is not likely to be a success on his eightieth birthday. Some bums may become centenarians, but Mozart became immortal at the age of thirty-five. In a nutshell, I realize there's no point in worrying about the future for sooner or later--and usually suddenly--someday will be forever." "What about religion?" Lorne thought aloud.

"Religion?"

"Yes, isn't that what you were leading up to?"

"No, and I'm surprised you bring it up."

"Well," Lorne explained, "yesterday the minister of Corine's church dropped in trying to make a Christian out of me." Doug smiled. "I wish I had seen that" he said.

"Do you believe there is a God?"

"A timely question," Doug observed. "Yes, I believe there is a God. Don't ask me to prove it, because I can't--at least not yet."

"I'm sorry I brought it up," Lorne said sincerely. "It was very thoughtless of me."

"On the contrary, Lorne. We almost got involved in an old fashioned discussion. Don't forget our friendship was forged by the heat of our first debate."

"Yes, I still remember," Lorne said warmly: "The pros and cons of a divided Germany."

"And the whole thing ended in a tie," Doug complemented, "but you've proved me wrong about your business. I still find it hard to believe that you actually made it in spite of all the odds against you."

"I haven't made it yet," Lorne said modestly. "The deeper you get into this game, the higher the stakes and the tougher the rules."

"Yeah, I guess so. Still, you've come a long way and I sure as hell hope you'll stick to your guns. Don't forget you've jumped the toughest hurdle already by surviving the beginning."

Lorne smiled appreciatively. A person would almost forget the impending tragedy, he thought. He's got a lot of guts.

There was a knock at the door and before Doug could utter a word, a nurse stepped in.

"It's five o'clock," she announced simply.

"Let's skip it for a few minutes, Helen," Doug said. "I'm getting the best form of medication right now."

"All right, ten minutes then." When she had disappeared he turned to Lorne and said: "That was one of four private nurses who take turns keeping an eye on me twenty-four hours a day courtesy of my honorable parents. They're very punctual. They comfort me with pills and needles every four hours. Gradually the frequency will be increased. When the crap will finally fail to still the pain, I'll know the end of the road is in sight. Until that happens I would like you to do me a favor, Lorne. Please drop in at least once a week. The kind of shot in the arm you give me doesn't come in a syringe. I want you to know I value your company above that of anyone else."

"You can count on it, Doug," he said, emotion choking his voice.

"If I had known I would have come sooner."

Doug faintly shook his head. "I'm glad you didn't," he said. "I couldn't have timed it better myself. Until a few days ago I was in a state of profound despondency and I could not possibly have appreciated your company. You must understand that for a girl-hopper like me it's quite a shock to be in bed for other reasons."

A few minutes later Lorne found himself aiming his car homeward. Somehow the world looked vastly different from earlier that afternoon: it seemed darker in more than one way...

Part V

XVII

It was a week later when Blackmoor phoned Lorne early in the morning. "Received my order yet?" he inquired.

"Got it in yesterday's mail."

"Swell. Have you got it handy? I've got some changes."

"Just a moment, please." And a minute later: "Okay, shoot."

"Where it says five hundred two-pound boxes of detergent, write seven hundred and fifty. As for the soap products, just double the figures."

"Holy Moses!" Lorne exclaimed: "you're really going great guns."

"Your stuff is catching on very nicely," Blackmoor said, audibly satisfied with the results. "Incidentally, Lorne, I want you to keep Saturday night open. I'm throwing a party and I expect you and your wife at eight."

The invitation sounded more like a command than a request, but Lorne would have jumped at it no matter what phraseology Blackmoor had used.

"Thanks, Ceis," Lorne said, addressing Blackmoor by his nickname for the first time. "We'll be there."

Lorne had barely returned the receiver to the set when there was a knock at the door.

"Yeah."

It was Esther, his secretary. "There is a gentleman to see you," she said formally. "A Mr. Beldan."

"Fred Beldan?!" he asked incredulously. "What the hell does HE want to see me for?"

"I don't know," Esther admitted, "but he insists it is very important."

For a moment he hesitated, then curiosity got the better of him and he said: "Okay, send him in."

Fred Beldan diffidently extended his hand. "How are you, Lorne?"

"Sit down, Frederick," Lorne said, declining the invitation to a handshake. And he added with a bitterness that five years had failed to eradicate: "Have you come to apologize?"

Beldan tried hard to smile but he merely produced a grimace. "I, I've come to ask for a job," he stammered.

"You must be kidding," Lorne snapped. "This is Vincent's Custom Chemicals - not Fentex."

A flash of pain swept across Beldan's face. The events following Lindhurst's abortive court action had left their marks on him. The lines in his face had been etched permanently into the grim expression of failure. His attire, an example of impeccability in the past, now bordered on the fashion representative of bums and derelicts. His hair had completely turned gray.

"You don't understand," Beldan said despairingly. "I had no choice."

"Balls!" Lorne exploded.

"Please," Beldan implored, "give me at least a chance to explain."

"All right," Lorne said, leaning back in his swivel chair: "Explain."

When Beldan had concluded his account of how Nithdale had forced him to take court action, Lorne looked at him reflectively.

Beldan's eyes betrayed the faint flicker of hope he felt in his heart.

"An explanation is not an excuse," Lorne said finally. "You tried to save your own neck by cutting mine. I can generate no enthusiasm for such strategy."

"I understand," Beldan said honestly. "I don't think I would feel any different if I were in your position. The point is I've got no one else to turn to."

"What about Fentex?" Lorne suggested, studying him closely.

"I may not have much pride left, but it's enough to stop me from stooping that low. They arranged my bankruptcy and sold my shop for a song to Darwin Fletcher. No, apart from the fact that they would never hire me, I could never set foot in that place again. But let me tell you that the real cause for my downfall was not Fentex but my wife."

Lorne bent forward with interest. "Your wife?" he echoed unbelievingly. "Where does she come in?"

"Elsie married me for my money," Beldan explained with a wan smile, "and she never missed an opportunity to rub it in. So, perhaps foolishly, I searched elsewhere for the affection I was denied at home and found it in the arms of a pretty young thing I had met at the Mocambo night club."

He paused as if to inhale the sweetness of the fading memory.

"Her name was Sylvia: Sylvia Sterling, and she provided everything Elsie did not: love, understanding and sympathy. I was so infatuated that I failed to see the ulterior motive behind Sylvia's kindness. But, looking back, I don't think it would have made a particle of difference if I had known. Isn't feigned love better than no love at all? Well, anyway, I put her up in a nice apartment, bought her fancy clothes and gave her enough money for her other needs. I didn't want her to work. I wanted her all for myself and I must say I never had any reason to believe she wasn't faithful to me. But the cost of providing for a wife and a mistress is a high one. My business simply couldn't carry the load and I gradually slipped into the red. In a desperate bid to save my skin I started to expand so I could increase my volume and thus my profits. I bought extra equipment from Fentex and you know the rest. After I had lost the shop, Elsie quickly filed for divorce. Somehow she had found out about Sylvia and consequently I didn't have a leg to stand on nor, after she was through with me, a pot to pee in. But the real heartbreak came later. You see, what kept me going at that time was Sylvia's promise to marry me. I was even grateful to my wife for making it possible. Then, on the night before we were to have been married, I dropped in at the apartment and found her gone. It was completely cleaned out. She had left nothing behind - not even a note. No explanation, no thank you, no good-by."

Fred Beldan sighed as if what he described had happened only a few days ago.

"Slowly it dawned on me that not I, but my money had been the main attraction. Too late I realized that Sylvia had more in common with Elsie than I had suspected. Women are parasites..."

"Not all of them, Fred," Lorne interjected, remembering how Corine had always helped him.

"No, not all of them," Beldan said bitterly, "but when you're penniless, love is awfully scarce. That's probably why even vultures leave a man alone when only the bones are left. Failure is a tough thing to get used to, Lorne. Nothing pushes a man closer to suicide than the knowledge that no one gives a damn what happens to you. The reason I didn't take my life was not because I thought there was still hope, but because I didn't have the guts. I scoff at anyone who claims that suicide is the way of the coward. I've been too close to it not to know better. I couldn't stay in Vancouver because it reminded me of everything I was trying so hard to forget. So I went to my brother in California. For three months I helped him in his coffee shop. I quit when it became obvious to me that I wasn't helping him, but that he was helping me. He could get two waitresses for the money he paid me and I knew I couldn't do the work of one. I don't want to bore you with the rest. I've slung beer, I've worked in lumber camps, I've done a thousand and one things: it's a long, drab story. But now I'm back in Vancouver. I love the place despite the past. I'm forty-nine now and I am confident I can still pull my weight. I've grown up in the dry-cleaning business, Lorne. I guess, it's like any other business: it gets into your blood. I want to get back into it. You're the only one who can make that possible."

Lorne saw Beldan meant it. "Have you got a car?" he asked.

"A fifty-two Plymouth," Beldan replied, and noticing Lorne's frown, he added eagerly: "It's in real good shape."

Lorne smiled for the first time since Beldan's arrival. "Come," he said. "I want to show you the plant."

Wayne Scott phoned from Kamloops just before noon. "I tried to get hold of you yesterday afternoon, but Esther said you had left," Wayne said. "I've got our man. Just a second I'll give you his phone number..."

"Don't bother," Lorne interrupted. "I just hired someone this morning."

"You're kidding," Wayne blurted, unable to conceal his annoyance. "Do I know him?"

"You should," Lorne said calmly. "He worked for Fentex once: Fred Beldan."

There was a tense pause at the other end of the line. "What do you want, Lorne?" Wayne finally said. "He double-crossed you once, isn't that enough?"

"I felt the same way when he asked me for a job," Lorne explained, "but Fred told me a lot I didn't know. I'm sure he won't cross me again. He paid a high price for trying it once."

"I hope you're right," Wayne said drily. "See you Saturday."

Corine reacted to his hiring of Beldan with no more enthusiasm. "It's kind, but I don't think it's smart," she said candidly. "The same move cost Julius Caesar his life."

"Fred could not possibly have worked for him, too," Lorne said facetiously.

"That's not what I mean, silly," Corine smiled, "but Julius Caesar also trusted a man twice. Once before he was betrayed by him and once after. The second time Brutus saw to it that there would be no chance for reconsideration."

"My, my, you flatter me by comparing me with the illustrious emperor," Lorne laughed. "Tell me my sweet little historian, whattcha cooking for supper?"

"Cabbage rolls."

"Hm," Lorne said: "Hamburger again."

"What's wrong with hamburger?"

"I hate to guess."

"You're just fussy."

"What time are Larry and Kathy coming back?"

"Stan said he would drive them over around eight. Apparently they're just having a ball. Kathy and Debbie have been playing with their dolls all afternoon and Ricky took Larry to a hockey game."

Stan Naylor stepped into the house shortly before eight o'clock, Larry and Kathy, their faces aglow, at his side.

"Daddy, can I have a pair of skates?" Larry asked before the door had been shut behind him. "I want to skate like Ricky and play hockey all the time."

"I'll see Santa about it," Lorne promised.

"But that's not until Christmas," Ricky protested. "That's enough," Corine interrupted. "To the bathroom: quick march!"

"I forgot to tell you," Stan said after Corine and the children had left the room. "Darwin Fletcher has joined our growing list of cash customers. I got his okay this morning."

"Good show."

"By next week we should have an extra three thousand dollars to work with."

"Can we ever use it," Lorne said gratefully. "Big Ceis doubled his soap order today. The stuff apparently is selling like hotcakes."

"You're over the hump, Lorne," Stan said in between puffs from his cigar.

"Uh, uh," Lorne said with his usual caution. "The bigger the volume, the bigger the risks. We're virtually operating without financial reserves. Any major difficulty could spell disaster."

"What could possibly screw us now?" Stan exclaimed unceremoniously.

"I don't know," Lorne answered simply.

"Neither did Caesar." Both men looked up in surprise. It was Corine.

Lorne noticed the puzzled look on his brother-in-law's face. "I hired Fred Beldan this morning to handle Wayne's territory," he explained. "Corine thinks I'll live to regret it."

Stan recalled the court episode well. "If you hired him despite the past, you must have had a good reason," he said diplomatically.

"I have," Lorne said, grateful for Stan's confidence. "A very good reason."

"He's a man with lots of experience," Stan added, "and that's what we need."

"His experience didn't prevent his bankruptcy," Corine commented with unusual persistence.

"His bankruptcy had nothing to do with his business qualifications," Lorne said mystifyingly. "His downfall was engineered by the person who should have been his best ally."

Stan, realizing the futility of pursuing the matter any further, rose from his chair. "Well, I've got to be going," he said. "I guess, we'll see you Saturday."

"Yes," Corine said. "We'll be over right after supper."

"I'm sorry, but we can't make it Saturday," Lorne intercepted, suddenly remembering. "Big Ceis asked us to come."

"But Saturday is Mary's birthday," Corine protested.

Lorne looked helplessly at his brother-in-law. He did not want to offend Mary by not coming, but to turn Big Ceis down seemed unthinkable. It would be tantamount to inviting repercussions he could ill afford. Already Lemton Distributors accounted for more than twenty five per cent of his total sales and all indications pointed to a higher figure before the year's end.

"In that case drop in during the afternoon," Stan said conciliatorily.

"When Cecil Blackmoor invites you, you don't argue: you just go. "Yeah, we'll drop in around two," Lorne said hastily, appreciative of the escape-hatch Stan had provided.

"It's a strange thing," Corine observed after Stan had left, "but progress in business has come to mean the opposite at home. Now even our social life is no longer our own. Why can't we be ourselves any more, Lorne? Don't you see we're drifting apart?"

Waldon Jefferson was beginning to get a pretty good idea what Henry IV must have felt like when Pope Gregory let him wait three days outside the gates of the Canossa castle during the winter of 1077 before forgiving his sins.

Jefferson did not have to brave the cold, for it was a beautiful spring day in New York, but he felt no more comfortable for it. He had been sitting in the anteroom for more than an hour, studying the ceiling tile, the secretary's tanned legs, his shoe laces and the lettering on the door that had remained closed: T.J. Sneldon. General Sales Manager. But his superior, who only the day before had instructed him by phone to take the first flight east, now obviously was in no great hurry to see him.

The bastard, Jefferson cursed under his breath. I wouldn't treat a janitor like that.

At last he heard Sneldon's suave voice over the intercom on the secretary's desk. A minute later he sat opposite him.

"You're looking well, Waldon," Sneldon started amiably. "The Canadian way of life must agree with you."

"I trust you didn't have me fly across the continent to discuss my health," Jefferson said with an impudence he normally reserved for his subordinates, but the humiliating waiting period had sharpened his tongue and evaporated his patience.

Sneldon's smile vanished instantly. "All right, we'll dispense with the cordialities and come right to the point. You're here to take charge of Inter-Office Communications."

"That doesn't sound like a promotion," Jefferson commented icily.

"It isn't."

"May I ask why I'm being transferred then?"

"You may, but I didn't think you'd find it necessary," Sneldon replied acrimoniously. "You see, Waldon, you weren't exactly a smash hit in Vancouver. In fact, you pulled the same stupid mistakes Nithdale did before you."

"I met my obligations," Jefferson protested. "I even saw to it that Fletcher got his precious press."

"A used model, fixed up to look like new," Sneldon observed, proving his usual thoroughness.

195

"Well, it was better than facing a suit for breach of contract," Jefferson said stubbornly.

"That's debatable. If Darwin Fletcher ever finds out what you pulled on him, he can cause more trouble than I care to imagine. But regardless, what good did that transaction do? Fletcher profited, Fentex lost and Vincent wasn't even affected by it."

"It looked like a worthwhile gamble at the time, but there is no such thing as a sure bet. I admit that the end result was not in Fentex's interest, but the intent was."

"Waldon Jefferson," Sneldon said disparagingly, "Fentex is an industrial giant - not a bookie joint. I have no admiration for your questionable tactics. There are more ethical ways to meet competition effectively."

"The only times I've heard objections voiced at Fentex about questionable tactics was when they failed to yield the desired results," Jefferson said recalcitrantly.

Sneldon narrowed his eyes as he studied the former division manager closely. This was obviously a case of gross insubordination. Not taking his eyes off him, he asked curtly: "Do I take it you're not interested in the position I've offered you?"

Jefferson slowly rose to his feet and placed his hands on the edge of the desk that separated them, his eyes boring into Sneldon's. Then he said with vitriolic passion: "I haven't got your talent for diplomatic phraseology, Teddy boy, but to put it in plain lingo: you can stick your job up your fat ass. If I want charity, I'd rather go to the Salvation Army. At least I'll know it's genuine."

XVIII

Lorne and Corine arrived at Horseshoe Bay shortly after eight. Except for a lone pedestrian the street that ran along the harbor was deserted. Driving right to the man, Lorne stopped the car and lowered the window.

"Could you tell me where I'll find Twin Spruce Cove?" he asked.

The eerie light of a lone street lantern revealed a toothless grin on the man's wrinkled face. The weather-beaten yachting cap, askance on his dirty gray hair, almost looked like a permanent fixture. He slowly took his pipe out of his mouth and raised his hand parallel to the car, the index finger, curved by arthritis, pointing to the inky darkness ahead.

"You drive straight ahead," he said in a strong Scottish burr, "and follow the road after it turns until you can see the water again. Mr. Blackmoor lives in the fourth house at your right."

"Thanks a lot," Lorne said. Then he put the car into gear again and followed the man's directions, the old fellow's grin lingering in his mind. It was as if he knew something important about Big Ceis that Lorne did not.

"I'm nervous," Corine said suddenly.

"Why in the world should you be nervous?" Lorne asked, trying hard to conceal his own apprehension.

"I don't know," Corine confessed. "That's what worries me."

"Nonsense, baby," he said, sounding more confident than he felt. "We'll have a great time."

Suddenly the splendor of light emanating from a huge ocean liner loomed up at their right, its festive appearance reflected in the calm water below the narrow road. A few moments later a sign spelling Twin Spruce Cove, basking in the brightness of a floodlight below it, sprang into sight.

Lorne piloted his car along the wide driveway which led sharply downward, the lights of the still invisible mansion mirrored in yellow splotches on the tall evergreens. Then, after negotiating a left turn, the majestic residence of Cecil Blackmoor stood suddenly exposed before their startled eyes. The parking area was crowded with several Cadillacs, Lincolns, two Jaguars, a Rolls Royce, an Imperial and about half a dozen sports cars.

"Our Studie will look a bit out of place here," Lorne laughed before parking the car as far away from the main entrance as possible.

"We can still go to Stan and Mary," Corine suggested diffidently.

"Not on your life," Lorne protested buoyantly. "This promises to be fun."

"I'm gonna look awfully conspicuous in this dress," she whispered as they walked toward the entrance.

"Don't be silly," Lorne smiled as he pressed an illuminated button. "If you smile you'll be the most attractive female in the house."

A young man in thin-legged pants and a blue blazer opened the door.

"My name is Jim Vance," he greeted pleasantly, "and if my memory serves me correctly you are Mr. Vincent."

"Yes, I am," Lorne said, wondering how he had been recognized.

"I remember seeing you at Lemton," Vance volunteered, and turning to Corine he inquired Henry M. Stanley style: "Mrs. Vincent, I presume?"

Corine smiled nervously. "How do you do?" she greeted stiffly. Vance returned the smile benignly and raising his hands, he asked: "May I take your coat?"

Lorne glanced in admiration at the palatial vestibule as he slipped out of his coat. A huge crystal chandelier cast a sparkling light throughout the richly decorated interior. At the left a painting showed in realistic colors the plight of a schooner in a seething sea, the dark gray sky alive with impending disaster. Just beyond, the still figure of a complete set of armor seemed to guard the split staircase: one part leading down, the other ascending. Thick-piled carpeting widened generously around the stairs in a warm embrace. At their immediate right was a small checkroom in which Vance hung their coats, creating an effect reminiscent of their jalopy among the automobiles outside. Corine cast a furtive glance at her coat now hanging forlornly among the largest collection of furs she had seen since her last visit to the Hudson's Bay Company.

Vance moved elegantly from behind the small counter of the cloakroom and said: "Please follow me."

At the top of the staircase he stopped, announcing:

"The men are downstairs at your left, Mr. Vincent." And addressing Corine: "I'll show you the way to the ladies."

Corine exchanged a meaningful glance with Lorne, her uneasiness heightened by their unexpected separation. Lorne managed to flash a confident smile just before she slipped out of sight. For a moment he studied the still shape of the shiny armor, the right gauntlet clutching the shaft of an awe-inspiring halberd, then he walked down, his steps cushioned by the softness of the red runner that covered the wide stairs. The animated sound of conversation which now reached his ears, ceased a minute later when he appeared in the doorway of a large lounge. About a dozen men turned their faces to Lorne as Big Ceis strode forward to welcome him. "Gentlemen," he said in his stentorian voice, "I want you to meet Lorne Vincent, Vancouver's most promising young businessman."

Lorne shook hands with the executives and tycoons as if the affair was an everyday routine for him. The youngest of them was at least forty-five years old. After the introduction Blackmoor led him to the bar.

"What will it be, Lorne?" he asked cordially.

"Rum and coke, please."

The conversations among the guests rapidly gained in decibels until Big Ceis again put an end to the verbal merriment.

"Fellows," he said, "tonight is primarily a family affair as you know, so there can be no live show. But before we'll interrupt the women in their latest gossip, I thought you might like to see some of my better home movies."

The men laughed approvingly, their knowing smiles puzzling Lorne.

"Ever seen them before?" a corpulent chap at his side inquired in a whisper.

Lorne confessed his ignorance.

"Man," the gent, earlier introduced as George Hewitt, continued, "You're lucky. I've seen them on several occasions and though I can't get enough of them, you can't beat the first time."

When everybody was seated in comfortable armchairs, the lights went out and the end wall of the room suddenly became alive with a young woman entering a richly furnished bedroom. Smiling in mock shyness she proceeded to undress herself until the wall shone with her lascivious nakedness.

"She's a real piece," Hewitt confided proudly.

As the girl moved to a bathroom, Lorne suddenly felt his clothes stick to his perspiring skin. He was grateful for the darkness hiding his reddening face. The scenes followed one another in a quick succession of obscenities, draining the self-assuredness Lorne had felt earlier. He stirred self-consciously in his chair, a reaction his neighbor mistook for a surging libido.

"Best tits west of Toronto," Hewitt commented excitedly.

Lorne remained silent. Later, when a young man joined the girl in the bedroom, he felt his heart pound in his temples, his mind now conquered by a strange mixture of lust and embarrassment.

The excitement of voyeurism swept violently through his brain when his eyes were initiated to the shattering image of the young couple copulating with a total lack of abashment.

When the lights were suddenly turned on again half an hour later, Lorne tried his damnedest to look nonchalant. Big Ceis slapped him roughly on the back, ruthlessly returning him to the realms of reality. "Beats soap, doesn't it?" he laughed raucously.

"Sure does," Lorne replied in a voice he did not recognize.

Blackmoor led his babbling and cigar-puffing guests upstairs and Lorne's eyes, still aching with the lewd display they had faithfully transmitted to the annals of the brain, widened anew in wonder. They had entered a room of enormous dimensions, the lights--like the background music--turned low. Near the end he could faintly perceive a cluster of chattering women, but it was the floor itself that filled him with the wondrous awe of a child in toy-land. Under his feet he saw hundreds of tropical fish swim magically under a thick glass floor. The brightly lit water seemed to set the floor ablaze and Lorne could not help envisaging the disaster that would occur if the glass should collapse under the shuffling feet. For an instant he saw himself struggle amid the tropical plants which were swaying slightly in the circulating water.

At the left the entire wall was covered with a huge display of coins, their backs reflected by terrace-style strips of mirror. The right of the elongated room furnished a spectacular view of Vancouver through a large picture window, overlooking Burrard Inlet. The city looked almost like something out of a fairy tale book: a multi-colored oasis ablaze in the vast desert of darkness.

As he followed the men toward the far end of the room, his eyes suddenly fell on a grotto-like formation of rocks which extended from the ceiling into the white sand at the bottom of the aquarium. A wrought iron balustrade served to keep inquisitive guests at a safe distance from a miniature waterfall that plunged audibly into a small pond which was partly obscured by ferns and other plants.

But the sight of the fascinating decor, fantastic as it was, failed to offset the impact of the thunderclap that was about to paralyze him.

Turning his eyes to the guests, he discovered Corine who composedly held a cocktail glass in her hand as she conversed with some of the women. Lorne envied her. She must have found the serenity I've lost, he inferred philosophically. As he walked to her, the women excused themselves and walked away.

"Did you have a good time, darling?" she asked sweetly. "Yes,"

Lorne lied. "How about you?"

"I'm really enjoying myself. Isn't it fabulous here?" "Sure is."

"I've been treated very nicely," Corine said appreciatively. "No one acts stuck-up."

"What's Mrs. Blackmoor like?"

"Very young and very pretty. She just left the room. I'll point her out to you when she comes back."

About ten chandeliers suddenly burst into bright light and the guests ringing the crystal punch bowl were now easily identifiable.

Big Ceis' voice exploded in Lorne's ears. "I'd like you to meet my wife," he said boisterously.

The guests parted respectfully as Mrs. Blackmoor came into view.

Lorne froze on the spot, his tongue sticking to his palate with the mucilage of emotion.

Terry Weldan did much better. "Pleased to meet you, Mr. Vincent," she said with a gracious smile. "My husband has told me a lot about you."

There followed an awkward silence, then with supreme effort he stammered: "I, I hope only good things."

"Naturally," Terry said gaily. "What else can there be said about a man as successful in business as you are?"

Before Lorne could formulate a comment, the room was filled with the magic rhythm of a rumba. Soon the transparent floor was crowded by dancing couples, the fish swimming stolidly beneath. Adding to his discomfort, he saw Corine twirl about under the guidance of George Hewitt. Big Ceis was getting his exercise from an attractive redhead.

"What's the matter, Lorne?" Terry asked bewitchingly. "Don't you like it here?"

"I admire your composure," Lorne complimented her drily.

"It's simple," she smiled naughtily. "I knew you were coming, so I was prepared. I figured you'd be surprised to see me, but I didn't think you'd be unhappy."

"I'm not unhappy," Lorne blurted, still not quite himself. "Just a bit shook up." Even in his boldest dreams she had not looked as stunningly beautiful as she did now. No wonder he had never forgotten her. And now? He was afraid to guess, but he knew the game was on again: only the rules had been changed and he had to be very careful. Bowing slightly, he asked facetiously: "May I have this dance, madam?"

His self-confidence quickly returned as they moved effortlessly to the beat of the Latin music.

"I'm glad you're doing so well for yourself," Terry whispered blithely.

"Can't kick," he said with a cockiness that surprised them both. "I see the same goes for you."

He pressed her closer to him.

"Easy, darling," Terry cautioned. "We're not alone." Lorne obediently loosened his grip and just noticed Corine giving him a dirty look as she brushed past him in the arms of a guy whose name he had already forgotten.

"Does Ceis know about us?" he asked *sotto voce*.

"No, and we'd better keep it that way," Terry replied, feeling his eyes burn on her cleavage.

"How long have you been married to him?"

"I'm not..."

Someone tapped Lorne on the shoulder. It was George Hewitt.

"Your wife dances marvellously," he smiled as he skilfully took Terry away from Lorne. Somewhat befuddled by Hewitt's proficiency in romantic piracy, Lorne walked towards the grotto.

"Down, boy, down," Corine greeted him, jealousy spilling over into her voice. "I'm beginning to see why you were so eager to come here. The way you danced with Mrs. Blackmoor you'd think you had known her for years."

That's a close guess, Lorne thought, but he said: "Am I complaining because you were dancing with some old slobs?" "At least I didn't cling to my partner," she snapped.

"May I offer you a drink?" It was Jim Vance. "The punch bowl is still patient. Or would you rather have something else?"

"No, punch will be fine," Lorne said, grateful for the interruption. And turning to Corine: "Isn't it, sweetheart?"

Corine forced a smile as she followed them to the side of the room. Vance adroitly filled the glasses, presenting them a moment later with a smile that showed signs of permanency. "Are you enjoying yourselves?" he asked.

"We're having a very good time Corine reassured him politely. And turning to Lorne: aren't we, darling?"

"It's a swell party," Lorne readily agreed. "A bit fishy below the surface though."

Vance erupted in a spasm of artificial laughter. "Very funny," he chortled. "Very funny."

Lorne gulped down his drink, suddenly envious of the fish swimming below Terry.

The next instant the condition of his eardrums was placed in jeopardy by Blackmoor's booming voice. "I saw you dance with my wife," he told Lorne accusingly. And directing himself to Corine, he added: "May I avenge myself by taking you for a dance?"

"I'd be delighted," Corine said, seeking to get even herself.

Poor thing, Lorne mused. The way I feel now she could not make me jealous if she were dancing with Prince Philip.

"You know," Vance startled him, "he likes you. He says you remind him of his son."

"I didn't know he had one," Lorne confessed.

"He hasn't anymore," Vance confided. "Bob was killed in a car accident. Ceis never quite got over it."

"I guess a person never really does," Lorne said sympathetically.

"That's right," Vance concurred. "Especially if it is your only child."

Their conversation was interrupted by a girl who seemed to have come from nowhere. "My gin fizz is all gone," she pouted. "Jimmy-boy make Connie another one?"

Lorne recognized her immediately: she was the receptionist with the knock-out figure at Lemton. Cocking her head slightly, she asked in her seductive voice: "Having a good time, Mr. Vincent?"

"Best time ever," Lorne smiled. Then he watched her walk suggestively beside Vance to the bar. What a night, he thought. All this sex appeal is hard on a man.

Scanning the dance floor, he spotted Terry with an airline executive. She brushed past Lorne several times, smiling at him across her partner's shoulder.

Lorne did not know whether it was Terry, Connie, the drinks or the film, but suddenly he felt like running away and let the cool evening air rinse the lecherous thoughts out of his mind. He tried to think of his business, of Larry and Kathy, and in final desperation of Doug, but he could think only of the bliss he had found in Terry's arms some seven long years ago.

So when Blackmoor returned with Corine a little while later, Lorne said resolutely: "We've had a wonderful time, Ceis. Thanks very much for everything."

"You're not thinking of leaving already, are you?" he inquired with feigned menace in his eyes. "I'm afraid we have to," Lorne said firmly.

"But it's only eleven," Blackmoor protested. "The party is just starting."

"Well, you see," Corine interjected dexterously, "we promised the baby sitter we'd be home before midnight."

"All right, I surrender," Blackmoor smiled benignly. "We'll do better next time."

"That's a promise," Lorne said automatically, but somehow he knew there never would be a next time.

Sunday Corine had been her former self again, reassured by Lorne's lovemaking after their return from Horseshoe Bay. But the passion she mistook for Lorne's devotion to her, had in reality been inspired by his reawakened desire for Terry. Though her ears had been caressed by whispered words of sweet intimacy, it was Terry he had secretly worshipped at the altar of Eros.

Now it was Monday and Lorne fought the feeble battle of reason versus libido in the privacy of his office. He knew, and he had told himself a thousand times, that he owed Terry nothing - that it was Corine who counted and Corine only. He realized that it was still not too late to prevent the past from destroying the future. He tormented himself by visualizing what it would be like if Corine should do to him what he considered doing to her. Adultery is so much easier to commit than to justify, especially for beginners. On the other hand, was it not natural for a man to escape the staleness of the marriage bed when a woman as beautiful as Terry promised new heights in sexual ecstasy? The double standard would not be so widely accepted if this were not so. Variety is the spice of life. No one expects you to wear the same suit day in day out or always drive the same car, so why should it be any different with women? A change is as good as a rest and he wasn't even tired. At least not of sex. Come to think of it, he wouldn't mind laying that Connie either. Besides, as long as Corine wouldn't know about it, it wouldn't hurt her. Boy, those cliché's were sure applicable in this sort of situation. Down with the puritans.

His hand reached for the phone, but it strangely stopped in mid-air as if by divine command. What about Fred Beldan's experience? He, too, had tried to eat the cake and have it as well.

Lorne remembered the price Beldan had paid for stepping out of line and he knew the risks in his case would be no different. Damn, damn, damn. The whole thing was driving him nuts. Why the hell was he so bloody indecisive? He was always quick with his decisions and now that more than ever was at stake he didn't know whether to fart or burp. His fist crashed angrily on his desk. Goddamn it all. Here he sat worrying his fool head off over a lousy piece of tail when he should be out in the plant. Terry obviously didn't have this problem or she would have called by now. Would she have the faintest notion what she was doing to him? She had not cared seven years ago, so why should she now? Where had she gone? Where had she been? What had she done? How had she met Big Ceis? When did she marry him? He paused. He remembered having asked her the last question, but he did not recall her answer. Lorne frowned, thinking hard. Then it came back to him. The mysterious smile on her face and the answer. Oh, yes: George Hewitt had interrupted them. Lorne could still feel the tap on his shoulder-piracy on the dance floor.

Now he had it. Why it was so simple: Terry was an old friend he had not seen for many years and what is wrong with looking up an old friend and talk about old times? Let's be fair: you can hardly call that improper. He was curious, that's all. He picked up the phone, looked up the number and dialed it briskly. What had all the fuss been about? He could hear her phone ring. He knew Ceis would not be home, because he had called him at his office only about ten minutes ago.

Good old Ceis: he had given Lorne another sizable order. The phone rang for the third time. Jesus! Then her soft voice sounded soothingly in his ear: "Hello?"

His newborn composure vanished like a snowflake in a campfire. "Terry," he blurted, "I've got to see you."

The silence that followed lasted a few eternal seconds. "I can meet you at the entrance of Capilano Park in an hour." she said.

"Thanks. In an hour then."

He hung up and leaned back in his chair. Casanova undoubtedly would have expressed himself more romantically, but hell, what de you expect from a beginner?

Walking past the switchboard, Esther Price startled him. "Will you be gone long?" she asked.

He had not thought of that. The answer obviously depended on Terry, but he could hardly say that.

"I think I'll be gone for the rest of the day," he said optimistically.

As he drove toward North Vancouver, doubt gnawed anew at his conscience. He could almost hear Corine's voice: "Why, Lorne?" she seemed to ask. "Why?"

And again it became clear to him that he stood much more to lose than he could possibly gain. This was a date with Fate. He realized that from now on he would have to lie to Corine, that one lie would necessitate the fabrication of another until in the end truth itself would seem a lie.

He stood divided against himself, but he drove on. He could not turn back. Not now. Not ever...

When he saw her, his heart pounded audibly in response. Her platinum hair splashed gaily across the collar of her mink jacket, and her shapely legs reminded him that she was a lot more than just an old friend.

"Hello, Lorne," she greeted him, a happy smile adorning her pretty face.

"Terry," he said. "It's so good to see you. Saturday was only a dream. Now it's real."

Suddenly all the premonitions of doom and dire consequences faded like snow in August. Suddenly the world was Terry and nothing else. Everything shrank to nothingness in the brightness of her smile.

They strolled silently side by side along a narrow path until in the privacy of a cluster of trees he abruptly drew her to him, feeling her lips part under his burning mouth.

"Oh, Terry," he whispered as his lips passed her ear on the way to the softness of her slender neck. "I love you so much."

"You poor baby. I've been so mean to you. Can you really forgive me?"

"Yes, sweetheart. As long as I have you I can do anything."

"I love you, too, Lorne. With all my heart I do. I've made such a mess of things, but I want to make up for it all."

He kissed her passionately, pressing hard against her responding body. After a few moments she pulled away from him. "This is no good," she said. "I know a much better place."

It was a ski cabin, the varnished logs glistening in the afternoon sun. The interior was equally rustic. Not a drop of paint had been used anywhere: everything was stained. In front of the stone fireplace lay a huge bear rug and overhead hung a mounted cougar head.

"I love skiing, so Ceis bought it for me last year," she explained. "Cozy, isn't it?"

"Just what the doctor ordered," Lorne quipped.

"In a few months everything around here will be white again. It's beautiful in the winter."

"It's beautiful here now," Lorne said as he joined her in front of the large window. The view was magnificent. The ruggedness of the mountain, the peacefulness of the inlet below, and in the distance the city, rendered noiseless by distance.

"Care for a drink?" she asked.

"I can get drunk just looking at you," he said happily, "but for good measure I'll have one anyway."

"Scotch all right?"

"That's fine. I'm easy to get along with today."

She walked away to the kitchen and Lorne heard her open a refrigerator hidden from his view. A moment later the room was filled with music. He was startled by the sound effects.

"Hey, this is almost as fancy as Twin Spruce Cove," he said.

"It's the latest thing," Terry explained from the kitchen: "stereo tape recordings."

"Pretty neat."

Later, their glasses emptied and refilled again, they danced. But dancing is an appetizer, not a substitute for sex. It doesn't still one's hunger--it only whets it.

"Yes, Lorne, hold me tight," she sighed.

"I've got a better idea," he said huskily as he lifted her up and carried her towards a chesterfield.

"No, not here," Terry whispered and nodding at a door in the hallway: "In there."

He managed to open the door without lowering her and carried her to the large bed where they found ecstasy in a passionate embrace.

XIX

Later, their passion spent, they lay quietly side-by-side. The climax had been followed by awkward silence. Lorne saw Corine's sad face on the planked ceiling as guilt rushed in where passion had departed. He had passed the point of no return. Life could never be the same again. He could never be himself again. He wasn't now.

"Are you sorry?" Terry asked sympathetically, as though reading his thoughts.

He turned his head towards her, smiling gently: "No, baby," he lied convincingly. "I've never been happier in my life." "Tell me you love me then," she challenged.

"I love you. Now and forever," he said, throwing in a kiss for good measure.

"Will you phone me again?"

"Of course, I will."

"We have to be careful. Ceis is very jealous."

"Husbands usually are."

A melancholy smile encircled her lips. "Ceis is not my husband," she said simply.

"But he introduced you as his wife," Lorne said, a look of incredulity on his face.

"I'm only his mistress, but he can't very well introduce me that way can he? It wouldn't sound respectable and Ceis loves to be respectable, at least on the surface. He was married once and acquired his initial capital that way, but he has gone through about a dozen women since his wife died in childbirth. He had a son, you know."

"Yes, I know," Lorne said. "Jim Vance told me."

"When Ceis tires of a mistress, he simply boots her out. With a wife that would be more complicated and certainly more costly, and Ceis is not the type of person who risks his money unnecessarily. He's a businessman all the way."

"How did you run into him?"

"I met him at a party in Las Vegas about a year and a half ago," she said. How well she remembered the party and the orgy that had concluded it. She had subsequently visited him at his hotel room on several occasions during his stay at the gambling capital and when he had asked her to become his make-believe wife, she had readily accepted. They had arrived in Vancouver the following day and it had felt great to be home again.

"Love at first sight," Lorne commented cynically.

"You don't understand," Terry said, ignoring his snide remark. "I was tired of wandering. Besides, I wasn't getting any younger and the kind of offer Ceis made is seldom repeated to older women."

"And during all the time you've been back, you never let me know," he thought aloud.

"I did want to see you, Lorne. As a matter of fact, I went to your old place on Lorenzo Street, but you had moved. When I found out you had married, I decided to let things rest."

"Why did you leave me in the first place?" Lorne asked, the hurt of that fateful Christmas burning anew in his heart.

"Let's not dwell on the past, darling. You can't set the old clock back."

"I realize that," he said, "but I still want to know why you left. The question has been nagging me for years."

Terry did not want to relate the painful confrontation with her father. That ugly incident was securely locked in her cerebral filing system with the label CLASSIFIED affixed to it. She had not forgotten, but she had succeeded in not remembering when she did not want to and she did not want to now.

"I left because I knew I wasn't good enough for you," she said. It was not the whole truth, but at least it was not a lie. "I'm too selfish to be a good wife. You would never have been where you are today if I had married you."

As the enormity of her words sunk in, he recalled the endless hours Corine had worked at his side typing invoices, filling bottles, mixing solutions and a thousand other things. She had returned to her job at the beauty parlor after their eventful honeymoon, helped him at the plant at night and somehow managed to do her household chores as well until Larry had been born and for nearly two years thereafter.

"But now we're together anyway," Lorne said sheepishly. "Why now, if not then?"

"Things have changed, Lorne. Everything has changed except my love for you." And turning on her side she kissed him lightly on the cheek, her fingers slowly zigzagging across his face. "I always knew I could not be a good wife to you, but now this no longer matters because you have a good wife.

I mean that sincerely, Lorne. I think she's very nice. But there is something else, too. Before we lived on two different planes; you were an idealist. I was not. Now you have come down to my level. Or is an adulterer less wicked than a whore?"

The words tore ruthlessly through his soul. The truth had never been so blunt.

He glanced at his watch. It was five-thirty. Too late for supper now. "Have you got a phone here?" he asked.

"In the kitchen," Terry replied. And as he stepped out of bed, she added: "Leave the door open. I want to hear what you're going to tell her."

Lorne flushed. She reads my mind like an open book, he thought. In the kitchen he paused to prepare his alibi. It quickly dawned on him that he was very much of a novice at this sort of thing. He had never had to lie to Corine before. Stalling would not solve the problem. He dialed the number with a quivering finger.

"Hello?"

It was Larry.

"Get your mother to the phone, will ya," he said gruffly.

Larry promptly dropped the receiver, the bang of it slamming against the wall piercing Lorne's ear. The rascal. He had told Larry a thousand times not to drop it but hang it on the side of the set.

"Hi, baby," he started, trying hard to sound casual. "I ran into Charley Renfield this afternoon and he invited me for supper. And guess what? It looks like Clayburn's is gonna give us their biggest order yet."

"What time will you be home?" Corine inquired with audible concern.

"I don't know yet."

"Try to make it not too late," she pleaded. "You need your rest, darling."

"I'll try, sweet," he promised before hanging up.

"Not bad for a first try," Terry complimented when he returned to the bedroom. "At least I take it this is the first time, or have you been unfaithful to her before?"

"No, this was the first time," Lorne said as he cuddled up to her, "but I don't think it will be the last. It's a strange thing, Terry, I thought I would feel guilty as hell, but I don't. I have no regrets at all. I just don't know whether that's a sign of maturity or depravity."

He got home just before midnight, but his hope that Corine would be asleep collapsed when he saw the living room ablaze with light.

"Oh, darling, what held you?" she greeted him. "I thought something had happened to you."

"What in the world could happen to me?" he said lightheartedly.

Suddenly Corine stepped back, a frown creasing her brow. Lorne almost had an apoplexy. He had inspected himself closely before leaving the cabin. Now he was sure Corine had discovered some telltale evidence of his amorous expedition. Some lipstick maybe or a blonde hair.

"Oh, Lorne," she said, tears suddenly flooding her eyes, "it has been such a terrible night. Doug died, darling. Dr. Marcus phoned earlier and said Doug wanted to see you one more time. Apparently you had told them yesterday you'd be by this evening and they had sort of counted on it. Poor Doug. He died just after nine."

Lorne looked at her as if he had been hit by lightning. "Oh, my God, what's happening to me?" he mumbled.

"You've got to slow down, sweetheart," Corine said sympathetically. "You are more and more losing sight of the things that really matter. No business in the world is worth that kind of sacrifice."

When Terry came home, Ceis was reading in bed. "Where the hell have you been all this time?" he greeted her, putting down the book.

"Uptown," she replied simply, taking off her shoes.

"Doing what?"

"Shopping."

"Till midnight?"

"Say what is this, a trial or something?" Terry asked testily.

"Let's just call it a preliminary hearing," Ceis said, observing her closely as she proceeded to undress.

Ceis couldn't see the fire yet, but he sure could smell smoke. "Well, what did you do besides shopping?"

"I went to see a movie."

"A double bill no doubt."

"Yes, how did you know?"

Ceis was only temporarily nonplussed by her remark. Then he remembered what he had been waiting for and he mellowed somewhat: "Well, next time give me a jingle, will you? I like to know where my girl is--beforehand."

He feasted his eyes on her naked splendor. "Don't bother with the nightie," he commented. "It'll just get in the way."

"Oh, Ceis, I'd rather not tonight. I'm awfully tired."

"Well, I'd rather anyway. The way I feel I don't think it'll take me long to wake you up."

Terry obediently submitted to him. It's a good thing I douched, she thought. Then she concentrated on her work, for with Ceis that's what it was: work! It takes a lot to please a spoiled rabbit...

The weeks passed in high gear. Doug had been buried, Fred Beldan did very well and Stan now worked full time for Lorne. Mother Nature worked around the clock painting autumn yellow, fuel sales were going up and people were coming down with the season's first colds.

Lorne had mastered his dual role as husband and paramour. Lies came easily and excuses came naturally. He had even convinced himself that he had never felt better in his life.

Leading a double life that had seemed irreconcilable only a month ago, now was as perfectly normal as turkey on Christmas. He had decided he loved Corine and Terry both, albeit in different ways. If it is acceptable to dislike more than one person, he reasoned, what's wrong with loving more than one? Doug had been right all along! Terry was very mature about the triangular affair. She wasn't jealous or anything like that. Neither was Corine, but then she didn't know the score and Lorne had no intention of enlightening her in that regard. She was quite happy, especially since Lorne spent more evenings at home lately. Practically all his rendezvous with Terry took place on afternoons when Ceis was safely at his office and would not question her whereabouts. Meanwhile Corine did not suspect a thing, although she had asked him about the decline in domestic bedroom activities. Lorne had pointed out that virility does not increase with age and that the workload at the plant wasn't getting any lighter. She had kissed him to show her understanding and fallen asleep with a peaceful smile on her face.

In a nutshell: it was a perfect set-up or so it seemed...

Jeff Humphries was listening patiently to his client's suspicions. He had heard the same story a thousand times before--only the data were different. He was still in his early thirties, but he knew enough scandalous information to fill a year's supply of lurid literature. He had only been in this racket five years, but he knew everything it takes to be a good private detective. Infidelity was a booming business.

"He drives a green 1948 Studebaker."

Humphries made a notation. This was pure nonsense, but it inspired confidence. Humphries had a photographic memory and seldom used notes, but he had discovered that a scribble now and then, especially when accompanied by an appropriate frown, helps promote the image of proficiency so valuable as an anesthetic during the fee quoting session. His fees were quite flexible, but always adjusted to whatever the traffic could bear. In some cases he played both sides of the fence: a very tricky undertaking demanding great skill and ingenuity, but extremely profitable. This case seemed to have the intrinsic ingredients for such an operation.

"Then there is that ski cabin I mentioned earlier..."

How much he had learned. He could laugh his insides out, while on the surface he appeared to be the epitome of concern. He could placate, reassure, boast or be modest and simultaneously calculate his profits. God, how he milked the suckers! There were other dividends as well, fringe benefits you might say. Sex for example. He had found women very generous with their favors, especially when they were in a pinch. Humphries often took advantage of such situations. Mixing business with pleasure was often very remunerative. He had lost count of the women he had seduced at their husbands' request. It takes gall to collect from the cuckolds later, but they always came through because with this proof of adultery they could junk their wives easily and cheaply.

In some cases he had accomplished such objectives by showing the wives photographic evidence of their husbands' infidelity. He had learned early on that nothing puts women faster on their backs than such pictures and invariably the husbands would catch them in--though preferably after--the act. The women always pleaded for the incriminating photos he had shown them earlier and a lively auction often followed with the husbands usually being the highest bidder.

Humphries could tell his client was reaching the end of his oration when his sentences were becoming coherent.

"I don't give a damn how you do it, Mr. Humphries, but I want positive proof one way or the other. I may just be imagining things, but it's your job to find out whether or not I am."

Humphries smiled his most confident smile. "Mr. Blackmoor," he said reassuringly, "I've cracked far tougher cases than yours."

"How long do you figure it's going to take you to find out what the score is?"

"That will depend on your wife," Humphries said professionally. "I think the sooner we start the better. There's no point in wasting time."

"Of course not."

"Now as for my fee..."

"I'll pay anything within reason," Big Ceis thundered. "Just get me the information I've asked for and I'll pick up the tab."

Two months of illicit love had made Lorne acutely aware of the ever-present and growing threat of discovery. So he arranged his dates with Terry using every possible precaution to prevent detection. They met during different parts of the day, never repeating their places of rendezvous and always on short notice. They parked their cars on separate parking lots, entered different department stores and used elevators extensively to shake possible shadows. Then they traveled in separate taxis to their meeting place. Afterwards they picked up their cars again and each returned to base. It was an elaborate procedure, but the stakes were too high to permit carelessness.

This time it was different: they had decided to meet and spend the night in Seattle. Ceis was on a week-long buying trip back east and Lorne had some legitimate business in the U.S. city. He had driven down and Terry was about to fly in under an assumed name.

Lorne killed time reading a magazine someone had discarded in the air terminal. He frequently consulted his watch, but time was crawling and the plane was late. He wondered what she would say about his brand-new car: a gleaming black Mercedes-Benz. Quite a difference from the old Studie! He snickered when it occurred to him that Big Ceis actually had paid for the car with his growing orders. You're a real sport, Ceis, albeit an unknowing one, Lorne mused.

The plane from Vancouver had arrived and Lorne felt his heart accelerate its beat as he scanned the new arrivals. A few moments later he saw her, an overnight case dangling meaningfully in her left hand.

"How did the dodging routine go?" he greeted her.

"Fine," Terry said, falling in step beside him, "but why did you come here? I thought we were supposed to meet at the Cayamin Motel." "I couldn't wait showing off my new car," he explained boyishly. "Besides, we're a long way from home. It's nice not to have to play hide and seek for a change."

Minutes later they were mobile. Terry, accustomed to the best of everything, did not seem overly impressed by his new conveyance. "It's a nice car," she said simply.

"It's a dream," Lorne corrected her, veering from one lane to another with the skill of a New York cabbie. "Please drive carefully," Terry urged with a trace of nervousness in her voice. Why do you keep switching lanes?"

"It's just an extra safety precaution," Lorne explained, "in case we're being followed."

"I thought you said we're safe here," Terry protested. "I think we are," he said, "but that doesn't mean we should let our guards down."

They had crisscrossed Seattle, absorbing the sights. Now they were undressing in their plush motel room.

"This has been a great day," Lorne said cheerfully as he flung his tie across the back of a chair. "I think we'll soon be exporting to the U.S."

"How romantic," Terry teased, her voluptuous breasts bursting provocatively free from her brassiere.

"I didn't mean to be disrespectful," he said facetiously. He still marveled at the sight of her gorgeous figure: her firm breasts, her narrow waist, her wide, inviting hips.

"Lights on or off?" he asked.

"Leave them on, darling," she said seductively. "I want to see all of you."

He mounted her with a skill that betrayed familiarity. Their passionate lovemaking made them lose awareness of their surroundings.

Suddenly the room was filled with a blinding brightness. Lorne tore himself loose, his eyes startled by a second flash. Ignoring his nakedness, Lorne lunged toward the intruder in a desperate bid to grab the camera, but the man whirled around and escaped.

"This is the end," Terry prophesied as Lorne angrily kicked the door shut.

"How the hell did he get in? I know I locked the door."

"He obviously had a passkey," Terry said, recalling similar experiences, but in her hustling days she had stood much less to lose.

"What are we going to do?" she asked, fear spilling into her eyes.

"What we had planned to do: make love," Lorne said, but his voice was too flat to be convincing. His words conveyed indifference, but his tone reflected the cold apprehension he felt in his heart.

"But what about tomorrow?" she protested, drawing her knees petulantly under her chin.

"To hell with tomorrow. Didn't you tell me that it is neither the past nor the future but the present that counts?" Lorne said. And recalling Doug's philosophy, he added: "Tomorrow may be forever." "I'm not going back to Ceis," Terry said resolutely.

"Of course, you are. The guy who took the pictures may not have been sent by Ceis. He may just be a free-lancer. In that case I'll pay him off and that's that. If my guess is right he'll contact me long before Ceis will be back."

"And if you're wrong?"

"Then we could be in for a bit of trouble," Lorne admitted. After all it takes two to tango but only one to turn the music off."

XX

Vancouver had not changed: only Lorne had. Everything was as he had left it and no one acted suspiciously. Still that night he snuggled closer to Corine than usual as if to find extra security and reaffirmation of her devotion.

When sleep finally came, Big Ceis awaited him.

"I'm glad you made it," Ceis greeted him. "I've got a dandy of a film to show you."

"Where's everybody else?" Lorne asked, his clothes fused to his body by clammy sweat.

"There is no one else here. Just you and me. Isn't that cozy?"

"Very," Lorne agreed obligingly, watching a school of fish gather below his feet. Suddenly the fish scattered away and an ominous shadow slid under his feet. "Sharky is my latest aquatic addition," Ceis explained. "I love sharks. I guess you do, too, being a bit of a shark yourself."

"It's sort of a private premiere," Ceis said as he aimed the projector at the screen near the grotto. "I'm sure you'll like it, because you're in it."

"I don't understand."

"Well, you will in a minute. I'm going to sell a lot of copies of this flicker. You'd be amazed what people are prepared to pay for anything as spicy as this one, but it's well worth it.

A moment later the screen came alive with the scene he had dreaded, but though he recognized Terry, he didn't recognize himself.

"I thought you said I was in it," he challenged.

"Well, aren't you? I'd say you couldn't be in it much more than that."

"That's not me," Lorne protested, missing the double-entendre. "You can't prove a thing."

"Why don't you take a closer look?" Ceis invited, his voice no longer cordial.

Lorne walked over to the screen. The next instant he felt the strangulating strength of Ceis' hands around his neck. He tried to yell, but panic had paralyzed his vocal cords. Suddenly he felt an excruciating pain in his back as he was pushed over the rod iron railing. Dazed he fell on the jagged rocks.

"It's Sharky's feeding time," Ceis announced, giving him a final shove.

Lorne sunk helplessly to the bottom of the aquarium. The shark swam swiftly towards him, baring a ferocious arsenal of pointed teeth. Lorne jumped like a frog, hitting the head board of the bed and awakening to the ringing of the telephone. Corine stirred at his side. He stealthily slipped out of bed and walked to the kitchen. It's about time we had an extension in the bedroom, he thought sleepily.

"Hello," he yawned. Suddenly he was wide awake.

The voice needed no introduction: Lorne knew.

"Sorry to disturb you, Mr. Vincent," the caller started, "but I thought this would be a good time to catch you home. I'm sure you're dying to know how the pictures turned out. Well, Mr. Vincent, they're terrific, simply terrific. Every detail is razor sharp, an excellent focussing job, I must say. There can be no doubt about your identity whatsoever. You both look very natural, if you know what I mean. Lovely pictures, really, but not too suitable for the family album. I could arrange a private showing at your office first thing in the morning or would you prefer me to dispose of them in the Horseshoe Bay area?" "I'll be at the plant at eight," Lorne said curtly."

When Lorne returned to the bedroom, Corine was sitting up.

"Who was that?" she asked sweetly.

"Ah, some jerk from an advertising company. Claims he's got a big promotion deal cooked up for me."

"And he calls you at this time of night?" Corine said more in surprise than doubt.

"Yeah," Lorne explained with feigned annoyance, "the guy is leaving at noon and he insisted on seeing me before then. Apparently he tried to get a hold of me while I was in Seattle."

In the morning Lorne left home hurriedly, skipping breakfast in fear Corine might discover his nervousness. Besides, he did not have much of an appetite knowing what was in store for him. Jeff Humphries walked into his office just before nine. Without any preliminaries he zipped his thin briefcase open and nonchalantly flung the pornographic prints on Lorne's desk. "Candid camera," he grinned.

A chill crept up Lorne's back as he glanced at the damning evidence. "How much?" he asked simply.

"Five g's."

"That's a lot of dough for two pictures," Lorne said, trying to size up his antagonist.

"It's a lot of picture," Humphries said drily.

"Well, I haven't got it," Lorne sighed. It was worth a try. "I'll give you two thousand dollars for the photos and the negatives."

"Three thousand, and that's a one-day special."

"Twenty-five hundred and that's final," Lorne bluffed.

"You're driving a hard bargain," Humphries said pensively, "but I guess, I shouldn't expect any different from a businessman as successful as you. All right, you win."

Lorne produced his cheque book, but Humphries stopped him cold before he managed to land his pen. "No cheque," he said firmly. "It's a cash deal."

"In that case you'll have to wait till the banks open at 10." Humphries grinned confirmingly.

"One more thing: it would be wise to remember that this is my first and final payment for your photographic services. So don't come back for an encore or try peddling your spares elsewhere, because you simply would not feel comfortable behind bars."

"I think we understand each other," Humphries agreed.

Blackmoor phoned two days later. "How was the trip?" Lorne inquired with feigned joviality.

"Excellent. I hear you've been away yourself."

"Yeah," he said, his voice no longer ebullient, "I spent a couple of days in Seattle. I am trying to get even with Fentex and it looks as though we'll be exporting to the States by the end of this month."

"Good show, but I hope you're not too busy filling an order for Lemton."

"Of course not," Lorne said, feeling a bit better again. "You've got preferential privileges!"

"I appreciate that. There are just a couple of things I'd like your view on. You see, the order may be too big for you to handle."

"What's involved?" Lorne asked with resurgent optimism. "Forty thousand dollars of packing and a week to do it in."

"Shea," Lorne whistled, "that's a lot of sauerkraut for a short fork." Ceis had never ordered more than ten thousand dollars' worth at a time before. "The usual products?" Lorne asked.

"Yes, but mostly compounds," Ceis clarified. "It's much like the last order, only about ten times that big."

If we work three shifts we should be able to swing it, Lorne thought. "Are the containers available?"

"Yes, they are. I've made arrangements that you can buy them direct from the manufacturer. They've got a good supply on hand and can deliver the works tomorrow if you'll order today."

"Fair enough," Lorne said. "To save time, I can drop in at your office later today and pick up your purchase order."

"Just get yourself something to scribble on and I'll hand you the dope over the phone."

When the week had passed, Lorne was on the verge of collapse. With the exception of a few catnaps he had worked around the clock supervising the mammoth operation. He had almost tripled his staff and for seven long, nightmarish days the lights in the plant had burned continuously, illuminating a film of sweat and a cacophonous pandemonium of industriousness.

His head throbbing with fatigue, Lorne looked at the countless cartons being readied for shipment to Lemton.

"How does it look, Lorne?" Ted Melville inquired.

Lorne smiled appreciatively at his foreman. "It's just great, Ted. I've never seen such excellent teamwork before."

Joe Tiflin, the shipper, walked up. "'When do you want us to start loading the trucks, Lorne?" he asked, beads of sweat glistening on his brow.

"Is everything ready?"

"Just about."

"I'd better phone Lemton and see what they've got to say about it," Lorne said. "They may want us to ship some of the stuff directly to their customers."

It has been a tough battle, Lorne mused as he headed for his office, but now that it is over, it feels great to have done it.

Victory seemed sweet indeed, for apart from the promise of profit, wasn't the order a clear indication that Ceis knew nothing about Lorne's affair with Terry?

God, how he missed her. He had not seen her since they had parted in Seattle two weeks ago and she had phoned him only once during that period. "We've got to lay low for a while, Lorne," she had said. "So don't expect any more calls from me for the time being and for God's sake don't try to phone me." Smart girl. She played it cool all the way.

Lorne entered his office, glancing at the unmade cot in the corner where he had taken his brief periods of rest during the past seven days: sleep on the installment plan!

He dialed the number wearily.

"Good morning, Lemton Distributors."

"Morning Connie," Lorne said, recognizing the girl's voice. "Is Mr. Blackmoor in?"

"Yes, he is," she sang sweetly. "Just one moment, please."

"Blackmoor."

"How are you this morning?"

"Fine, Lorne. How about yourself?"

"We have completed your order, Ceis. Where and when would you like to have it shipped?"

"Ship it anytime and anywhere as long as you don't send it to me." "But you ordered the stuff," Lorne blurted, his head reeling.

"I did? My memory must be slipping: I don't remember a thing about it."

"No, but...Oh, hell, cut it out, Ceis. I'm too beat to appreciate a joke."

"I'm not trying to be funny," Ceis said with dead earnest. "I'm just trying to get something across to you."

"I don't understand what you're getting at."

"Well, it's really quite simple: you screwed Terry and now I'm screwing you. I am gonna rub you out. With no more orders from me, and the cancellation of the one you're now stuck with, this won't be tough to accomplish."

Lorne listened dumbfoundedly, the receiver seemingly glued to his reddened ear. When the connection died Lorne pushed his face into his hands. "My God," he mumbled, "what am I going to do?" But the more he thought about the dilemma, the clearer it became that the situation was irreversible. He was trapped. There was no escape. He owed more than twenty thousand dollars for chemicals alone, chemicals which had been mixed in the preparation of solutions for which only Ceis had a market and which now crowded the plant with thousands of bottles and cans bearing the Lemton label as a colossal monument to Lorne's stupidity.

The price of fleeting bliss which sex provides now had assumed astronomical proportions. Without further orders from Lemton, which accounted for nearly half of his total sales, he could not possibly meet his financial obligations. The mortgage payments alone were now beyond his means.

Bankruptcy was clearly inevitable: it was just a matter of time. The irony didn't escape Lorne: How he had considered Fentex the greatest threat to his enterprise. How he had lambasted American business ethics. How he had cursed Nithdale and Jefferson. How he had even worried about Fred Beldan. But he had dealt victoriously with all his rivals. He had survived, grown and prospered. But what for? To be crushed by his own libido! He stared morosely at his desk calendar. November 24 He suddenly realized he had not even talked to Corine on the phone for two days. He dialed the number quickly.

"Hello?"

It was Larry. Everything was still all right then. She wouldn't leave the kids behind. Lorne hung up with the speed of lightning. What was there to talk about? He had found out what he wanted to know. His thoughts turned to Terry and he realized that Ceis would deal no less harshly with her. It was a mess all the way around. Yesterday he had been sitting on top of the world. Today years of toil had been nullified and tomorrow he would face the threat of having his family swept out of reach. But the most painful aspect of his downfall was that he had no one to blame but himself. He could never expect Corine to understand what he did not even fully understand himself. How can this be explained, let alone be justified? Still, while he regretted the consequences of his affair with Terry, he did not regret the affair itself. There is no profit in self-delusion. His feelings towards Terry had not changed: he knew he would always love her.

> Life knows no certainty 'xcept death
> For all must exhale that final breath;
> Whether they be strong, rich or clever
> Someday every person faces forever

Doug Marcus

Made in the USA
Charleston, SC
15 April 2014